BYGONES

Cover Design: Müllerhaus Publishing Arts, Inc., www.mullerhaus.net

Cover Photo: Matt Swaggart

Published by Barbour Publishing, Inc., P.O. Box 719, Uhrichsville, Ohio 44683, www.barbourbooks.com

Our mission is to publish and distribute inspirational products offering exceptional value and biblical encouragement to the masses.

ecpa Member of the
Evangelical Christian
Publishers Association

Printed in the United States of America.

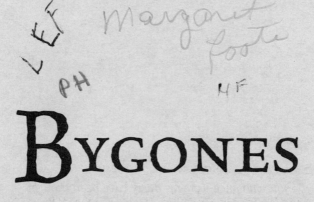

BYGONES

KIM
VOGEL SAWYER

BARBOUR
PUBLISHING

But now in Christ Jesus
you who once were far away have been brought
near by the blood of Christ.

EPHESIANS 2:13 NIV

ONE

Henry Braun paused outside Jimmy's Dinner Stop and pressed his hand to his abdomen. Beneath his neatly tucked shirt his stomach churned. He couldn't decide if it was nervousness or excitement that had his belly jumping like a trout on a line. Either way, it didn't matter.

He hadn't seen Marie in more than twenty years. In his jacket pocket he carried a snapshot of her—one she'd enclosed in a Christmas card to her aunt Lisbeth three or four years back. But he didn't need it to remember her. A man never forgot his first love.

His hand trembled slightly as it connected with the smudged silver door handle of the café. As he tugged open the door, a wave of stale tobacco-scented air washed across him. Stepping inside, he allowed the door to drift shut behind him. He removed his hat, held it against his stomach with both hands, and stood silently, taking in the busy scene.

Nearly every booth and table was filled with noisy patrons, most of them men, probably truckers like

Jep Quinn. Two waitresses, wearing pale blue knee-length dresses and white aprons, bustled between tables, pouring coffee from tall plastic containers and bantering with customers. Although both women appeared to be middle-aged, he picked out Marie right away. That nutmeg hair of hers, even cropped short into mussy curls, was unmistakable.

He remained beside a tall counter that held a cash register, waiting for someone to show him to a table. Curious gazes turned in his direction, and one man jabbed another with his elbow, pointing rudely before making a comment that brought a laugh from the other members of his group. Henry was accustomed to this treatment when he stepped out into the world. He averted his gaze and maintained his stoic expression.

After several minutes of waiting, the unfamiliar waitress waved a hand at him and hollered, "Hey honey! There's a spot over here. C'mon in!"

Henry pointed to his chest, his eyebrows high, making certain she meant him. When she smiled and quirked her fingers at him, he moved forward on legs still stiff from the long drive. He slid into the empty booth.

"You new around here? I don't think I've seen you before."

The woman's bright smile, meant to put him at ease he was sure, made him feel like recoiling instead. But it would be impolite not to reply, so he said in an even tone, "I'm just passing through."

She gave a nod and a wink. "Well, welcome to

Cheyenne. Enjoy your stay." Slopping coffee into a thick mug and whacking a menu on the table in front of him, she added, "Just look that over, honey, and I'll be right back to take your order."

He raised a finger to delay her. "I don't wish to order a meal, I only want to—" But she took off, and his request died on his lips. Leaving the coffee and menu untouched, he followed Marie with his gaze. How comfortable she appeared as she moved among the tables, smiling, sometimes teasing, laughing. . . . He had been so certain when she climbed into Jep Quinn's semi she would quickly realize her mistake and return to Sommerfeld. To him. Now he felt foolish. Marie had obviously found her niche in the outside world.

Disappointment struck him, and he pondered its cause. Had he expected to find her cowering in a corner somewhere, overwhelmed and repentant? No. He had read the letters she'd sent to her aunt Lisbeth over the years. He came here knowing Marie had adopted the worldly lifestyle. The disappointment was personal.

His fingers twitched on the tabletop. Why hadn't she recognized him at once, as he had her?

❄

"Hey Marie, got a live one in booth thirteen."

Marie balanced three plates on one arm and grabbed a basket of rolls with her free hand. Sally was fond of pointing out the most handsome men who entered the roadside café, figuring Marie needed a man in her life. Marie didn't second the opinion. But she sent her friend a brief grin. "Oh yeah?"

"Yeah." Sally released a light chuckle and reached past Marie for the plates Jimmy handed through the serving window. "From the way he's dressed, he must be a preacher or somethin'. Check him out."

Marie gave a quick nod. "When I've got a minute to spare." She weaved between tables to deliver Friday's special—fried fish, hush puppies, slaw, and fries—to the truckers at table three. She placed the plastic basket of rolls in the middle of the table, scolding when one of them made as if to pat her bottom. She served him first and quipped, "That should keep your hands busy." All three men roared. Smirking, she moved around the table and plopped plates in front of each customer. Hands on her hips, she asked, "Anything else I can get you fellas?"

The one with the roving hand grinned. "What I want probably isn't on the menu."

"You behave," Marie warned. Although she'd had plenty of opportunity over her years of widowhood, she'd never engaged in flirtation with customers. Sally said she wasn't the flirty type. Marie had always taken that as a compliment.

She backed away from the table. "If you think of something I missed, just wave a hand in the air."

The men hollered their thanks and dug into their food. As Marie turned to head for the serving window, she remembered Sally's comment and glanced toward booth thirteen. Her feet came to an abrupt halt right in the aisle between tables.

That was no preacher. Just a man. A Mennonite man. The plain blue shirt, buttoned to the collar, and black jacket with missing lapels identified him as clearly as advertising on a billboard. Her gaze bounced from his clothes to his face. His brown-eyed gaze met hers squarely, and she gasped. Her knees buckled. She reached for something—anything—to keep herself upright. Her hand connected with the shoulder of the nearest patron, and she heard a gruff voice call, "Hey darlin', whatcha need?" Her gaze remained pinned to that of the Mennonite man's, who sat unmoving in the booth, his brown eyes unblinking.

"I–I'm sorry," she managed, removing her hand. The customer shrugged and went back to eating. Sally dashed by, and Marie caught the sleeve of her dress.

Sally paused in midstride, her face crinkled in concern. "Hey, what's wrong? You look like you've seen a ghost."

"I think I have."

Sally shifted her gaze toward the booth, then back at Marie. "You know that preacher?"

Marie nodded slowly. "I need a minute. Can you—"

Sally smiled and patted Marie's hand. "Sure, honey. Go ahead. I'll cover you."

Her gaze still on the man in the booth, Marie mumbled a thank-you. Her sluggish feet didn't want to move. Go. *Walk. Have to see what he wants*. Finally her feet obeyed, and she moved as if wading through cold molasses.

He rested his palms on the blue-speckled tabletop

and looked up at her. He was older now. His close-cropped dark brown hair was speckled with gray, and lined sunbursts marked the corners of his eyes. But he was still undeniably handsome. Unmistakably Henry.

His Adam's apple bobbed in a swallow. Her throat felt dry, too. One of her hands, as if of its own volition, smoothed her unruly curls. The touch of her hair made her conscious of her uncovered head, and embarrassment struck at the thought of her bare knees and the tight fit of her bodice. Things that had become commonplace over the years now left her feeling exposed and vulnerable. She felt her cheeks flood with heat, and part of her wanted to run away and hide. Yet her feet turned stubborn once more, refusing to move.

What was he doing in Cheyenne, Wyoming—hundreds of miles from Kansas? How had he known where to find her? Had her family sent him? A dozen questions threaded through her mind, but when she opened her mouth, only one word squeaked out. "Hi."

"Hello." His voice had deepened with maturity, but the timidity she remembered still underscored the tone. "You"—he glanced around the bustling café—"are very busy right now."

She licked her lips. "Yes, I am. I—I can't really take a break, but—"

His nod cut her off. "I understand. When are you finished here?"

"Four."

Another nod. "I'll wait."

The simple statement flung her back nearly two

dozen years. She heard, in her memory, his pain-filled voice whisper, *I will wait for your return, Marie.* Now she wondered. . .had he?

"Marie?"

Sally's voice jarred her back to the present. She looked over her shoulder. Sally stood in front of the cluttered serving window, her arms held out in a silent gesture of *I need you.* Marie nodded, then spun back to Henry. "Don't wait here." She dug in her apron pocket, retrieved her keys, and twisted her apartment key from the ring. Slipping it into his hand, she said, "You can go to my apartment. The Woodlawn. Take the Broadway Avenue exit off the highway, then go ten blocks north and two east. The apartment building is on the corner of Carson and Twenty-third. I'm in Apartment 4B. Go in, make yourself at home. I'll be there as soon as I can."

She started to turn away, then looked at him again. "How did you get here?"

He pointed out the window. "I drove myself."

She glanced out to the parking area. A solid black four-door sedan waited, dwarfed by semi trucks. Her eyebrows flew high in surprise, and she caught a hint of a grin twitch his cheeks.

"I've worked on cars all my life, and now I drive one."

"Marie!"

Sally's frantic call spurred Marie to action. "I'll be home sometime after four." She dashed to the counter and took the waiting plates. Out of the corner of her eye, she watched Henry exit the café, then followed

11

his tall form as he crossed in front of the window. Moments later, his car backed out of the parking lot and disappeared between semis.

"You gonna deliver those meals or hold 'em till the food is cold?"

Jimmy's sardonic voice captured Marie's attention. Her face flooded with heat once more.

"Sorry." Turning toward the waiting table, she called, "Food's comin' right up, boys."

After serving the men, she sneaked a peek at her wristwatch. Still two and a half hours until quitting time. Her breath whooshed out. *I hope I last that long. . . .*

The brown-brick apartment complex was clean but showed signs of age. Concrete slabs, some cracked, served as porches to each unit. The grass, mostly brown and brittle, was sparse in places, exposing patches of dirt. Henry stepped onto the slab in front of the door marked 4B and shook his head. On the corner of the poor excuse for a porch, a clay pot held a clump of drooping plastic tulips.

So Marie still liked flowers.

Henry couldn't help but think of the large, rambling farmhouse that had been Marie's childhood home, its thick grassy yard scattered with bright marigolds, zinnias, and morning glories. After all that space and beauty, how could she live in a place like this? He sighed, sadness weighing on his chest.

Despite having a key, Henry felt like an intruder as

he opened the door and stepped inside. The apartment was quiet except for a ticking clock and a funny noise—a *blurple-blurp*—he didn't recognize. For long minutes he stood on the little rug in front of the door and allowed his gaze to drift around the small area, uncertain what to do.

A long sofa, draped with a bright-colored quilt, stood sentinel along the north wall. In front of the sofa crouched a small chest. Its top held a short stack of magazines, a small black box with white push buttons, and two crumpled napkins. A spindled rocking chair heaped with pillows rested in the corner.

Across from the couch, on the opposite wall, stood a shelving unit with a large center section flanked by open shelves. He crossed to it, his fingers reaching to stroke the surface. He shook his head. At first glance, the unit appeared to be wood, but closer examination proved it to be wood-printed paper glued to a solid base. Artificial wood. . .and artificial flowers. Sadness pressed again.

From the center portion of the shelves, a large television set stared blankly at the sofa. The glass front was coated with fine particles of dust. On a shelf above the television, he located the source of the blurping—a small fish aquarium, with a bright-colored castle and three goldfish. Every now and then a little tube at the back of the square glass box sent up a series of bubbles, which burbled as they rose to the top.

He watched the fish for a little while, his heart aching at the silent message they presented. Marie loved animals, but she probably wasn't allowed a pet in this apartment. Had she purchased the fish as a way to replace the memories of the dogs, cats, and lambs from the farm?

Shifting his gaze from the fish, he turned his attention to the photographs on the shelves. Each frame was unique—some wood, some metal, some pasted with beads or carved with flowers. A few of the pictures he'd seen before, in Lisbeth Koeppler's small sewing room, arranged in a simple album that rested next to the little woven basket that held every letter Marie had sent over the years. All of the photos featured the young girl Henry knew about but had never met.

He leaned closer, examining each photograph in turn, analyzing the girl's features. She had Marie's cleft chin and blue eyes, but not Marie's hair. A shame. That had always been Marie's best feature.

Now that hair was cut short into curls that waved helter-skelter on her head. So many changes. But what had he expected? Shaking his head, he turned from the photographs and crossed to the couch, seating himself on the edge of the soft cushion. Off to the side of the room were two open doorways. One led to the kitchen—he glimpsed a chrome-and-Formica table-and-chairs set—and the other to a hallway that, he surmised, ended with bedrooms. Such a tiny space compared to what she'd left behind. . .

Looking over his shoulder at the clock on the wall, he realized he would have a long wait. He clasped his knees and sighed, wishing he had brought along a book to read. His gaze found the television, and his reflection stared back from the large blank screen. Curiosity struck. What might be showing at two thirty in the afternoon on the television? But he didn't move to turn it on.

Except for the clock's *tick, tick* and the fish bowl's *blurple-blurp*, he sat in silence. Another sigh heaved out. At home he always had things to do, which made the time go quickly. *Blurple-blurp.* He looked at the clock again. *Tick, tick.* Sighed again. "I suppose I could look at one of these magazines."

Suddenly a noise intruded, a scratching outside. He rose as the door swung open and a girl—the one from the photographs—stepped through. She was humming, her head down, fiddling with something in the oversized brown leather bag that hung from her shoulder. She bumped the door closed with her hip and brought up her gaze, swinging her hair over her shoulder at the same time.

The moment she spotted him, she let out a scream that made the fine hairs on the back of his neck rise. Her hand plunged into her bag, and she yanked out a tiny spray can, which she aimed at him. "Don't come any closer. I'll shoot you. I swear I will!"

He brought up both hands in surrender, although he could see no threat in that little aerosol can.

"Who are you?" she barked, her blue eyes wide in her pale face. The hand holding the can quivered, but she didn't back down.

"My name is Henry Braun." He kept his voice

low and soothing. The girl's wild eyes made his stomach turn an uneasy somersault. "I drove over from Sommerfeld to see your mother."

"How'd you get in here?"

"Your mother gave me the key. See?" He pointed to the chest in front of the couch, where he'd placed the house key.

Still scowling, the girl inched forward and snatched up the key. Keeping the can aimed at him, she growled, "You stay right there. I'm going to call my mother. Don't you move!"

The girl backed through the doorway that led to the kitchen and disappeared behind the wall. He heard some clicks, then the girl's voice. "Jimmy? This is Beth. I need to talk to Mom."

Henry crept to the front door and let himself out, then perched on the concrete stoop. He would wait out here for Marie. That girl of hers was crazy. For the first time since he headed out on this journey, he wondered if Lisbeth Koeppler had made a mistake.

Two

Although she normally left her sunglasses in the car, today Marie kept them on her face when she walked from the carport toward her apartment. Why she felt the need for the small shield, she couldn't be sure—she just knew she needed it.

Rounding the corner of the apartment complex, she spotted Henry sitting on the stoop in front of her door. Marie's heart caught; her steps slowed. His pose—elbows resting on widespread knees, head down, fingers toying with something on the concrete between his feet—reminded her of when they were teenagers and he would come to visit. Henry's bashfulness always kept his head lowered, his fingers busy spinning a blade of grass or twiddling a small twig.

Long-buried memories rushed to the surface, clamoring for attention. She shoved them aside and focused on the present. Why hadn't he gone in? She had assured Beth he had permission to be there. She stopped several feet short of the porch. Her shadow bumped against his right foot, and he looked up. The slash of shade from his hat brim hid his eyes.

"You didn't wait inside." A foolish statement, considering where she'd found him.

A slight grin twitched one side of his lips. "No."

She took a step closer, her shadow swallowing his foot and the pebbles he had been lining up on the sidewalk. "Why?"

Pushing to his feet, Henry shrugged. "With your daughter home, I thought it best to wait out here."

Of course. He wouldn't be comfortable in the apartment alone with Beth. Remembering Beth's panicked phone call, Marie nearly chuckled. Her daughter had no idea how harmless Henry was. "Let's go inside and we can talk."

He moved aside and allowed her to step onto the stoop, then waited on the sidewalk while she knocked on the door. Three clicks sounded—all three locks. Hadn't Beth believed her when she'd said Henry wasn't dangerous? The knob turned and Beth yanked the door open.

Normally Marie would have greeted her daughter with a cheery hello and a kiss on the cheek. But today, with the clicks of the locks still ringing in her ears, she moved through the doorway and called over her shoulder, "Please come in, Henry."

He followed, his hands clamped around the brim of his hat. He stepped past the little throw rug and waited silently under Beth's scowling perusal.

Marie closed the door, then gestured toward the couch. "Go ahead and sit down." She crossed to the entertainment center and removed her sunglasses, placing them on top of the television. In the glass, she watched Henry's reflection as he crossed to the couch in three long strides, sat, and laid his hat on the seat beside him.

Shifting her gaze, she caught a glimpse of her tousled curls in the fish tank's glass. She smoothed a hand over her hair, feeling exposed and vulnerable in front of Henry without the head covering of her youth. Her hand itched to grab the sunglasses again, but how silly she would look, wearing them in the house. Clasping her hands together, she turned to face her daughter.

"Beth, bring Henry a glass of water. He's been sitting out in the sun for quite a while." She hoped Beth heard the admonition in her tone.

Her mouth in a grim line, Beth disappeared into the kitchen. Soon the rattle of ice in a glass and running water let Marie know her daughter was following her instructions. She sat in the rocking chair in the corner and offered Henry a weak smile.

"It was a big. . ." Shock? Accurate, but too strong. ". . .surprise to see you in the restaurant today."

Beth entered the room, moved stiffly to Henry, and held out the water without a word.

"Thank you." He took a long draw, giving Marie a dizzying sense of déjà vu that quickly disappeared when he wiped his mouth with the back of his hand. "I probably should have called, but—"

Marie drew back, startled. "You know my number?"

He set the half-empty glass near the stack of magazines. "Lisbeth had it."

At the mention of her aunt, Marie's heart melted. Images of the sweet-faced, gentle woman filled her head. Of all the people in Sommerfeld, Marie missed Aunt Lisbeth the most. Leaning forward, she spoke eagerly. "How is she? It's been weeks since I've heard from her."

Henry dropped his gaze. "Your aunt Lisbeth is why I'm here."

His voice sounded strained. Marie's chest constricted.

"I'm going to my room." Beth turned toward the hallway.

Henry jumped to his feet. "No. Please. I need to speak with both you and your mother." He waved his hand clumsily at the couch. "If you'd care to sit, I'll explain why I've come."

Beth sent Marie a puzzled look, but she sat on the arm of the couch near the rocker. Henry remained standing at the other end, and for a few minutes he worried his lower lip between his teeth. Marie knew he was gathering his thoughts, but she sensed her daughter's impatience. She touched Beth's knee—a silent plea to sit quietly and wait.

Henry cleared his throat. "There is no good way to share bad news. I'm so sorry, Marie, but your aunt Lisbeth passed away six weeks ago."

Marie covered her mouth with her fingers, holding back the words of anguish that rushed to her lips. Dear Aunt Lisbeth. . .dead?

Beth dropped to her knees beside the rocking chair and placed her hands in Marie's lap. Tears glittered in her blue eyes. "Oh Mom, I'm sorry."

Marie blinked rapidly, managing to give her daughter a wobbly smile of thanks. Beth knew what Lisbeth meant to her. She'd named her baby Lisbeth Marie for her great-aunt. Even though the two Lisbeths hadn't seen each other since Beth was only two weeks old, Beth had read the letters that had arrived over the years, had listened to her mother's stories of time with her favorite aunt. Beth would mourn, too.

Looking at Henry, Marie choked out a single-word query: "How?"

Henry sat back on the couch. Sympathy shone in his eyes. "Her heart."

Marie nodded. The Koeppler bane.

"She'd been ill for the past two years," Henry continued in a tender voice. "The doctor warned her to slow down, but. . ." He shrugged. The gesture communicated clearly, *You know Lisbeth.*

Yes, Marie knew Lisbeth. Always busy, always giving, always smiling. Closing her eyes, she allowed a picture of her aunt to fill her mind. . .Aunt Lisbeth at the table in her kitchen, wrinkled hands kneading a lump of dough, her eyes sparkling beneath her white prayer cap. Marie swallowed the lump of sorrow that filled her throat and gave Beth's hands a squeeze. Beth slipped onto the couch, still holding one of her mother's hands.

"Thank you for coming all this way to tell me." For a moment, Marie longed to reach out and clasp Henry's hand, too. Instead, she coiled her hand into a

21

fist and pressed it to her lap. "Lisbeth always informed me of family deaths in the past, and it was hard to get news like that in a letter. It was kind of you to break this to me gently. Six weeks. . ." She shook her head. "Of course, no one in my family bothered to let me know." She made no attempt to mask the resentment in her tone.

Henry ducked his head. A few moments of silence ticked by before he met her gaze. "There's more." He glanced at Beth, his brow furrowed. "This word is for you."

Beth shot her mother a startled look.

"Your mother's aunt Lisbeth ran a little café in Sommerfeld."

Beth released a little grunt of irritation. "I know. Mom and I talked a lot about Great-Aunt Lisbeth."

Henry's gaze bounced quickly to Marie, an unreadable expression in his eyes, before returning to Beth. "I guess you also know Lisbeth never married, so she has no children."

"Yes."

Henry swallowed, scratching the hair behind his left ear. "Lisbeth and I were. . .close friends."

Marie wondered briefly if they had bonded after her unexpected departure from Sommerfeld—perhaps sharing their heartache at her decision to leave and marry Jep.

"I spent a great deal of time with her, especially when her health began to fail," Henry went on. Beth sat with pursed lips, her fingers tight on Marie's hand. "She asked me to see that her things were cared for after her death. I promised her I would. My sister, Deborah, and her daughter, Trina, have kept the café running, and I've checked her house each day to make sure nothing has gone wrong."

Beth held up her hand. "What does all this have to do with me?"

Henry continued in a calm voice, as if he had rehearsed the words a certain way and they must be delivered as planned. "Two weeks ago, at the prompting of your grandfather. . ."

Beth's fingers convulsed on Marie's hand, and Marie tightened her grip.

". . .I began to clean out the house in preparation for sale of the contents. In Lisbeth's desk, I found her will, written in her own hand. She bequeathed all of her earthly belongings to you, Beth."

Beth jerked back, her hand yanking free of Marie's. "W–what?"

Marie's heart pattered so loudly it nearly covered Henry's quiet statement.

"The café, the house, and everything inside has been left to you."

Beth's wide-eyed gaze met her mother's. "But— but what do *I* want with all that?"

Marie ignored her daughter and looked at Henry. "Do my parents know this?"

Henry's gaze dropped briefly, his forehead creasing, before he offered a nod. "I showed them the will. They couldn't deny it was what she wanted."

"They aren't protesting it?" Marie held her breath. Surely her father would fight to his own

23

death the bestowment of anything to this unclaimed grandchild.

"No, they're not."

Marie released her breath in a *whoosh*.

Beth broke into a huge smile, jumped from the couch, and clapped her hands. "Mom, this is a real windfall. Now maybe Mitch and I won't have to take out a loan to start our business after all. It's like Karma or something!"

Spinning to face Henry, she fired off a rapid explanation. "My boyfriend and I want to open an interior-design shop with one-of-a-kind antiques and specialty items. We were going to get a small-business loan, but now. . ." She paused, licking her lips. "How much do you think you'll get for the house and café? I mean, I know it's in a small town and all, but surely it'll raise at least—what?—thirty thousand? Maybe more?"

Henry rose, holding his hand toward Beth. "You need to sit down."

"I'm too excited to sit!"

Her smile lit the room, but it also cut Marie's heart. This "windfall," as Beth had called it, was at the loss of someone Marie held dear. Beth seemed to have lost sight of that.

The girl paced across the small room. "After everything is sold, go ahead and keep a little for your trouble—maybe 3 or 5 percent—then send me a check for the rest. I trust you."

Henry shook his head. "That won't do."

"Okay," Beth huffed. "Eight to 10 percent."

Henry drew in a breath. "It's not about the money."

Beth tipped her head, scowling. "Then what?"

Once more Henry gestured toward the couch. "Please, will you sit down?"

Beth sent Marie a wary look, then seated herself on the edge of the couch. Looking up at Henry, she flipped her palms outward. "Well?"

"Lisbeth included a condition in the will. Before any of the property can be sold, you must reside in it for a period of no less than three months."

"What?" Beth's voice squeaked out shrilly. She leaped up again and placed her hands on her hips, glowering at Henry. "You must be joking!"

Henry remained calm. "It's not a joke."

"Oh, this is rich." Beth laughed, but the sound held little humor. "These people I've never met kicked my mom and me out of their lives, and now I'm supposed to drop everything, move to Sommerfeld, and live with them for three months? That's the biggest farce I've ever heard of."

"Beth. . ." Marie rose and touched her daughter's arm.

The girl pulled away. "I'm sorry, Mom. I know you loved that old lady, and maybe a part of me loved her, too, just because you did. But what she's asking me to do. . . I won't do it." She pointed at Henry. "You figure some way around that ridiculous *condition*. I don't care how you do it, but get me the money without forcing me to live in that awful town."

Before Marie or Henry could respond, she dashed

down the hallway. The slam of her door echoed through the apartment. For long moments, neither of them spoke. They just stood at opposite ends of the couch, looking past each other.

Finally, Henry sighed. Without looking at Marie, he said, "If Beth doesn't fulfill the condition, the property transfers to Lisbeth's brother and sister."

A bitter taste filled Marie's mouth at the thought of her father and her aunt Cornelia sharing the proceeds. Marie wished Lisbeth had just left everything to Aunt Cornelia rather than involving Beth. It was a kind gesture, but that condition. . . It guaranteed heartache. Aunt Lisbeth must have known it would be met with resistance. Why would she place such a requirement on the acquisition?

"I'm reasonably certain you can proceed with splitting the property between Aunt Cornelia and. . ." She couldn't say the word *Dad*. She hadn't had a dad in more than twenty years. Swallowing, she finished, "Beth is very headstrong."

A brief smile flitted across Henry's face. "I can see that."

Marie laughed ruefully. "She won't give in." Even though Beth had never known her father, she had inherited many of Jep Quinn's characteristics. The tendency to act first and think second was very much like him. But even after a lot of thought, Beth was unlikely to concede to Aunt Lisbeth's requirement.

Marie didn't know what to say. There had been a time when she and Henry had spoken freely with each other. But those days were long gone, buried under years of separation. Standing in his presence now was uncomfortable. And sad.

"I'll mail you a copy of the will." Henry's low-toned voice carried a hint of regret.

"Thank you." Marie finally met his gaze. His velvety eyes locked on hers, causing an unusual patter in her heart. "It was kind of you to make the long drive," she blurted out. "I hope your family didn't mind you taking the time off."

Henry blinked twice, his sooty lashes momentarily shielding his eyes. Then he swallowed and picked up his hat, putting it on his head. "Lisbeth was my only family." Without another word, he slipped out the door.

THREE

M itch, it was the most aggravating thing!" Beth slammed her fist against her pillow. Clicking the hands-free button on her cell phone, she held the phone like a microphone and continued to vent her frustration. "Can you imagine the nerve of that guy? Standing in my living room, telling me I have to live in some tiny little backwoods town for three whole months just to claim an inheritance. It is so totally stupid!"

She jumped up from her bed and stomped back and forth across the small bedroom. "And Mom just stood there, saying nothing." A pang of guilt struck. "I mean, I kind of understand. She got a shock, finding out her favorite relative died." The ire rose again. "But still, she knows as well as I do that we aren't welcome there. Why didn't she just tell him to get out?"

From the other end of the line, Mitch's husky chuckle sounded. "Maybe because your mama is a lady, and a lady doesn't holler 'Get out' at a visitor?"

Flopping across the bed, Beth threw one arm

over her head. She pictured Henry Braun standing uncertainly beside the couch while she aimed her mace can at him, and she laughed. "You should have seen the way he was dressed—straight out of *Little House on the Prairie*."

"Oh yeah?" Mitch's voice held humor. "One of those bowl haircuts and a beard that hangs down to his chest?"

"No." Beth twirled a strand of hair around her finger. "Real short, neat haircut. And no beard. Actually a pretty decent-looking man for an older guy, except for those clothes. They made him look so. . .backward." She snorted. "Did he really think I'd go live with a whole town full of people like him? No thanks!"

Mitch's husky laughter sounded again.

She sighed. "I told him to figure out some way to sell the property and send me the money. But I doubt he'll do it. Mom said if I don't meet the condition, my *grandfather*"—she managed to make the title sound like a dirty word—"will get it all instead."

"Is that what you want?"

Beth's throat felt tight. "No! He shouldn't get anything after what he did to Mom—sending her away in disgrace, like she'd done something terrible by marrying my dad and having me." *What kind of a father disowns his child?* Beth wondered for the hundredth time.

"Listen. . ."

Beth's fingers tightened on the phone as Mitch's tone turned wheedling.

"Maybe you ought to back up and look at the big picture."

"What do you mean. . .'big picture'?"

"Now don't get riled."

"I'm not riled!"

Mitch's laugh did nothing to soothe Beth's jangled nerves. Sitting up, she growled into the phone, "I'm going to hang up."

"No, Lissie, come on—listen to me."

Beth crossed her leg and bounced her foot.

"That guy said you'd have to live in. . .what's the name of the town?"

"Sommerfeld." The word was forced between gritted teeth.

"Sommerfeld. But just for three months. You'd be out of there by Christmas. You'd have the money in hand to start our business right after the first of the year."

"But Mitch—"

"Besides, that town full of. . .what's the religious group?"

Beth huffed. "Mennonites."

"That town full of Mennonites has to be loaded with antiques. I mean, those people don't buy new stuff very often. There's bound to be tons of things you could pick up—probably for a song—to put in our boutique."

Beth stood, her stomach fluttering. "You want me to *go*?"

"Like I said, it's only three months. Drop in a bucket." His chuckle sounded again. "I could live in an igloo in Antarctica for three months if it meant gaining a pocket full of cash and a storehouse of goods for our business."

"Fine." Beth grated out the word. "I'll book you an igloo in Antarctica, and you can leave in the morning."

Mitch's full-throated laughter rang. "Oh Lissie, you are too cute."

Dropping back to the bed, Beth sighed. "I'm not trying to be. I really don't want to go to that town."

"Not even for the money?"

"No."

"Not even for the antiques?"

"No."

A slight pause. "Not even for us?"

His persuasive undercurrent melted a bit of Beth's resolve. "Mitch. . ."

"Three months, Lissie. That's not such a huge price to pay for our future, is it?"

Beth fell backward, bouncing the mattress. "You are so annoying."

Another chuckle. "But lovable, right?"

Despite herself, Beth released a short giggle. "So. . . if I go, will you come, too?"

A snort blasted. "Yeah, I can imagine how well I'd fit in there. As inconspicuous as a snake in a jar of jelly beans."

Beth giggled, thinking of Mitch's hair that curled over his collar in the back and stuck up in gelled spikes on top of his head. Not even one of those flat-brimmed black hats would make him blend in with the Mennonites if they all dressed like Henry Braun.

"But," Mitch continued, "I think you should take your mom."

Beth released a low whistle. "No way. Mom will never set foot in Sommerfeld again." Flat on her back, she stared at the ceiling, remembering the pain in her mother's eyes when she explained to eight-year-old Beth why she had no grandparents to visit at Christmastime like her friends had.

"But it would give you some company." The persuasive tone returned. "And surely she knows how to run a café after all the years she's spent working in restaurants. A working café would bring in more money than one that's sat empty for a while. She'd help you out, wouldn't she?"

"I couldn't ask her to!" Beth rolled onto her stomach and propped herself up with her elbows. "She hasn't seen her family since I was two weeks old. That's more than twenty years. Imagine how hard it would be for her to go back."

"Aw, let bygones be bygones." Mitch's flippant tone raised Beth's ire. "For the chance at maybe thirty thousand smackers, she can set aside her differences."

Beth set her jaw, allowing her lack of response to communicate her displeasure at his uncaring attitude. After a long pause, Mitch's voice came again, more subdued.

"Lissie?"

"Yeah?"

"At least ask her. There's not much mothers won't do for their kids."

Beth knew that. Mom had given up her entire life for her—sometimes working two jobs to be sure they had a decent place to live and the extras like braces and gymnastics lessons and a vacation every summer. Beth hadn't had to pay a penny for college—Mom had squirreled away enough money over the years to cover the cost of her associate degree in interior design. If Beth asked, Mom would go. But was it fair to ask?

"You gonna think about it?"

Mitch's voice jarred Beth back to the present. "Yeah." She drew in a long breath and let it out slowly. "I'll think about it."

"Good girl."

The approving tone sent a shiver down Beth's spine. He seemed to be counting the money already. "No guarantees, Mitch," she reminded him.

His chuckle, which was becoming annoying, rumbled one more time. "You know, Lissie, I think I know your mama better than you do. 'Bye, babe."

Beth stared at the blank screen on the cell phone for a long time before flipping it closed. She sat up, placed the phone on the whitewashed nightstand, and replayed Mitch's arguments. Maybe he was right. Three months wasn't that much, considering the payoff.

Beth looked around her simple bedroom with its secondhand furniture. Mom had always given her the best she could afford, even if it meant doing without something herself. How many of the clothes in her mother's closet came from Goodwill? Even though she was on her feet all day, she never bought the expensive, cushy shoes but chose discount stores so she could do more for her daughter. Mom gave and gave and gave. Maybe it was time for Beth to give back.

If Beth went to Sommerfeld and met the condition of the will, she'd be in a position to pay her mom back. Take her shopping and let her pick out an outfit that didn't come from the clearance rack. Or maybe take her on a vacation. Mom had told her how Dad promised to show her the United States from shore to shore, but she'd gotten pregnant and couldn't travel. And then of course, he'd died.

Even though Beth had never met her father, she still missed him. Mom had tried so hard all her life to be both mother and father. . .to keep Beth from feeling as though her life was incomplete. She'd done a great job, but there was that constant spot in her heart where a father's love should have been.

Beth rose and moved to her dresser, picking up the framed snapshot of her parents, taken when Mom was about halfway through her pregnancy. Dad stood behind her, his chin on her shoulder, his hands cupping the gentle mound of her belly. A lump filled Beth's throat. Her daddy would have loved her. She just knew it. And he would never have cast her aside, the way Mom's dad had done.

She set the picture down, her lips pursed, forehead creased. That old man should not get the money meant for her.

"Well," she mumbled, turning toward the

bedroom door and sucking in a big breath, "the only way to find out what Mom thinks about all this is to ask her." She headed for her mother's bedroom.

Henry pulled into the first gas station he encountered when he entered Kimball, Nebraska. Dusk had fallen, and the air had a nip in it as it whipped around the pumps and pushed at his hat. The odor of gasoline filled his nostrils, reminding him of the smell that surrounded the truck stop where Marie spent her days.

She was still pretty, he acknowledged, as he forced the nozzle into the opening of the fuel tank and clicked the handle. The modern clothing and short hairstyle hadn't been to his taste, but her blue eyes still had their sparkle, and the cleft in her chin was as appealing as it had always been.

As a young man, courting Marie, he'd wanted to kiss that little cleft, but bashfulness had held him back. Looking at her today, he'd had the same impulse. His stomach clenched. Who would have thought a man of his age would harbor such a boyish whim? It was best to put those thoughts aside. Marie had made her choice. She made it twenty-three years ago when she climbed into Jep Quinn's semi and rolled down the highway without waving good-bye.

Lisbeth had meant well, but her good intentions would accomplish nothing. Henry remembered the brief message enclosed in the envelope with Lisbeth's will, a message meant only for Henry's eyes.

If we can bring her home, home will find its way back to her heart, and she will be ours again. Yes, Lisbeth had known how Henry still felt about Marie. But Henry knew how Marie still felt about Sommerfeld. He'd seen it in her eyes when he'd given her daughter the condition for receiving Lisbeth's inheritance. Marie would not come home again.

The pump clicked off, signaling a full tank. Henry removed the nozzle, hooked it back on the pump, and closed the gas cap. Leaving the car at the pump, he went inside the convenience store. He selected his supper—a plastic-wrapped sandwich and a pint bottle of milk—and paid for it and the gasoline at the register. Ignoring the curious stares from two teenagers at the magazine rack, he returned to his vehicle, climbed in, and aimed his car east on Interstate 80. He estimated that tomorrow morning's sun would be creeping over the horizon when he arrived in Sommerfeld.

Sunrises. . . New beginnings. . . *My dear heavenly Father, being near Marie again has given my heart funny ideas. It would not bother me a bit if You were to remove all memories of her from my mind.*

Despite his prayer, the image of Marie's tousled hair, blue eyes, and delicate cleft chin refused to depart.

Marie's bedroom door cracked open and Beth leaned in, only her head and one shoulder appearing.

"Mom?"

Marie set aside her book and removed the discount-store reading glasses from their perch on the end of her nose. Patting the patch of mattress next to her knees, she invited, "Come on in, honey."

Beth crossed the floor on bare feet, her head down, long hair hanging in tousled curls over her shoulders. Maternal love swelled up, creating a lump in Marie's throat. In spite of all the regrets she carried, having and raising Beth made them all worthwhile.

Beth sat on the edge of the mattress and picked up Marie's discarded glasses, twirling the plastic frame between her fingers. "I was just talking to Mitch."

As always, mention of Beth's boyfriend made Marie's scalp prickle. She couldn't pinpoint a reason for it—the young man was intelligent, polite, and treated Beth well. But there was. . .something. "What about?"

"Aunt Lisbeth's will."

Marie nodded. "Quite a surprise, wasn't it?"

"I'll say." Beth sighed. Her head still low, she peeked at her mother through a fringe of thick lashes. "Mitch thinks I'm foolish for not meeting the condition."

Marie listened as Beth outlined all of Mitch's arguments. When Beth had finished, she asked, "And how do you feel about it?"

Throwing her head back, Beth huffed at the ceiling. "It makes me mad. I mean, it's not really fair to say, 'I'll give you this if you do that.' It's like what your dad did to you."

Marie tipped her head. "What do you mean?"

"You know—saying you weren't his daughter anymore because you chose to marry my dad and leave the community. It's putting conditions on love."

Marie nodded slowly, lowering her gaze to her lap.

"I guess what makes me madder than the condition on the will," Beth continued, her voice quavering with fervency, "is the idea of your father getting the money that should be mine."

Marie jerked her chin upward, looking at Beth's profile.

Beth turned her face, meeting her mother's gaze. She blinked several times, licking her lips. "Mom, if I decided to do what your aunt Lisbeth said—if I decided to go to Sommerfeld—would you come with me?"

Marie pressed backward against the pile of bed pillows, her hand on her chest. Beneath her palm, her heart pounded like a tom-tom. "Go. . .to Sommerfeld?"

Beth nodded. "I don't know how to run a café, but you do. We could keep it going, which would give us a little income during the months we have to stay there, and Mitch says a functioning business will raise a better price." She set the glasses aside and took her mother's hand. "Mom, I know it's hard for you to think of going there. I know there are bad memories. But the money from that café and the house can give me my dream business and let me do things I wouldn't be able to otherwise."

Marie felt as though something blocked her voice box. She couldn't find words.

"I don't expect you to answer now." Beth squeezed

Marie's hand. "Just think about it. If you say no, I'll understand, but. . ." She paused, sucking in her lips for a moment. Giving Marie's hand a final squeeze, she let go and stood.

She zipped across the room and left, closing the door behind her.

Marie stared at the closed door, all the points Beth had made ringing in her ears. Money to start the business, possibility of accumulating items for the boutique, putting Lisbeth's money into the hands she chose. . .

How Marie wanted to help her daughter. But return to Sommerfeld? A rush of memories cluttered her mind—memories she hadn't allowed to surface for years. She closed her eyes, smiling at recalled funny moments, feeling the prick of a tear at touching times. Then one picture loomed over the rest. Her father, his face set in an angry scowl, his finger pointing toward the door, his voice booming, "You made your bed, young woman. Go lie in it!"

Her eyes popped open, sweat breaking out over her body. She trembled from head to toe. Return to Sommerfeld? How could she do it? Then she thought of Beth's pleading eyes.

Marie's head drooped, as if the muscles in her neck had given way. She could not deny her daughter the means to achieve her dream. As difficult as it would be, she would return to Sommerfeld. For Beth.

Oh Lord, help me. When the words formed in her heart, she wasn't sure if they were a prayer or a command.

FOUR

Henry parked his vehicle behind Lisbeth's Café, in the alley beside the empty storage shed. There had been no room out front, all the parking spaces taken by highway visitors. He wondered briefly if Marie had been gone so long she would fail to recognize the differences between Sommerfeld residents' means of transportation and the vehicles driven by those who lived in the nearby cities.

Her little red car with the white pinstripes would certainly stick out among the Mennonites' plain, black cars. He shook his head, clearing his thoughts. What difference would it make? Marie wouldn't be seeing any of these vehicles. She and Beth had made their choice. His heart felt heavy at his failure to bring them here. Lisbeth would be so disappointed.

With a sigh, he swung open his car door and stepped out. He stood in the V made by the open door and stretched, straightening his arms over his head. His shoulders ached, and he emitted a low groan.

The slam of the café's back screen door caught his attention, and he glanced toward the simple beige block building. His niece, Trina, bustled across the ground toward the trash bins, a black plastic garbage bag in her hands. The white ribbons on her prayer cap lifted in the gentle breeze, twirling beneath her chin. She reached the bins and paused, poising her body for a mighty throw.

"Trina!" He trotted toward her in an awkward gait. His stiff legs didn't feel like moving so quickly. "Let me get that."

Trina grinned at him, her freckled nose crinkling. "Thank you, Uncle Henry. I hate hefting that thing over the edge. Sometimes I dump it on my head!"

With a chuckle, he swung the bag into the high bin, then rubbed his shoulder. "I'm too old to be sitting behind a steering wheel all night."

Trina grinned as she fell in step with him and they headed toward the café. "You aren't old, Uncle Henry."

His lips twitched as he quirked a brow. "Oh?" He touched his temple. "And all this gray hair is just pretend, huh?"

The girl laughed, slipping her hand through the bend in his elbow. "It makes you look distinguished."

Henry shook his head. "I think you're a flatterer, but thank you just the same."

They stepped into the café's kitchen, and Trina scampered to the sink, where she soaped her hands. Based on the sounds carrying in from the dining area, Henry guessed Trina and Deborah were having a typically busy Saturday morning. Deborah stood at the long stove, where she deftly scrambled eggs on the built-in grill.

Trina snatched up two waiting plates from the serving counter behind Deborah and disappeared through a swinging door that led to the dining area.

Henry crossed to Deborah. "Do you need my help?"

She barely glanced at him as she lifted two slices of ham from a tray and placed them next to the eggs. A sizzle sounded, followed by the delicious scent of smoked ham. Henry's mouth watered.

"You look like you need a long rest."

His sister's blunt comment made him grin. "Yes, I suppose I could use one. I've been up for"—he consulted the round clock hanging on the wall—"almost thirty hours now."

"Then go to bed." Deborah poked the ham slices with a fork and flipped them to the other side, then scooped the eggs from the grill with a metal spatula, sliding them onto plates.

Henry shook his head. "Not if you need me."

Trina burst through the door, her cheeks flushed. "Three orders of hotcakes, Mama. One with sausage, one with fried eggs—sunny-side up—and one with sausage and scrambled eggs."

Deborah gave a brusque nod and spun toward the tray of sausage links. Her elbow collided with Henry's midsection. She pursed her lips, shaking her head. "You're no help standing in my way. Go home and go to bed."

Trina's dark eyes sparkled as she took the plates of

ham and eggs. "She's right. You look like you're about to fall over. Get some sleep."

Henry opened his mouth to protest, but the telephone by the back door jangled.

Deborah jerked her chin toward the sound. "If you want to help me, answer that. I have hotcakes to pour."

Henry reached the phone as it began its third ring. Pressing the black plastic receiver to his ear, he said, "Lisbeth's Café. May I help you?"

After a pause, a woman's voice—soft, hesitant—carried through the line. "Is—is this Henry?"

He frowned, the café clatter making it hard to hear. He plugged his open ear with his finger. "Yes, this is Henry Braun. May I help you?"

"Henry, this is Marie."

He nearly dropped the receiver.

"Do I need to take that?"

Deborah's strident tone made Henry spin around, tangling himself in the spiraling cord. He shook his head. "No, it's for me." At Deborah's nod, he turned his back on her and hunched forward, an attempt for privacy.

"Are you there?" Marie's voice sounded again, still timid.

"Yes, I'm here." Henry cleared his throat. "What—what can I do for you?"

A self-conscious laugh sounded. "Well, they say it's a woman's prerogative to change her mind, and Beth has exercised that prerogative."

Henry's heart began to pound.

"Have you notified my. . .parents yet?"

"No." Henry swallowed. "I only just now got into town. I haven't had a chance to talk to them yet."

"So it isn't too late for Beth to meet Aunt Lisbeth's condition?"

The lump returned to his throat. "No, it isn't."

"She'll be relieved to hear that."

"I–I'm sure she will," Henry's voice squeaked. He cleared his throat. "When does she plan to arrive?"

"I expect it will take at least a week to get things squared away here, probably more like two. Do you need to know a specific arrival day right now?"

Henry shook his head, his thoughts racing. "No, of course not. But the house will need airing and a few groceries brought in. If—if you let me know a couple of days ahead of time, I'll make sure things are ready for her."

"Thank you." Her warm tone coiled through Henry's chest. "But don't go to any extra trouble. We'll bring food from our cupboards here, and I'm capable of airing a house."

Henry jerked upright. "Y–you're coming, too?"

"Yes." The word was nearly whispered. "I plan to keep the café running."

Henry looked over his shoulder at Deborah, who stood with her hands on her hips, scowling at the shelf above the grill. A satisfied smile creased her face as she yanked something down and sprinkled it over the sizzling eggs. He pictured Deborah and Marie side by side at that grill. An involuntary snort blasted.

"Henry?"

Marie's questioning tone brought him back to reality. "Yes?"

"Should I use this number to reach you?"

He rubbed his chin. He could give her the number for his shop, he supposed, but for some reason he felt the need to distance himself a bit. "Yes," he said, a niggle of guilt he didn't fully understand twisting his heart. "Deborah will get the message to me."

"All right. Thank you. I—I suppose I'll see you soon."

He wished he could guess what she was thinking. "Yes."

"Good-bye."

The line went dead. Henry held the receiver for another few seconds before slipping it onto its cradle. He looked across the room to Deborah.

She shifted her gaze to meet his, then frowned. "Henry, you're about to fall asleep leaning against the wall. Go get some rest."

He nodded, covering a yawn with his hand. "If you're sure you don't need me."

She flapped a hand at him. "Go. We'll be fine. Trina and I have found our stride."

"All right then. I'll see you later." He didn't wait for her reply, simply exited through the screen door and headed to his car. Not until he was backing out of the little parking area did he realize that Deborah hadn't even asked how his visit had gone.

"So you're really going to do it." Sally sat across from

Marie, a coffee cup hooked to her finger. "You're going home again."

The restaurant was blessedly empty after its normally frenzied Saturday. The women sat in a secluded corner booth, away from the two teenage busboys who mopped the floor on the opposite side of the large dining room.

Marie slipped off her shoes and tucked her feet beneath her. She ducked her head at Sally's comment, chuckling ruefully. "I'd hardly call it going home. That denotes some sort of waiting welcome. I doubt I'll have that."

Sally shook her head, her bleached-blond curls bouncing. "Then why do it? That girl of yours is twenty years old—plenty old enough to make the trip alone. Why put yourself through it?"

Over the years of working together, Marie had confided in Sally many times. They had both raised daughters alone, although Sally was alone due to divorce rather than widowhood. Still, the pair had shared woes and worries and laughter. Marie saw genuine concern in Sally's eyes now, and her heart expanded in gratitude.

"If she's going to keep Aunt Lisbeth's café going, she'll need me."

"Didn't you say that man's sister was running it?" Sally placed her mug on the table and played with the handle, running her finger in a circle inside the loop. "She could keep running it. You don't really *need* to go."

The feeling that had plagued Marie for the past

two weeks as she packed items and made the dozen arrangements that precede a move now returned. She didn't understand the odd longing; she only knew she had to answer it.

"Yes, I do."

Sally huffed. "Because Beth can't do without you?"

"No." Marie's voice lowered to a husky whisper. "Because I need to. . ." But she couldn't finish. Need to what? Put things to rest? Exorcise a ghost? Burn a bridge. . .or build one? She wasn't sure.

Sally reached across the table and gave Marie's hand a pat. "Listen, honey, you think I don't understand? My daddy did to me exactly what my Cindy's daddy did to her—walked out the door and never looked back. Even though yours didn't leave you physically, he left you emotionally when he sent you away."

Pain stabbed Marie's heart. Even after all the time that had passed, the heartache of that moment—when she stood in her parents' doorway with her fatherless baby wailing in her arms and saw only condemnation in her father's eyes—was as sharp in remembrance as it had been in the living.

Sally tugged her hand. "You're going back there to see if he's changed his mind, aren't you?"

Marie sighed. "Maybe."

Sally took another sip of her coffee, her lowered gaze pinned to Marie. "Well, three months isn't so long, I suppose. A person can bear just about anything for three months."

Marie smirked. "Even handling this place without my help?"

"Humph." Sally plunked her empty mug on the table. "Did you see the replacement Jimmy hired? Can't be more than nineteen and barely a hundred pounds dripping wet. I'll be doing all the lifting and serving while she stands at the counter and flutters her eyelashes at Jimmy all day."

"Oh Sally." Marie shook her head, smiling at her friend. "At least I know you'll miss me."

"You know I will."

"Thanks for letting Cindy sublet my apartment."

Sally flapped a hand in dismissal. "Oh, that was nothing. It was time for her to spread her wings a bit, find out what it's like not to have Mom around to pick up her dirty socks and pay her phone bill. It'll be a growing experience for her."

"I wouldn't trust anyone else to feed my fish and take care of my furniture." Marie quirked one brow. "She *will* feed my fish and take care of my furniture, won't she?"

Sally laughed. "She's not perfect, but she is kind to animals and isn't a vandal. I'm sure your fish and furniture will be fine."

"Good."

Sally's brow creased. "Marie, can I give you a word of advice?" All teasing had left her tone.

Marie shrugged, offering a silent invitation.

"Be careful. I know it's been a long time, but those hurts haven't completely healed. If you go there with the expectation of being brought back into the fold, and your daddy tosses you aside again, you're going to have open, bleeding wounds."

Marie shook her head, forcing a smile. "Now didn't I just say I don't expect a big welcome?"

"Yes, that's what you said," Sally countered, her eyes flashing. "But saying and believing are two different things." She leaned back, pinning Marie with her steady gaze. "And I know you pretty well, my friend. You and me—we're a lot alike. Underneath, we're still little girls looking for our daddies' approval."

Even though she tried not to think about it, Marie knew Sally was right. The absence of her father's love was a hole that had never been filled.

"Does he know you're coming?"

A weight settled on Marie's chest. "I'm sure he does. Henry told both my father and my other aunt that Beth would be claiming her inheritance. As to knowing *when* I'm coming. . ." She shrugged. "That depends on whether Henry shared my arrival time with my parents. I only called him at noon today. I didn't want him going to a lot of extra work to get things ready for us." A smile tugged at her cheeks. "You see, in Sommerfeld, people don't do physical labor on Sunday. And I didn't leave him anything but Sunday to prepare for us."

"Sneaky." Sally winked, grinning impishly; then her expression sobered. "So. . .what time will you pull out tomorrow?"

"By six, if I can get Beth out of bed." She sent Sally a knowing grin. "It's a ten-hour drive without stops, and I want to be there before it's dark if possible."

"Well, I can see why!" Sally whistled. "Living in a house with no electricity. . ." She patted her hair.

"I'd never survive without my blow-dryer and hot rollers."

"Oh, but a person can bear *anything* for three months." Marie threw out the teasing comment, her lips twitching in a grin.

Sally laughed, reaching across the table to clasp Marie's hand. "And I forgot—you don't need to worry about your hair because the ladies all wear those little bonnets." She tipped her head, examining Marie's hair. "I just can't picture you in one of those things."

Marie touched her head, trying to recall the feel of the starched organdy cap. Too much time had passed—the memory eluded her.

"Can I take those?" One of the boys approached their table, pointing at the coffee mugs. "Gonna do the last load of dishes now."

"Sure." Sally handed them over, then sighed. "We should get out of here anyway. It's been a long day, and tomorrow promises to be longer. At least for you."

Marie nodded, locating her shoes beneath the table. She slipped her feet into the comfortable leather loafers and rose, extending her arms toward Sally. The women embraced, the hug lasting several seconds, with Sally rocking Marie back and forth.

When they finally pulled apart, Sally tweaked Marie's chin. "Now, do like I said—take care of yourself. Don't expect too much. Bide your time, get that inheritance for your girl, and come on back here and rescue me from that bodacious young'un Jimmy brought on board."

Marie laughed as Sally slipped her arm around

her waist. They walked to the parking lot together. At Marie's car, they hugged again. "I'll see you shortly after the new year," Marie said, a lump in her throat.

Sally nodded. " 'Bye, Marie."

The words were delivered on a light note, but something in Sally's expression as she backed away from Marie's car left Marie feeling as though her friend believed the good-bye was not a temporary one.

FIVE

Henry closed the window over the kitchen sink. Turning around, he leaned against the counter, raised his face, and sniffed deeply. He gave a brief, satisfied nod. Allowing in the crisp fall breeze had done wonders. The house no longer held the scent of neglect.

Heading into the small dining room, he walked through the path made by the late-afternoon sun slanting through Lisbeth's hand-sewn lace curtains. The glow highlighted the layer of dust that coated every surface. The open windows had freshened the air, but now he had a new problem to fix.

With a sigh, Henry returned to the kitchen and scavenged under the sink for a dust rag. He shook his head as he dusted Lisbeth's furniture, wishing he'd used better sense. Uncovering all the furniture had felt like such an accomplishment, but if he had left the sheets in place until after airing the house, he could have simply carried the dust away when he removed the coverings. That was something a woman would have considered, he was sure.

Despite having been the caretaker of his own home for the past twenty-some years, he still found little joy in housekeeping. But complaining didn't make the work go any faster. With another sigh, he turned from the sideboard, which housed Lisbeth's plain, white dishes, to the oak table and chairs. Pulling out one chair, he swept the dust rag over every inch of its surface, humming to fill the quiet. Trina, bless her heart, had asked permission to help him ready the house, but her father had firmly denied the request.

"Sunday is a day of rest," Troy Muller had scolded his daughter. Then he'd given Henry a stern look, as if he should know better.

Henry squirmed, remembering the embarrassment of the moment. Yes, Sunday was a day of rest—and he rarely abused the fourth commandment—but what else could he do? Marie hadn't let him know until yesterday noon that she and Beth would be leaving the next morning. That had only given him Saturday evening to prepare for her arrival. It wasn't enough time.

Besides, he assured himself as he headed down the short hallway to Lisbeth's sewing room, he had waited until after church service to come finish the tasks. Certainly the Lord understood he was performing a mission of mercy. Two women, tired from a long drive, wouldn't have the energy to do the cleaning necessary to make the house livable.

Running the rag across the top of the waterfall

bureau, he scowled. Turning a slow circle, he looked for the photograph album and basket that used to rest on the bureau. They were nowhere to be seen. He opened drawers and peeked into the closet, but the items weren't there. His brow puckered as he contemplated where they might be.

A knock at the back door interrupted his thoughts. His heart skipped a beat as he trotted to the kitchen. Was Marie here now? He began forming words of greeting, but when he peeked through the curtain, he recognized Deborah.

Surprised, he swung the door wide. "What are you doing here?"

She held up a casserole dish covered by an embroidered tea towel. "I brought you our leftover supper." Charging past him, she plunked the dish on the counter. Hands on hips, she glared at him. "I'm sure you haven't taken the time to eat."

He pushed the door closed. "Not yet. I planned to eat when I finished here."

"Men." Deborah shook her head. "What were you doing?"

Henry waved the dust rag, creating a cloud. He sneezed. "Dusting."

Deborah's eyebrows raised. "With that?"

Henry looked at the rag, then back at his sister. He shrugged.

Heaving a sigh, Deborah held out her hand. "Give me that. All you do with a dry rag is push dust around." When he handed the rag over, she pointed at the casserole and said, "You eat while I dust."

After slamming a few cupboard doors, she located a can of furniture polish. Turning, she spotted him still standing beside the counter. "I said eat!"

Henry laughed. "Does Troy know you're here?"

"Of course. As if I would take off without telling him where I was going."

"Does he know you're working?"

With a sour look, Deborah marched through the door that led to the dining room. He heard her muttering, and he couldn't help smiling. Deborah had always been like a toasted marshmallow—crusty on the outside but soft underneath. Although he felt a twinge of guilt, he appreciated her taking over the dusting task. He retrieved one of Lisbeth's forks from a drawer, pulled a stool to the edge of the counter, and helped himself to the creamy chicken-and-rice casserole.

While he ate, he let his gaze rove around the homey kitchen. Lisbeth's penchant for bright colors was showcased in the embroidered muslin curtains bearing red strawberries and green vines. A matching stamped pattern of berries and vines decorated the white-painted cupboards and walls. He frowned when his gaze encountered the little table crunched in the corner of the kitchen. It had always worn a red-and-white-checked cloth. Where might that have been tucked away?

And where were those photographs? Raising his voice, he called, "Deborah, do you remember the picture album and the little basket Lisbeth kept on the bureau in her sewing room?"

A grunt came in response. Henry interpreted it as a yes.

"They aren't there now. Do you know where they went?"

Deborah stuck her head through the doorway. "How should I know? Ask her family—they're the ones who arranged the service."

Henry nodded, thinking back to the day of Lisbeth's funeral. Had the album and letters been there that day? He couldn't remember.

"Where's Lisbeth's broom and dustpan?"

Deborah's brusque question brought him back to the present. He swallowed and stood. "On the inside of the door leading to the basement. I'll get it."

"No. Stay there and finish. I just want to sweep the front room."

"I did that last night," Henry said.

She raised her brows but didn't speak. Obviously he hadn't done it well enough. She disappeared again.

Henry ate as quickly as he could, rinsed the casserole dish and fork, then headed to the front room in time to catch Deborah shoving the couch against the wall. He moved her out of the way and repositioned the couch himself. "You even swept under this thing?"

"Well, certainly. Those dust bunnies always manage to come out of hiding when you least want them to."

Henry brushed his palms together and glanced around the room. In the minimal sunlight remaining, the room looked as neat as it had when Lisbeth Koeppler lived. How many evenings had he spent in this room, visiting with her? She'd been like a second mother to him. His heart twisted as a pang of loneliness struck.

Deborah headed toward the back of the house, broom in hand. She called over her shoulder, "Do the sheets on the bed need to be changed?"

Remaining in the front room, Henry replied, "No. I took care of that yesterday."

"Where did you find clean ones?" The sounds of running water and a cupboard door opening and closing accompanied her words.

"In a chest in Lisbeth's bedroom."

There was an odd clatter, and then Deborah's voice came again. "If they were shut up in a chest, they probably smell musty."

"I took them outside and threw them over the line to air them first."

Deborah didn't respond. He plodded through the house to the kitchen, where he found her washing the casserole dish. She glanced up when he stopped beside the counter. "Light a lamp. I can't see in here anymore."

"Will you need it? There's only that one dish and fork."

Wordlessly, she reached into the soapy water and held up a handful of silverware. "I dumped the drawer full in here. Hated to waste the water."

Henry lit the lamp he had set on the small kitchen table and carried it to the counter.

Deborah released a little snort. "How do you think our city dwellers will survive without electricity?"

Henry opened a drawer, seeking a tea towel. On top of the neat stack of towels, he found the checked tablecloth. He draped it over the table while answering his sister. "Marie's family didn't have electricity when she was growing up, so it won't be new to her." Returning to the drawer, he grabbed a towel and began drying the silverware Deborah placed in the dish drainer.

"Maybe, but it's been awhile. And that girl of hers. . .she won't know how to act."

Henry remembered Beth's reaction when she found him standing in her living room. He smiled. "Oh, I suspect she'll find a way to adapt."

"Where will she sleep? Lisbeth only had one bed."

"I put a cot in the sewing room." The cot had come from his own basement—he kept it on hand for when he hosted summer sleepovers with his nephews. "It doesn't look too bad with one of Lisbeth's quilts over it." He had chosen the red-and-white patchwork quilt with calico hearts embroidered in the centers of selected white squares. It had always been Marie's favorite of the stack in Lisbeth's linen closet.

Deborah shot him a pointed look. "You look forward to their arrival, don't you?" Her voice held a note of accusation.

Henry shrugged, dropping dry forks and spoons into the plastic tray in the silverware drawer. "I don't know what I feel. I just know it's what Lisbeth wanted."

Deborah slammed another handful of silverware into the drainer. "What Lisbeth wanted. . . It would have been better if she'd just given everything to J.D. and Cornelia rather than stirring up this trouble."

Henry paused, leaning against the counter to stare at his sister. "What trouble?"

Deborah didn't look at him. "You know what I mean." She swished her hand through the water and grabbed another spoon. "That girl of Marie's coming here to sell the house and café. I think it's shameful."

"J.D. and Cornelia would have sold it, too," Henry pointed out. "How is that different?"

"It just is!" Deborah snapped out the words. "J.D. and Cornelia had a right to it. This girl. . .Beth. . . she's never even been here!"

Henry could have reminded his sister that it wasn't Beth's fault she hadn't been here, but he knew it would only cause an argument. Instead, he repeated softly, "It's what Lisbeth wanted."

Deborah jerked up the sink plug and watched the water swirl down the drain.

Henry dropped the last fork into the drawer, hung the damp towel on a rack above the sink, and gave Deborah a one-armed hug. "Thank you. Marie and Beth will appreciate this."

She stepped away from him, her expression grim. "I didn't do it for Marie and Beth. I did it for you." She pointed at him. "And you remember something, Henry. Marie has been in the world for a long time. She's not the girl we once knew. I know what Lisbeth was trying to do here, but I have every confidence that three months in Sommerfeld will do little more than make her all the more determined to get away again. Don't—" Her voice cracked, her expression softening. She dropped her hand and sighed. "Don't let yourself get hurt a second time, Henry. Please?"

"Deborah—"

She snatched up her casserole dish and headed for the door. Over her shoulder, she ordered, "Things look fine in here now. Go home."

***

"Mom, stop at the next gas station, huh? I need a break."

Marie stifled a sigh. "Honey, it's less than an hour to Sommerfeld. Can't you last that long?"

Beth huffed. "I need to go to the bathroom, okay?"

"Well, if you'd lay off the sodas, maybe you wouldn't need a bathroom every half hour." Marie tried to inject humor into her tone, but she was aware of a biting undercurrent.

Apparently Beth heard it, too, because she snapped, "I also need to stretch my legs. I'm tired of sitting."

Marie was tired of sitting, too. She and Beth had traded off driving during the day, but most of the time she'd been behind the wheel. The tug of the small trailer of belongings attached to the back of their car made Beth nervous. Marie's nerves had been frayed, as well—mostly from the early-hour last-minute packing and from having to listen to Beth's lengthy cell phone conversations with her boyfriend. Marie was just about ready to snap.

She held her tongue, however, recognizing that

a large part of her unease was due to what waited at the end of their journey. The closer they got to her childhood home, the more the knot in her belly twisted. Despite Sally's warning, she recognized a small glimmer of hope that someone—Mom or Dad, or one of her brothers or sisters—would be waiting at Lisbeth's to welcome her back. She knew it was unlikely, maybe even ridiculous, and she did her best to squelch the niggling thought. But it hovered on the fringes of her mind, increasing her stomachache with every click of the odometer.

"There's a station." Beth pointed ahead.

Marie allowed the sigh to escape, but she slapped the turn signal and pulled off the highway into the station. Beth hopped out the moment the car stopped and dashed inside. Marie got out more slowly and walked to the hood of the car. She stretched, glancing across the landscape.

An unwilling smile formed on her lips. In the west, the sun had slipped over the horizon, but the broad Kansas sky gave her the final evidence of its bright presence. Deep purple clouds, undergirded with fuchsia, hung high on the backdrop of cerulean blue, and airy wisps with brilliant orange rims hung close to the horizon.

Beth stopped beside her mom's shoulder. "What are you looking at?"

Marie pointed. "The sunset. I'd forgotten how beautiful they could be. Aunt Lisbeth always said there was nothing like a Kansas sunset. She was right."

Beth smirked. "You're not going to get all sentimental on me now, are you?"

Marie shot her daughter a sharp look. "There are worse things than being sentimental. Being insensitive is one of them."

Beth rolled her eyes, and Marie's gaze dropped to her daughter's hand, where she held a super-sized fountain drink. "You said it's just another hour. This won't kick in until well after we get there." Beth's teasing grin eased a bit of Marie's tension.

She gave her daughter a playful tweak in the ribs. "Let's go. We're almost there."

SIX

"Well, there it is."

Beth sat up straight in the passenger seat, blinking rapidly to clear the sleep from her eyes. Peering out the window through the dusky light, she caught a glimpse of a sign advertising harness making—*harness* making? Then the vehicle made a sharp left off the highway. Sure enough, there was the town. Sommerfeld. Hardly a town at all, really.

"This is Main Street." Mom sounded as though her tonsils were tied in a knot. The car slowed to a crawl. The headlights illuminated the double-wide, unpaved street.

Main Street. . .unpaved. Beth swallowed a disparaging comment.

Mom pointed to the first building on the left-hand side of the street. "There's Lisbeth's Café. . . now Beth's Café." She grinned, then shook her head, sighing. "My, the hours I spent there when I was a teenager. . ."

My unexpected inheritance. Beth leaned down to

squint through the driver's-side window. The evening gloaming and absence of streetlights made it difficult to make out details, but the café appeared to be a rock building, two stories high, fronted by a brick sidewalk. Startled, she glanced right and left. All the sidewalks were brick.

And not a soul was in sight. Anywhere.

She whistled through her teeth and fought off a shiver.

"What's wrong?" Mom's voice dropped to a whisper, adding to the eerie feeling of being in a ghost town.

"Where is everybody?"

Mom shrugged. "It's Sunday. They're all at home. I told you Sunday is a day of rest."

"Yeah, but. . ." Beth shook her head. The highway traffic less than a half mile to the south, contrasted against the absolute inactivity of the town, was too bizarre.

"Over there is my brother Art's business." Mom pointed to the right.

Out loud, Beth read the sign above the door of the large wooden building. "Koeppler Feed and Seed— Quality Implements and Agricultural Products." Turning to her mother, she whistled through her teeth. "This is wild, Mom. It's like being on a movie set for a Western."

Mom laughed softly. "Well, it is unpretentious. But it's hardly the thing movies are made of."

Beth nearly wore out her neck looking back and forth as Mom made a left turn followed by a second turn one block farther. They drove in silence past two blocks of residential houses, most of which appeared to have been constructed in the earlier part of the twentieth century, increasing Beth's sense of stepping back in time.

The car finally pulled into the dirt side yard of a quaint bungalow with a high-peaked roof and a railed porch that extended halfway across the front and around the north side.

At first glance the house appeared dark, but as their car pulled around to the back, a pale yellow light glowed, gently illuminating the window at the northwest corner. Mom stopped the car behind the house and shut off the ignition. Then, with a huge, heaving sigh, she stared at the building.

"Well, this is it. Your new home sweet home." She sat, unmoving, her hands gripping the steering wheel.

Beth frowned. "Are you okay?"

Mom's laugh sounded forced. "As okay as an old lady can be after driving thirteen hours straight." She rubbed the back of her neck and yawned. The action seemed feigned. "I sure hope that light in there means somebody has made up the bed. I'm not sure I have the energy to do it myself."

Both women climbed out of the car and walked toward the back porch. A black iron gaslight stood along the grassless footpath from the dirt driveway to the house, but it wasn't burning, leaving the path dark. Mom stepped onto the wood-planked porch and twisted the doorknob. "Locked."

Beth tipped sideways, trying to peek through the door's window. "What'll we do?"

For a moment Mom stood there, staring at the knob. Then she bent over to lift the corner of a plastic mat in front of the back door. She held up a key and offered a weak smile. "Just like always."

Beth gaped. "Outside? Where anyone could find it?"

Mom laughed again, the sound more authentic this time. "You're not in the city anymore, Beth. Things are. . .different here." She turned the key in the lock, pushed the door open, then gestured for Beth to enter.

Beth stepped into a dimly lit, narrow room with doorways springing in all directions. She slid her hand along the wall beside the door. "I can't find the light switch."

Mom stepped in and closed the door. "Honey, I told you. No electricity. Follow the glow."

The glow, as Mom called it, came from the open doorway along the north wall. Beth walked through the doorway and found herself in a simple kitchen with white painted cabinets and a small, round table covered with a cheerful red-and-white-checked cloth. A cordless lamp sat on the countertop, sending out a meager amount of light. The only light in the entire house.

Beth shook her head. "Primitive."

Mom moved past her but stopped at the table. She fingered the cloth, her face pinched. After a moment, she released the tablecloth and picked up the lamp by its handle. Smiling in Beth's direction, she said, "Shall we explore?"

With a shrug, Beth followed her mom around a corner and into the dining room. A square wooden table flanked by four chairs filled the center of the uncarpeted floor. A glass-front cabinet holding simple white dishes stood along the west wall—the only other piece of furniture in the room.

Beth resisted another shiver, her feet echoing on the hardwood floor as she trailed behind her mother through a wide doorway to what was obviously the living room. A couch sat beneath one window, with a small wood table on spindly legs at one end. Beside the little table sat a curved-back rocking chair. Mom crossed to it and sat down, placing the lamp on the table. The lamp clearly lit Mom's face. Although she seemed pale and her eyes looked tired—or sad?—a smile curved her lips.

"This was Aunt Lisbeth's favorite seat." Mom's hands caressed the worn arms of the rocker. "When I was little, I used to run in here and climb into it before she could, just to see her put her hands on her hips and scowl at me. She could make the fiercest face while her eyes just twinkled, letting me know she was only teasing. And I would scowl back." She laughed softly. "I wouldn't have dared to scowl at any other adult, but Aunt Lisbeth was different." She stared across the room, seemingly lost in thought.

Beth sank onto the couch. It was stiff and the fabric scratchy, unlike the cushiony velvet sofa at home. "Mom?"

A few seconds passed before her mother turned to look at her.

"If there's no electricity, how will we get heat in here?"

Her mother looked disappointed by the question. Another lengthy pause followed before she pushed off the rocking chair. Picking up the lamp, she said, "Follow me."

She led Beth back through the dining room, through a different doorway, ending in the utility porch. Swinging open a door, she pointed. "There's a coal-burning furnace in the basement. That's what heats the house." She sniffed, and Beth did the same, inhaling a thick, musty odor. "Someone already has it going, but if you're cold, I'll go put in some more coal."

Beth peered down the dark, wooden stairs and shook her head. "No, that's okay. I'll just put on a hoodie." She hugged herself, knowing the chill came from something more than the temperature of the house. "It looks creepy down there."

Mom smiled. "We'll have to go down eventually anyway. Want to see how the furnace works?"

Beth gave an adamant shake of her head. "No thanks!"

"All right, then." Mom closed the door and faced Beth. "Let me show you Lisbeth's bedroom—there's only one bedroom, so we'll have to share the bed."

Beth made a face. "Great."

Mom sighed. "Beth, I tried to prepare you for all this before we came, but you didn't want to talk about it, remember? You said you preferred to find out everything when you got here rather than get scared enough to change your mind. Now that we're here, I'd rather you didn't complain constantly."

Beth threw her hands outward. "Who's complaining?"

Mom looked at her with one eyebrow raised and her mouth quirked to the side.

"Okay, okay, I'm sorry. I know you said it would be simple, but I had no idea. . . . How did you live like this? Coal-burning furnaces, no lights, everything so. . .bare."

"I suppose when you don't know any different, it doesn't seem like a hardship." Heading for the back door, she said, "Why don't we get our suitcases and then I'll show you the bedroom? And the bathroom. I imagine by now your pop has kicked in."

Beth recognized the teasing note. She matched it, clasping her hands beneath her chin in a mock gesture of supplication. "*Pleeease* don't tell me the bathroom is actually an outhouse."

Mom laughed, and her curls bounced as she shook her head. "Oh no, we have indoor plumbing."

"Well, let's be grateful for small favors." Beth followed her mom outside. The cool air nipped at her, carrying a fresh scent very different from that of home. A rustle overhead followed by a flapping indicated some kind of night bird took flight from the trees, and Beth involuntarily ducked. Yet when she looked upward, seeking the location of the bird, she found herself mesmerized by the endless expanse of sky.

She'd never seen so many stars, and the plump

three-quarter moon appeared as bright as a halogen against the velvety black. "Wow."

Mom swung a suitcase from the back of the trailer and paused, peering upward. She smiled. "Oh yes. With all the city lights, a person forgets how brilliant the stars truly are." She took in a deep breath, released it slowly, and said, " 'The heavens declare the glory of God; and the firmament sheweth his handywork.' "

At her mother's wistful tone, Beth jerked her gaze to look at her. Mom's eyes glittered as brightly as the stars. Suddenly uncomfortable but not sure why, Beth forced a hint of mockery into her voice. " 'Sheweth'?"

Mom gave a start, looking at Beth sheepishly. "Oh." She laughed lightly. "Something I memorized as a child. Funny. . ." She nibbled her lower lip, her gaze returning to the sky. "I haven't thought about that in years."

Beth waited, her arms folded around her middle. Her mother stared upward, a smile barely tipping the corners of her lips. What was Mom thinking— remembering? For some reason, Beth felt afraid to ask.

After a long while, Mom released an airy sigh, then aimed a bright smile in Beth's direction. "Well, let's get these suitcases inside and unpacked, huh? The rest can wait until tomorrow and sunlight."

Marie pulled the stiff sheet and chenille spread to her chin and stared at the ceiling. From down the hall, a series of squeaks indicated Beth wiggled on the cot. An odd warmth filled her face as she thought about that cot. The second, smaller bedroom had always been Lisbeth's sewing room. Someone had taken down the folding table she'd used to cut fabric or lay out quilt squares and put up the cot, obviously for their use. And she knew who had done it.

When she'd called yesterday, Henry had been eating lunch in the café, so Deborah had called him to the telephone. He had sounded dismayed when she'd said she and Beth would be coming the next day. She could still hear his startled, "But there's no time for preparation." That had been her intention— she hadn't wanted him to feel obligated to get things ready for her. Then he'd asked, "Do you remember Lisbeth only has one bed in her house? Will it work for you and your daughter to share?"

Marie's hesitation before replying that it would be fine no doubt communicated her true feelings about having to bunk with Beth. He must have brought in the cot. And covered it with the bright heart-appliquéd quilt Marie had always loved. Did he remember her preference for bright colors when he'd fixed up the cot?

Her chest felt tight, and she pushed that thought away. How silly to take a trip down Memory Lane. Yet she couldn't deny being in Lisbeth's house, being in Sommerfeld, was tugging her backward in time.

She closed her eyes, her body tired, yet her mind refused to shut down. Outside, under the stars, the Bible verse from Psalms had slipped from her mouth so easily. She couldn't remember the last time she'd quoted a scripture. Yet it had happened effortlessly, as if it had been lying dormant, waiting for an opportunity to present itself.

When she'd first pulled into the yard and seen the light glowing from the kitchen window, her heart had leaped with hope that maybe—*maybe*—someone would be in the house waiting to greet her, to hug her, to welcome her back. But the locked door had let her know no one was around.

The disappointment of that moment stabbed like a knife. Hadn't Sally told her not to expect too much? Yet underneath, an ever-so-hesitant glimmer of hope resided, only to be snatched away by a locked back door. No, no one had been waiting.

Except God.

Marie's eyes popped open. What made her think that? " 'The heavens declare the glory of God.' " She whispered the words into the quiet room. A feeling of comfort followed. A feeling she little understood and was too tired to explore.

"Well, if You're around, God," she muttered with a touch of belligerence, "You might let me get some sleep. It's been a long day, and I've got my work cut out for me tomorrow with cleaning this house and carting in the stuff Beth and I brought."

How strange it felt to speak to God that way, the easy way Lisbeth had always spoken—out loud, without pretension. The way one would talk with a neighbor over the fence. Another constriction grabbed her chest, making her breath come in little spurts. Squeezing her eyes shut, she pushed aside the emotions straining for release and willed herself to sleep.

"Mom?"

The soft voice brought Marie to full attention once more. A shadowy figure stood beside the bed, reminding Marie of the days when Beth was little and would wander in, awakened by a nightmare. "What's wrong, honey?"

"I can't sleep. I'm tired, but it's so quiet here. It's creeping me out."

Marie understood. She scooted over. "Climb in. We'll share tonight, huh?"

Beth slipped in and curled onto her side, facing her mother. "I heard you talking."

Marie's heart caught. "Oh?" She chuckled softly. "I guess I was planning out loud. Lots to do tomorrow."

In the muted shadows cast by moonlight, Marie saw Beth nod. "Do you think I should go to the café tomorrow, or can it wait?"

"It can wait if you want to. It's never open on Mondays."

A long sigh came from Beth's side of the bed. "I guess I should have asked questions before we came. But I was right—I wouldn't have come if I'd had any idea. . . ."

"You know, it really isn't that bad," Marie's voice snapped out more tartly than she'd intended. Why was she so defensive? Sommerfeld was no longer her home. Based on the fact that no one was here to greet them, her family was no longer hers either. So why tell Beth it wasn't bad?

More kindly, she added, "It's only three months, honey. Think of it as. . .an adventure." She smoothed Beth's hair away from her face. "Who knows, maybe someday you'll write a book about all this."

Beth laughed, pressing her fists beneath her chin. "Who would believe it?"

"Truth is stranger than fiction."

Another laugh. "Oh yeah."

Marie sighed. "Close your eyes, honey. Get some sleep."

Beth's eyes slipped closed. They lay in silence for several minutes before Beth's voice came again. "Mom?"

"Yes?"

"Thanks for coming with me."

Marie smiled and gave Beth's hair another stroke. "You're welcome."

"I wouldn't want to be doing this alone."

"Well, no worries. You're not alone."

Although Beth finally drifted to sleep, Marie lay awake, gazing out the window at the starry sky, her words to her daughter echoing through her heart. *"No worries. You're not alone."*

SEVEN

Marie carried in a box of groceries and set it on the cluttered counter. Looking at the boxes already there, she realized she had been responsible for bringing in each one. Aggravation rose. Was Beth on her cell phone. . .*again?*

Hands on hips, she bellowed, "Beth!"

"In here."

Marie followed the voice and found her daughter in the dining room, lying under the table, flat on her back. Bending forward and propping her hands on her knees, she peered at her. "What in the world are you doing?"

Beth's ponytail lay across the floor in tangled disarray. "Checking out this table. It's solid wood, Mom. I can't even find any nails—just pegs. It's amazing!"

Marie squatted down between two chairs to peek at the underside of the table. "Do you see a brand anywhere—symbols burned into the wood?"

Beth twisted her head, her gaze seeking. Her face

lit up. "Yeah! Right there!" She pointed. "It looks like a K with an O at the bottom right-hand edge." Looking at her mom, she wrinkled her brow. "What does that mean?"

"It means your great-grandfather and great-great-uncle constructed it." Marie straightened and got out of the way as Beth scrambled from her hideaway. "My mother was an Ortmann. Her father joined forces with my father's uncle to open a furniture-making shop." Marie headed through the kitchen, Beth on her heels. "I would imagine if you went door to door around here, you'd find quite a few pieces with that brand."

"When did they start their business?" Beth followed Marie outside to the trailer.

Marie handed a box to her daughter and scowled thoughtfully. "Hmm. Grandpa Ortmann was born in 1907, I believe, and he started the business in his early twenties. . .so maybe the late 1920s?" It felt good to share a bit of family history with Beth. She picked up a box and turned toward the house.

Beth plodded up the back porch stairs and through the utility porch door, which Marie had propped open. "Then that table would be more than seventy years old." Beth's tone turned calculating. "Definitely antique, and certainly unique. I need to do some exploring on the Internet to figure out its value."

Marie put her box on the kitchen table, staring at her daughter. "You're planning to sell it?"

Beth gawked over the top of the box she held. "Well, yeah. I mean, that's why I'm here, remember?

To claim all this stuff, sell it, and open my antique shop." With a light laugh, she added, "Duh!"

"Don't get sassy." Marie spun on her heel and headed outside again.

Beth trotted up beside her. "What are you getting so huffy about?"

Marie stopped and whirled on Beth. She opened her mouth, but nothing came out. Beth was right—what was she getting huffy about? The only reason they were here was to meet the condition of Aunt Lisbeth's will, lay claim to everything, sell it for whatever Beth could gain, and get out. Why was she feeling territorial? She sighed and touched Beth's cheek.

"I'm sorry, honey. I didn't sleep very well last night, and I'm tired and cranky. I didn't mean to take it out on you."

Beth's smile returned. "That's okay. I understand." She moved to the end of the trailer, her ponytail swinging. "This afternoon, while I get my computer set up and figure out how to connect to the Internet, you can nap." Then she spun around, her face set in a frown. "I just realized. . .no electricity and no phone line, so no way to connect." She released a disgruntled *uh*. "This really stinks!"

Marie put her arm around her daughter's shoulders and gave a squeeze. "There's a phone line at the café and all the electricity you could need. We'll rig it up over there, okay?"

"Whew!" Beth brightened again. "Thank goodness the café is halfway modernized." Grabbing a box, she moved toward the house. "Speaking of the café, I'm hungry. Can we find something to eat?"

Marie followed Beth into the kitchen. "Let's get some of this stuff put away so we have moving-around room, and we'll have some cold cereal. We'll have to do simple meals until I can remember how to operate Aunt Lisbeth's stove."

The sound of a knock made both women spin toward the utility porch. Marie's heart leaped into her throat. They'd come! Her family was here! She raced through the utility porch to the back door to find Henry Braun in the open doorway. Her hopes plummeted once more.

"Henry."

He took off his hat and offered a smile, apparently unaffected by her flat greeting. "Good morning, Marie. I see you're hard at work."

She took in his neat appearance—crisp twill trousers and dark blue shirt tucked in at the waist, clean-shaven chin, and hair combed smoothly into place. She ran a quivering hand over her tousled waves, aware of how disheveled she must look in faded jeans and an old sweatshirt. As heat filled her face, she decided it was good it wasn't her father at the door— he'd surely disown her a second time if he saw her like this.

A worried frown creased Henry's forehead. "Are you all right?"

Ducking her head, she released a rueful chuckle. "I'm fine. I just. . ." Shaking her head, she pushed aside the jumble of emotions her disappointment had inspired, met his gaze, and forced a smile. "Come on in. I can't offer you coffee or anything. . . ."

Henry remained in the doorway between the kitchen and utility porch. "That's fine. I've had my breakfast."

"Well, we haven't," Beth said, transferring cans of vegetables from a box to an upper cabinet. "And we won't be able to eat decently until Mom figures out the stove."

"It's powered by propane." Henry took a step into the room. "I'm sure there's still some in the tank. Do you want me to get the stove started for you?"

"That would be great. . .if we have something here to cook." Marie looked at Beth. "Have we brought in the ice chest?"

"I haven't."

Henry turned and headed for the back door. "I'll bring it in."

Marie hurried after him. "You don't have to do that."

He didn't look back as he tromped down the porch stairs. His broad shoulders lifted in a brief shrug. "It's not a problem. I came by to see if you needed anything. Carrying in an ice chest is a simple thing to do."

Marie stood at the tail of the trailer while Henry ducked and stepped inside. He took hold of the ice chest and dragged it to the opening. Back outside, he stood upright and grinned at her. "That's heavy. Did you put your refrigerator in there, too?"

Marie slapped a hand to her face. "Refrigerator!

Is Aunt Lisbeth's still—"

"In the basement," Henry said. "And it operates on a generator, same as always."

"Beth will love that. She's so fond of the basement." Marie grabbed one end of the ice chest and Henry took the other. She grunted as they lifted it.

They struggled up the stairs and into the house. Henry turned backward to get through the doorways. In the kitchen, his gaze bounced from the tabletop to the counter; both were scattered with boxes.

"Let's just set it on the floor," Marie suggested.

"Are you sure you don't want it downstairs, by the refrigerator?"

Marie lowered her end. "I'm not carrying that heavy thing down the basement stairs. And neither are you. I'd rather make several trips."

Henry released his end with a nod. "I can help you."

They both straightened, their gazes connecting. Marie felt a blush building again and wished she felt less self-conscious. She wouldn't feel comfortable until he left. "That's all right. I'm sure you have things to do."

She was right—Henry did have things to do. Albrecht's tractor still didn't sound quite right when he fired up the engine, and Henry's fingers itched to fiddle with the carburetor until the engine purred. But, he reasoned, Mr. Albrecht could wait another day or so. Who else would help Marie?

He had been so certain when he pulled into the yard he would find other vehicles here—family members come to assist in unloading the women's things and getting them settled. Her parents and siblings knew she was back. He'd made sure he told all of them after she called on Saturday. So where were they? Indignation built in his chest at their standoffish behavior. Had J. D. Koeppler forgotten the parable of the prodigal son? Where was Marie's hug of welcome, the fatted calf?

"I have nothing more important than helping you right now," he insisted, offering a smile to let her know he meant it.

"Have him show you how to start the stove," Beth inserted, "or I'm heading down the highway until I find a McDonald's."

Henry kept his smile aimed at Marie. "I'm afraid it would be a lengthy drive. Salina and Newton are the closest towns with fast food, and they'd both seem pretty far away when you're hungry." He stepped around Marie, heading for the stove. "Did you try to light a burner?"

"Yes." She leaned against the doorframe. "I do remember how to start a propane stove. When it wouldn't light I just assumed it was out of propane."

He nodded. "I turned it off at the valve. I didn't want propane leaking into the house." With a heave, he tugged the stove forward a few inches. The feet screeched against the linoleum floor, and Beth covered her ears. He sent her an apologetic smile. "Sorry." Reaching behind, he found the valve and gave a few twists. Then he pushed the stove back into place. "Hand me a match, please."

Beth removed a match from the tin matchbox holder hanging above the sink and gave it to him. He twisted the knob to start the front left burner. A hiss let him know gas crept through the lines. He struck the match, held it to the burner, and was rewarded by a circle of blue flame.

"Hurray!" Beth clapped her hands. "Okay, Mom, I'll have eggs over easy and toast."

Marie and Henry exchanged grins. Marie said, "Then Henry had better start the oven."

"Oven?" Beth pulled her brows low. "For eggs and toast?"

Henry's lips twitched with amusement as Marie explained.

"For the toast. I'll have to put the bread under the broiler—we can't plug in a toaster, you know."

The girl's eyes rolled upward in a manner Henry had witnessed from his nieces. He turned his back and opened the ice chest, pretending to hunt for an egg carton, before he let loose the chuckle that pressed at his chest.

"Isn't there some way to get electricity here?" Beth pulled out a kitchen chair and sat. "I saw power lines in town, so *somebody* has power."

"Many of our residents have electricity," Henry said. "None of our Amish neighbors do, but nearly all of the Mennonites have chosen to use it."

Marie lifted Lisbeth's iron skillet from the drawer in the bottom of the stove and set it on the burner. Moving to dig through one of the boxes, she glanced at him. "Well, then, how hard would it be to have an electrical line run to the house for this former Mennonite's use?"

The words "former Mennonite" pinched Henry's heart. He was glad Lisbeth didn't hear it—it offered proof that Marie had fully released her childhood faith. He watched Marie pour a scant amount of oil into the pan and spread it around with a metal spatula. "The line to the house would be simple. Wiring the whole house to receive the current would be the hard part."

Marie grimaced, her lips pooching into an adorable pout. "Of course. How foolish of me." She broke eggs into the skillet and a cheerful sizzle sounded. "I'm sorry, honey, but we're going to have to put up with things the way they are. It hardly seems worth the expense and effort to wire the whole house for three months."

Henry ducked his head at Marie's blithe words.

"But won't we get a better price for the house if it's wired for electricity?" the girl argued.

Marie sent her daughter a frown. "That's an expense we don't need right now, Beth. Let the next owners worry about it."

Beth sighed. "Oh all right. But don't plan on me hanging around here much. I'll spend my days at the café, where at least I can access the Internet and listen to a radio." Another sigh released. "No television for three months. Torture!"

Marie laughed, but Henry thought it sounded strained. He looked at Beth. "I'm sure you'll stay busy enough with the café that you won't miss television too much. But if you need entertainment—"

"Oh please!" Beth held up both palms as if warding off a blow. "Don't tell me there's cow-milking and corn-shucking contests!"

Marie spun around, her face flaming. "Beth!"

The girl's wide, blue eyes blinked in innocence. "What? It was just a joke."

Turning back to the stove, Marie flipped the eggs, but her lips remained set in a grim line.

Henry glanced between the two before completing his statement. "Once or twice a month, the young un-married people of our community rent the skating rink in Newton and spend the evening there. Maybe you'd like to join them. You could get to know your cousins that way."

Beth opened her mouth. Marie shot a warning look in her direction. The girl closed her mouth for a moment, her eyes sparking, then gave Henry a sweet smile. "I'll give that some thought."

"Butter the bread, Beth. The eggs are done." Marie scooped eggs onto plates and put them on the table. "Henry, would you like me to fix you an egg, too?"

"No thanks." Henry backed up to get out of Beth's way as she bustled across the kitchen with a loaf of bread and a butter knife in her hand. He reached into the ice chest and pulled out the butter tub.

"Thanks." Beth took the butter and sat at the table.

Henry remained near the doorway, waiting until Marie sat next to Beth. They didn't pray before they picked up their forks. He cleared his throat. "Tell you what, while you eat, I'll empty the rest of your trailer."

Marie half stood, holding her hand toward him. "You don't need to do that."

He waved at her. "It's not a problem. There doesn't seem to be much left. Sit for a while. You've earned it." He hurried out the door before she could offer another argument.

Most of the boxes left in the trailer were labeled either Mom or Beth. Those with Mom, he stacked outside Lisbeth's bedroom; those with Beth outside the sewing room. The few with no label he left on the utility porch. With each journey between trailer and house, his frustration with Marie's family grew. Why hadn't any of them shown up to help?

Based on J.D.'s scowling response when he'd been informed his long-lost daughter was on her way, Henry wasn't surprised that Marie's father wasn't here. But neither her brother, Art, nor her sister, Joanna, had responded negatively. In fact, he was sure Joanna's eyes had lit with happy expectation. So where were they?

He put the last box on the utility porch, then returned to the trailer to close it. After snapping the latch into place, he turned and found Marie standing a few feet away. The morning sun slanted across her face, highlighting her creamy complexion and bringing out the strands of gold in her tousled nutmeg curls. She looked tired.

"Do you have to take the trailer back today?" he asked, to keep from asking something more personal.

"Yes. By noon to avoid another day's rent. But I

only have to take it to Newton, so I have time yet."

He nodded, then lowered his gaze. They stood silently for a few minutes. He shifted his foot, digging his toe into the dirt. Head still down, he said, "I can unpack some boxes for you if you'd like."

"No. No, you've done plenty."

He glanced at her. She met his gaze directly. A shy smile played on the edges of her lips. "Did you fix up that bed for Beth?"

"Yes."

"That was very thoughtful. Thank you."

He shrugged. "It wasn't so much. Just a cot and some bedding I found in Lisbeth's linen closet."

"The quilt—"

"—was on top of the stack," he said, watching the toe of his boot make an indention in the dirt. "I hope it was all right."

A slight sigh sounded. He sensed disappointment, and he thought he understood the reason for it. She needed remembrances from someone. But it was better if they didn't come from him. She needed her family.

Backing up a step, he waved at his car. "I'd better get out of your way so you can get this trailer out of here."

"Thank you again, Henry. For everything."

He read gratitude in her fervent gaze. Swallowing, he nodded. "You're welcome. Oh!" Digging in his pocket, he retrieved a key ring and held it out to her. "This is for the café. The key with a number one on it unlocks the front door, two unlocks the back door, and three is for the storage closet inside."

She took the ring and fingered each key in turn, seeming to examine the numbers etched into the metal. Eyes downcast, she said, "Thank you."

"You're welcome. Have a good day, Marie. And welcome home."

Her cheeks flooded with pink, and she ran her hand through her curls. He was sure he saw a glint of tears before she blinked and the shimmer disappeared. "Thanks. You have a good day, too."

She turned and headed back toward the porch, her shoulders slumped. Henry slid behind the steering wheel and shook his head. Before he went to his shop, he had another errand to run.

EIGHT

Beth looked up when her mom returned to the kitchen. Wordlessly, Mom dropped a silver key ring next to Beth's plate, the keys sending out a subtle *ting* as they hit the table. Beth picked them up and turned in her chair to follow her mother's progress to the sink, where she washed her hands.

"What are these for?"

"The café. Front door, back door, and storage closet."

Beth smirked, dangling the ring from one finger. "Oh. So they don't keep the café's keys under the doormat?"

Mom offered a weak smile in response. Drying her hands on her pant legs, she faced Beth. "I've got to take the trailer to the rental place in Newton. I can drop you off at the café with your computer so you can get started trying to connect to the Internet. No guarantees you'll find anyone who will provide service here, but I'd think at least one of the dial-up companies would be able to help you."

Beth rose slowly, holding out her hand to indicate the unpacked boxes. "Don't you want me to stay here and get this mess cleaned up?"

Mom shrugged. "We can do that this evening. I know you feel cut off from the outside world. Wouldn't having Internet connection help?"

Beth bounced across the floor and gave her mother a hug. "You're the best, Mom! Thanks."

Mom returned the hug, then set Beth aside. "Yeah, well, you'll be rethinking that this evening when I'm cracking the whip to get all this stuff put away."

Beth laughed and followed her down the hallway to the bathroom. Mom picked up her hairbrush from the edge of the old-fashioned porcelain sink and ran it through her locks, creating some semblance of order.

"Seems kind of silly to get it all put away when we won't be here that long," said Beth.

Mom sent a brief scowl in Beth's direction. "I will not live out of boxes—not even for three months. While we're here, we might as well make things as homey as possible."

Beth shrugged. "Whatever. Should I change before going to the café? Do you think anyone will be offended by my stunning attire?" She struck a pose in her long-sleeved T-shirt and trim-fitting blue jeans.

Mom quirked her brow, her lips twitching. "I doubt anyone will stop in. It's never been open on Mondays. Besides, you should do whatever feels comfortable."

Beth tugged at the hem of her shirt. "This is comfortable."

"Okay, then." Mom moved past her to her bedroom and came out again, purse in hand. "Grab your laptop."

"And my boom box!"

Mom shook her head, chuckling. "Let's go."

An hour later Beth had put the café's telephone to good use by arranging service with an Internet provider that was delighted to finally have someone from Sommerfeld as a customer. They guaranteed she'd be up and running by the middle of the week. Her cell phone was recharging, and her boom box provided background noise. Her telephone calls done, she puttered around the café, becoming acquainted with her new property.

Everything was so *plain.* Walls painted white, with not even a wallpaper border or paneling to break the monotony. White square tiles bearing gray speckles covered the floor. The wide glass windows that stretched across the front of the café at least wore curtains—blue gingham café-style, with little gold plastic loops attaching them to the gold metal rods that divided the windows in half. She stepped onto the front walk to check out the front of the café in the sunlight, but the curious looks from passersby sent her scuttling back inside.

Perched on the edge of the black vinyl seat of one of the high-backed wood booths that lined both sides of the eating area, Beth kept her back to the window. Fifties-style tables and chairs filled the center of the room. Leaning forward, she skimmed her fingertips over the sheeny surface of one table, thinking of a diner back in Cheyenne that had similar tables. In that restaurant, with LPs and music-industry memorabilia decorating the walls, the tables had seemed retro. Here they just seemed out-of-date.

"I suppose," she mused aloud, "someone might consider these trendy. Maybe I should cull a few for my boutique."

The back screen door slammed.

Beth jumped up. "Mom, I'm glad you're back," she said, charging toward the doorway that led to the kitchen. "Guess what? I got—"

She came to a halt when she spotted a teenage girl in the kitchen. Her pulled-back hair covered with a little white cap and the yellow gingham dress that hung just below her knees marked her as Mennonite. Beth nearly giggled when she spotted the girl's white athletic socks and leather sneakers. The footwear seemed out of place with the rest of the outfit. Of course, despite her shoes, she fit the whole town better than Beth ever would.

Beth caught the hem of her shirt and pulled it over the waistband of her low-slung jeans. Meeting the girl's gaze, she offered a self-conscious smile. "Hi. The café isn't open."

The girl giggled, her brown eyes sparkling. "Oh, I know. I waited tables for Miss Koeppler before she died. And my mom and I have kept it going the last couple months. But I saw the lights on and figured someone must be in here, so I thought I'd come introduce myself. I'm Trina Muller." She crinkled her nose. "Well, actually Katrina. But I've always preferred Trina. My grandpa calls me Katrinka." The girl looked toward the radio as an inappropriate lyric blasted.

Beth scuttled over and flicked the OFF button. "Sorry about that." She grimaced.

The girl shrugged. "You didn't select the programming, did you? So don't apologize." She stepped closer to Beth, a warm smile lighting her face. "You must be Marie Koeppler's daughter, but I don't remember your name."

Beth slipped her fingertips into her jeans pockets and leaned against the counter, hunching her shoulders. "Mom named me Lisbeth after her aunt, but I've always gone by Beth."

"Ah." The girl giggled again. She sure was a happy thing. "So you have a nickname, too."

"My boyfriend calls me Lissie," Beth blurted out.

Trina's brown eyes nearly danced. "Did you know my uncle was your mom's boyfriend before she left town?"

This was intriguing. "Who's your uncle?"

"Henry Braun."

Beth's jaw dropped. She straightened, her hands slipping from her pockets. "You mean the Henry who came to tell me about. . . ?"

Trina nodded. The little ribbons that dangled from her cap bounced with the movement. "He and Miss Koeppler—your great-aunt Lisbeth—were very good friends. They both loved your mom a lot. Neither one ever seemed to get over her leaving with that truck driver and not coming back after he died."

That truck driver has a name, Beth's thoughts defended. *Jep Quinn*. She folded her arms across her chest, her heart pounding. "She would have come back if it weren't for my grandfather."

Trina lost a bit of her sparkle. "Oh, I know. My uncle Henry always hoped—"

The screen door slammed again. A tall woman in Mennonite attire stepped across the threshold. Trina looked over her shoulder, and her face flamed pink. She linked her fingers together and pressed them to her ribcage, a smile quivering on her lips. "Hi, Mama."

"It's like Grand Central Station around here," Beth muttered. *Hadn't Mom said this place would be empty on Monday?*

The woman stormed in, her chin held high, her gaze pinned on Trina. Without so much as a glance in Beth's direction, she let loose a tirade that made Beth's ears burn. "Katrina Deborah Muller, you were to go directly to the grocer and home again. I can see from your empty hands that you never even made it to the grocer. What are you doing in here talking to. . ." She waved a hand in Beth's direction, still without looking at her.

Some deviltry made Beth reach out and shake that waving hand. "Hi. It's nice to meet you. I'm Lisbeth Quinn, but you can call me Beth."

The woman jerked her hand free. A brief upthrust of her lips masqueraded as a smile. "I am Deborah Muller." She spun back to her daughter. "To the grocer's, Trina, and then home. We'll discuss this more thoroughly later."

Trina scurried toward the door.

"Good-bye, Katrinka," Beth called. "It was very nice meeting *you*." She emphasized the last word enough to give Trina's grumpy mother a not-so-subtle message.

Trina sent a quick, impish grin over her shoulder before slipping through the door.

Her mother started to follow but then turned back. "Will you and your mother be handling the café starting tomorrow, or do you prefer to have some help?"

Beth wanted to snap back that she and her mother would be just fine, thank you very much, but she managed to think before she spoke. "If you and Trina are willing to continue for a few more days—to give Mom and me time to settle in and learn the ropes—it would be very helpful." She didn't add a thank-you.

Deborah Muller nodded brusquely. "Very well. The café opens at 6:00 a.m. I am always here by five. I'll see you then." She zipped out the door before Beth could reply.

Five a.m.? Beth groaned. She stomped to the door and peeked out. The alley was empty. Good! Maybe that would be the last of the visitors. She smiled, remembering Trina's grin. How old might the girl be—fifteen? Sixteen at most, probably. A little too young to become a friend, Beth decided, but good to talk to. . .if she would keep her comments about "that truck driver" to herself. And not mention Mom's old boyfriend. Henry Braun and Mom. . . Beth closed her eyes for a moment, remembering Henry's attentiveness and offers to help this morning. Mom had greeted him warmly and invited him in. . .which was more than Beth could remember her mother doing with any man in all of her growing-up years.

A frightening thought straightened Beth's spine. Surely Mom didn't still harbor feelings for that Mennonite man. The idea left her vaguely unsettled, but she snorted and pushed the notion aside. Mom was here to help her, plain and simple. Beth puffed out a breath and shook her head. No sense getting worked up over nothing.

The café seemed too quiet after the Mullers' brief visit. She clicked the radio back on, turning up the volume loud enough so the dining room vibrated with the beat of the music. She grinned. That should keep anyone else from venturing in! Leaning on the counter that held the cash register, she plucked up a menu and examined the café's offerings, humming with the music. When someone tapped her on the shoulder, she released a squawk and nearly threw the menu over her head.

Mom's laughter rang. "I wouldn't have been able to sneak up on you if you didn't have that noise cranked so loud." She covered her ears with her hands. "Can you turn it down?"

Beth zipped around the counter and slid the volume bar to the lowest level. "I'm so glad you're back." She gave her mother an impulsive hug. "It's been lonely here, except for my intruders." Briefly, she described her visits by Trina and Deborah. "That woman!" Beth huffed. "She acted like I had leprosy or something. I know we'll need her help for a while— at least until we get the hang of things here—but I wanted to just drop-kick her out the back door."

Mom stretched her lips into a grimace. She sat on a stool next to a long, metal counter and sighed. "We'll need to continue using Deborah, if she'll stay. We won't be able to run the café ourselves."

"Why not?" Beth slumped against the counter. It felt cold against her hip, and she shivered.

"Honey, I can wait tables and order supplies. But I can't do the cooking. I've never cooked in a restaurant before. And unless you want to learn how to do it. . ."

"Oh boy." Beth heaved a huge sigh. "You mean I'm going to be with her every day?"

Mom chuckled softly. "Deborah isn't that bad. She's just always been a little. . .bossy."

Beth raised one eyebrow and tipped her chin.

Mom laughed. "Okay, a lot bossy, but we'll need her expertise if you're serious about keeping the café going. Or"—she lifted her shoulders—"we can close it and bide our time."

Beth sighed. "It's tempting, but Mitch said a working café will bring in more cash. One that has sat closed will have to rebuild its customer base."

"Are you sure about this?"

Beth grinned. "Since when do you let me make such important decisions?"

"Since you became the recipient of an extensive estate."

"Oh yeah." Beth grimaced, flipping her hands outward to indicate her surroundings. "Quite the estate."

Mom rose from the stool and turned a slow circle, her gaze wandering around the quiet kitchen. "Actually, honey, this is a precious gift. This was Aunt Lisbeth's life. Essentially, she's given you everything she valued." Her tone turned wistful, her eyes misting. "It might not seem like much by the world's standards, but to her. . ."

Beth put her arm around her mother's shoulders. "It's hard for you to be here, isn't it?"

Mom blinked rapidly and shook her head. "No. I have a lot of good memories from here. I spent nearly every day with Aunt Lisbeth from the time I left eighth grade until I married your dad. In fact"—she quirked a finger—"come with me."

Beth followed her mom to the dining room, to the table closest to the front door. Mom pressed both palms against the tabletop. "Right here is where your dad was sitting the first time I saw him." She closed her eyes and arched her neck, smiling as she relived some important moment. "He caught my eye. . . ." Opening her eyes, she grinned at Beth. "Even though I knew better than to flirt, I was human enough to enjoy boy-watching. And your dad made boy-watching a pleasure."

Beth sat at the table and rested her chin in her hands. "Tell me about it."

"Oh honey, I've told you a hundred times how I met your dad."

"So make it a hundred and one." When Mom

still hesitated, Beth affected a pout. "Pleeease?"

With a deep-throated chortle, Mom sat across from Beth and imitated her pose—elbows on the table, fingers cupping her face. "Well, when he came in, he was all sweaty. Hair drenched, clothes soppy. . . I could tell he'd been in the sun far too long."

"And you brought him a glass of ice water, which he guzzled in three seconds."

"Yes. So I immediately brought him a second glass, and he looked at me—"

"—and winked and said, 'A girl who knows a man's mind—what a rare find.' "

Mom pulled back, lowering her brows. "Hey, who's telling this story?"

Beth giggled. "Okay, I'll be quiet."

Mom rested her chin in her hands again and grinned. "Even though fraternizing with outsiders was frowned upon, he was impossible to resist. He was so handsome and friendly. . .and so *stuck*." She laughed, her eyes twinkling. "His semi had broken down, he had no way to leave, and the café was the only place in town to hang out."

Beth, remembering the next part of the story, frowned. "Mom, why didn't you ever tell me Henry Braun was your boyfriend?"

To her amazement, Mom's cheeks blotched red. "Who—who told you that?"

"Based on your reaction, it must be true." Beth folded her arms on the tabletop. "You told me Henry fixed Dad's engine, but you never mentioned you were dating him."

Mom dropped her gaze, running her fingertips along the chrome edge of the table. "It wasn't important. And we weren't dating." She shook her head, wrinkling her nose. "At least, not the way you and Mitch are dating. We were just. . . He and I. . ." Releasing a huff, she said, "There was never any formal agreement between us."

Beth thought about Trina's statement that Henry never got over Mom's leaving. Maybe there hadn't been a formal agreement, but Henry must have been serious. "Still, it had to have been weird for him. You know, fixing Dad's semi so he could get back on the road, then seeing you leave, too."

"I suppose." Mom shifted her gaze, seeming to peer out the window.

Suddenly curious, Beth leaned forward. "Do you ever wonder what your life would have been like if you'd stayed? You know, if you'd married Henry instead of Dad?"

Mom jerked her gaze around, her eyes wide. "No."

Beth snorted. "Oh, come on. Be honest."

Mom became very interested in a scratch on the tabletop, her brows furrowed as she ran her fingernail back and forth in the furrow. "In all honesty, Beth, no. When I left Sommerfeld. . .the second time. . ." Briefly, her gaze bounced up to meet Beth's before returning to the scratch. "I never looked back. I didn't *let* myself look back. It was too painful, I guess. I wouldn't be here now if—"

The sound of a clearing voice intruded. Beth looked toward the kitchen. Henry Braun had pushed back the swinging door that separated the kitchen from the dining room. He stood framed in the doorway, and a second man—older, with bushy gray eyebrows and a stern face—stood behind him, peering over Henry's shoulder with a frown. The older man stepped around Henry and took a step into the dining room.

Mom gasped, and Beth shifted her attention to her mother. Her face had gone white. One hand rose to smooth her hair, and her throat convulsed.

Beth looked again to the gray-browed man and understanding dawned. She stood. "Hello, Grandfather."

NINE

Henry waited for J. D. Koeppler to move fully into the room, to return Beth's greeting. But the man stood as if rooted to the tile floor, glaring at his daughter.

Marie stood slowly, her palms on the tabletop as though she needed its support. She licked her lips and blinked several times. "H–hello. . .Dad." Her glance flitted toward her daughter, then returned to J.D. "I'd like you to meet your granddaughter, Beth."

J.D. gave a single nod, his face impassive. Henry considered grabbing the man's shirtfront and propelling him across the floor with a command to say something. But J.D. was known for his stubbornness—any pushing would only make him resist more. The tension in the room increased with every second that ticked by, and a silent prayer filled his heart. *Please, Lord, let someone speak. Let someone reach out.*

But the prayer went unheeded. Instead, it appeared that everyone had turned to stone, resembling a tableau—*Family at Impasse*. Beth stood with her head at an arrogant angle, her narrowed gaze aimed somewhere to the left. Marie seemed to hold her breath, her wide-eyed gaze on her father's face. And J.D. stared back, his carriage stiff.

Beth shifted, an odd grin creasing her face. She approached the doorway, swaying her blue-jean-covered hips in a way that emanated defiance, and held out her hand. "How nice to finally meet you. It's been. . .what? Twenty-one years? Yes, that seems to be about right, give or take a month or two. I believe I was all of two weeks old when you saw me last." She released a brittle laugh. "Of course, I have no memory of that, and since you've made no effort to be a part of my life, well. . ." She raised her shoulders in a shrug that lifted the hem of her shirt, showing her belly button and a tiny silver ring.

Marie jerked to life as J.D.'s frown deepened. She rushed forward a few feet, her hands clasped at her waist. "Beth, please. . ." Her whisper carried over the sounds coming from the radio in the kitchen.

Beth swung her gaze in her mother's direction and held her hands out. "Did I say something untrue? This *is* the man who refused to help you raise me after my dad died, isn't he?"

J.D. finally took a step forward, his eyes blazing beneath his bushy, gray brows. "If I had helped raise you, you would have more respect for your elders." Wheeling on Marie, he gestured to Beth with one hand. "Haven't you given your daughter any training?"

Marie opened her mouth, but Beth jumped in. "My mother has given me plenty of training. She's taught me to always do my best at whatever I do, to be truthful at all times, and to treat others the way I want to be treated." The girl crossed her arms and tipped her chin up, sending a saucy look in J.D.'s direction. "Seems to me you forgot that third one when Mom came to you needing help twenty years ago."

Marie put her hand on Beth's arm. "Honey, this isn't the time—"

Beth pulled away. "Then when is the time, Mom? Look at him!" Beth pointed to J.D., her finger mere inches beneath the man's firmly clamped jaw. "Look at his face. He doesn't want us any more now than he did then."

Henry glanced at grandfather, daughter, and granddaughter. Three different emotions displayed on three faces. Stoicism on the eldest's, resentful anger on the youngest's, and what could only be defined as deep hurt on that of the one caught in the middle.

Marie's throat convulsed as if she fought tears, and Beth snorted. Crossing her arms again, she glared at her grandfather. "Well, don't worry, *Grandfather*. We're not here to stay, so you won't have to put up with our unwanted presence for long. As soon as our time is up and I've got the money from the sale of the house and this café in my pocket, we'll be out of your life. And I guarantee we'll never bother to darken your doorstep again."

The girl charged for the doorway, forcing J.D. to

move aside or be run down. She paused at the back counter just long enough to snatch a little silver telephone from its cord, then stormed to the back door. There, she spun briefly to send one more glare in J.D.'s direction. "I'm going back to my house to put a big X on the calendar." Her lips twisted into a snide leer. "One day down. Eighty-nine to go." Then she slammed out the door.

Marie started after her. "I'd better show her the way back."

Henry caught her arm. "It's a small town. She'll find it. And it will do her good to walk off some of that anger."

Tears welled in Marie's eyes, but she blinked them away. "You don't understand. That isn't anger. I know it seems like it, but underneath it's. . ." She looked at J.D. Recrimination flashed in her eyes. "It's a lifelong hurt. From being rejected."

J.D. raised his chin. His eyes narrowed into slits. "*You* rejected *us*."

Marie's jaw dropped. "What? Dad, I didn't reject you."

"You chose that truck driver over your family!"

"I fell in love!"

J.D. reared back at the volume of her statement. Henry's heart launched into his throat.

Marie took a deep breath, and when she spoke again, her voice was under control. "I fell in love with Jep. I wanted to spend my life with him."

Henry shifted backward, a feeble attempt to separate himself from Marie's earnest words.

"I didn't leave with him to get away from you. I just. . .left."

In an instant, a scene from the day of Marie's departure flashed through Henry's mind. A rumbling semi, a man waiting behind the wheel, and Marie beside the open door, confusion on her face.

"Yes, you left. You left your family, your home, and your faith." J.D.'s growling accusation dispelled the memory.

Marie shook her head. A tear slid down her cheek, and she dashed it away with a swipe of her hand. "I didn't. Not at first. I went to a meetinghouse; I honored my beliefs. Yes, I lived somewhere other than Sommerfeld—I was with my husband. But you know all that because I wrote to you. I tried to include you in my life. I didn't *leave* anything until you made me." Sadness underscored her weary tone. "Not until after Jep died and Beth was born and I asked for your help. And you refused to give it. You gave me no choice but to leave, Dad."

"And this is what you choose?" J.D. flicked the short curls over Marie's right ear with work-worn fingers, a contemptuous sneer on his face. "Shorn hair and an uncovered head? Clothing that—"

Henry held up both hands, unable to stay silent a moment longer. "Stop this! What are you accomplishing here?"

J.D. pointed at Henry. "You brought me here. You said I should go see my daughter. Well. . ." His gaze swept from Marie's head to her feet and back again. "I've seen. I come here, out of the goodness of my heart, and all I receive is disrespectful backtalk and blame for her foolish choices." He shook his head, releasing a snort that sounded very much like the one Beth had made. "This is not the girl I raised. This is a woman of the world—a woman who intends to return to the world. And I have no reason to stay here."

He spun on his heel and thumped to the back door. He slammed through without a backward glance.

Henry looked at Marie. He expected tears, but none came. Her face was white, her blue eyes wide, her chin quivering. But she held her emotions inside. His heart ached for her. "Marie, I'm sorry."

She moved stiffly to the noisy box on the counter. She clicked something, and the raucous tune halted midscreech, abandoning them to an uncomfortable silence. Her shoulders slumped. For long seconds she remained beside the counter, head down. He stayed in his spot beside the dining room door, uncertain what to do.

With her back still to him, she finally spoke. "You have no need to apologize, Henry. You meant well, bringing him here. And I admit, when I saw him, I hoped. . ." She sighed, lifting her head as if examining the ceiling. Her nutmeg curls graced her tense shoulders. Turning slowly, she met his gaze. All sadness was erased from her expression. She simply looked resigned.

"I'd better go check on Beth. Thank you for. . ." She swallowed, giving a shake of her head. "Thank you." Moving toward the door, she said, "Would you lock up when you leave?" She didn't wait for his answer but slipped out the door. In a moment he heard her car's engine fire up and then the rumble of tires on gravel as she pulled away.

Henry remained in the middle of the silent café, hands in pockets, heart aching. "Lisbeth, it isn't working."

* * *

Marie found Beth at Lisbeth's house. As Henry had predicted, she'd found her way just fine. But judging from the way she was slamming clothes onto hangers and smacking them into the closet, the walk had done nothing to drive out her hurt and anger.

Marie understood Beth's pain. Her chest felt laid open, her heart lacerated and bleeding. She leaned against the doorframe of Lisbeth's sewing room and crossed her arms. "Hey."

Beth barely glanced at her mother. Her lips were pressed in a tight line. She whammed another hanger onto the wooden rod. "Don't tell me I shouldn't have spoken to him like I did, because I won't apologize."

"You're an adult, not a child. You can decide when you believe you owe someone an apology."

"If anyone owes anyone an apology, *he* owes *us* one. Standing there looking at us as if we were scum." She rolled a T-shirt into a wad and slam-dunked it in a dresser drawer. "Couldn't even say hello after two decades of ignoring us. Who does he think he is anyway, some sort of god?"

Beth paused, hand raised to place another hanger in the closet, and released a huge sigh. Plunking the hanger into place, she turned to face her mother. Tears glistened in the corners of her eyes. "Why does he hate me so much? What did I do to him?"

"Oh honey." Marie rushed forward, her arms outstretched. But Beth eluded her, sidestepping to reach into a box and pull out a sweater. Marie folded her arms across her middle, giving herself the hug she longed to give her daughter. "He doesn't hate you, Beth. How could he? He doesn't even know you."

"And he doesn't want to." The harsh undertone returned. She held the sweater at arm's length, frowning at it. "At least I have a few memories of Grandpa Quinn. Of course, after Grandma died and he moved to Florida, we didn't see much of him. But he was around for a while anyway. It's not like he *disowned* me."

Beth's flippant tone spoke clearly of the hurt she tried so valiantly to conceal with a facade of anger. Marie battled tears as she listened to her daughter share her thoughts.

"But your father. . .and the people in this town. . . That's a different story." Beth popped the sweater onto a hanger but then just stood, holding it two-handed against her ribs. She sucked in her lips, her brow creased. Suddenly she whirled to face Marie. "It's because Dad wasn't Mennonite, isn't it? I'm like a. . .a half-breed to them."

Marie sank onto the cot, causing it to squeak with her weight. She ran her finger around the edge of the neatly appliquéd heart nearest her hip. In her mind's eye, she saw Aunt Lisbeth's veined hand guiding the needle through layers of cloth. A smile tugged at her lips. And then another hand flashed in her memory: her father's hand reaching for her head to flick her curls. She flinched, pushing aside the thought.

"There's so much. . .history. . .behind my father's feelings, Beth. I'm not sure I can explain it in a way that will make any sense."

Beth put the hanger in the closet, then sat on the floor cross-legged. Folding her hands in her lap, she turned her hardened gaze on her mother and barked a one-word command. "Try."

Marie pursed her lips, organizing her thoughts. "I suppose the simplest explanation is this. Outsiders bring in new ideas that don't match the teachings of the church. The church's doctrine is very important. We are to be separate from the world—peculiar, even. When others look at us, we want them to see an outward difference that leads them to the heart, where Jesus resides."

"I don't like it when you say 'us,' like you're a part of them, too."

Marie's heart turned over at her daughter's belligerent tone. "I say 'us' because it's my heritage. Yours, too, even though you weren't raised with it." Beth's frown didn't encourage Marie to continue that line, but she added, "It isn't the doctrine that's wrong here, honey, but the extreme to which it's carried by a few."

Beth scowled. "What I remember about Jesus from

Sunday school is that He was loving to everybody. If Jesus resides in a heart, shouldn't a person's behavior show that? I sure didn't see much lovingkindness in the way your dad treated us today."

Marie turned away, pain stabbing with the reminder of her father's stern, condemning posture. She sighed. "Yes, *Christian* means *Christlike*. And sometimes people don't do a very good job of emulating Him." Turning back to Beth, she leaned her elbows on her knees and clasped her hands together. "But you can't let the way my father treated us today make you think ill of all Christians or all Mennonites. That wouldn't be fair."

Beth pushed to her feet. She flipped her ponytail over her shoulder and reached for another sweater. "Of course not. That would be like your father thinking all non-Mennonites are horrible people. I sure wouldn't want to be like that."

Marie sat in silence, watching as Beth emptied the box of clothing, then reached for a second box. When Beth continued to work without looking in her direction, she finally sighed, rose from the cot, and moved to the doorway. "Well, I guess I'll go make us some sandwiches."

"I'm not hungry."

"Well, then—"

"My phone's recharged. I'm going to try to reach Mitch again." Beth closed the door in her mother's face.

Marie stood for a moment, staring at the wooden door, battling with herself. She understood Beth was upset. Angry. Hurt. When Beth was little and had a problem, Marie had always insisted she talk it out until they reached a workable solution. But now? She wasn't sure they would find a solution to this situation if they talked from now until New Year's. Her father was set in his ideas and unlikely to change.

She'd never thought about it before, but J. D. Koeppler and Beth were a lot alike—both headstrong, unwilling to bend. A humorless chuckle found its way from Marie's chest. She supposed neither would appreciate the comparison. Through the door, she heard Beth's voice and assumed the cell call had gone through. With a sigh, she headed to her own room to put away her clothes. She really wasn't hungry either.

TEN

Marie wiped her hands on the calico apron that reached from her bodice to below her knees. As had been the case more than twenty years ago, commuters from the surrounding smaller communities on their way to their jobs in the larger cities pulled off the highway to enjoy breakfast at Lisbeth's Café. The place had bustled with activity from six on. Now, at nine thirty, the breakfast rush was over, and she welcomed a moment to lean against the counter and catch her breath.

Her denim midcalf-length skirt felt scratchy against her bare legs, and she shifted a bit so the fabric wasn't brushing her skin. When Beth had spotted her this morning, dressed in the straight denim skirt and button-up blouse, she had raised her eyebrows. Marie had raised hers, too, at Beth's rattiest pair of jeans and skintight baby T that left a half inch of midriff showing. "Wouldn't you like to at least put on a sweater?" The suggestion had been made gently, but Beth immediately flared.

"You told me I could be comfortable, and this is comfortable."

Marie had held up her hands in defeat, but she'd wondered over the course of the morning just how comfortable Beth really was. She'd spent the entire morning hiding in the supply closet, "doing inventory," with her cell phone pressed to her ear, talking in hushed tones with anyone she could rouse.

She could hardly blame Beth for wanting to stay out of sight. Of course, the customers from out of town hadn't reacted oddly to her presence, but the handful of Sommerfeld citizens who came in for morning coffee and conversation had stared unabashedly, their gazes darting away when she met them directly. Their only comments to her had been those necessary for ordering—no friendly greetings or idle chitchat.

Deborah hadn't greeted her or Beth cheerfully either. Even now, with no customers in the café and the opportunity to visit, Deborah sat on a stool on the opposite side of the kitchen, her back to Marie, her nose buried in the *Mennonite Review*. The only communication with her this morning had been brisk instructions on how things were done. If Marie had her druthers, she'd be hiding in the closet, too, but someone had to wait tables and run the cash register.

A stack of dishes awaited washing. Marie sighed as she stared at the towers of white and blue ceramic plates, bowls, and cups. They'd need to be finished before the noon traffic came in, which Deborah had indicated was so light they might consider closing the café for the midday hours. She and Beth would discuss that later, but whether they decided to close or not, the dishes had to be washed.

Marie decided she wasn't going to be the one to do them. Waiting tables and making sure the café stayed stocked with the needed items for serving was enough of a task without adding dishwashing to the list. Beth would have to carry a share of the load.

She marched to the supply closet and stepped inside, closing the door so their conversation wouldn't carry to Deborah's ears. Beth, engrossed in a cell phone exchange, held up her hand in a silent bid for patience. Marie waited, leaning against the closed door.

"Okay, I'll start checking. Yes, I'll give it my best shot—you know how persuasive I can be." Beth's soft, intimate chuckle raised the hairs on the back of Marie's neck. "Well, listen, Mom's in here, so I'll talk to you later. Love you, too. 'Bye." Beth flipped the phone closed and smiled. "Mitch has some great ideas for adding to our boutique's inventory. I'm going to start visiting the farms this afternoon, asking if the farmers have any items to sell. He said he'd get a small business loan to pay for the stuff, then we'll pay that back when we sell the café."

"Sounds reasonable." Marie crossed her arms and gestured with her head toward the kitchen. "Honey, Deborah cooks, I serve customers and take the tabs. We need someone to run the dishwasher."

Beth tipped her head, her brows low. "Trina told me she'd been working here with your aunt. I'll bet she knows how to work the dishwasher. I wonder where she is."

"I wasn't speaking of Trina," Marie chided. "I was speaking of you. I need *you* out there."

Beth crunched her face into a scowl. "I don't think I can stand working with that woman. She's such a sourpuss."

"You won't have to work with her. As I said, she's cooking. The stove and the dishwasher are on opposite sides of the kitchen."

Beth huffed. "But I'd really like to start making those visits."

Marie quirked one brow. "Beth, you asked me to come with you and help, which I'm very willing to do, but you've got to help, too." At Beth's grim expression, she suggested, "Maybe you can ask Deborah if Trina can come in tomorrow and operate the dishwasher for you, but for today, I need you."

"I'm not asking Deborah anything."

Marie released a laugh.

"What's so funny?" Beth scowled.

"You. You look exactly like your grandfather with that stubborn set to your jaw."

As Marie had suspected, the reference to J. D. Koeppler provided the impetus for action. Beth tucked the cell phone into her jeans pocket and pushed past her mother. Marie remained in the closet doorway and watched Beth stalk to Deborah's side.

"Mrs. Muller." The use of the respectful title made Marie's chest swell with pride.

Deborah turned her head, meeting Beth's gaze.

She didn't smile. "Yes?"

Although Beth folded her arms over her chest in a battle stance, she maintained an even tone. "I wondered if it might be possible for Trina to come in tomorrow and run the dishwasher."

Deborah set the newspaper aside. "Will you be here?"

Beth shrugged. "I'll be in and out."

"Trina is at an impressionable age. Her father and I wish to keep her focused on those things we feel are important to her spiritual and emotional well-being."

Beth glanced at Marie. Irritation flared in her eyes, and Marie held her breath, hoping her daughter would think before speaking. Beth dropped her arms, slipping her fingertips into her back jeans pockets, then faced Deborah again. A slight smile curved her lips. "I assure you I have no intention of corrupting Trina. She's a cute kid, and I wouldn't want to do anything to hurt her. She'll be safe here."

Deborah seemed to examine Beth's face. Beth stood still under the scrutiny, waiting. Finally Deborah gave a brusque nod. "I'll ask her father. If he says it's all right, she can come tomorrow."

Beth shot Marie a triumphant grin before turning back to Deborah. "Thanks."

Deborah returned to reading her paper, and Beth skipped across the tile floor to Marie's side.

"Piece of cake." Slinging her arm around her mother's shoulders, she said, "Okay, show me how to work this big ol' monstrosity."

Beth held her cheerful mood the remainder of

the day, much to Marie's relief. Although Deborah never openly spoke to either of them, she lost a bit of the tight look around her mouth as the day progressed, giving Marie hope that she might soften in time. She had no desire to walk on eggshells the entire duration of their three months together. She doubted she and Deborah would return to their old friendship, but she would be satisfied with the loss of tension between them.

Henry was among the supper patrons. When Marie delivered his plate of pot roast, potatoes, and seasoned green beans, he smiled. "When the place is closed, I'll come by."

Marie's eyes flew wide.

His cheeks, wearing a slight shadow of whisker growth, blazed red. "To show you the books from the past several weeks while Deborah has been in charge. She asked me to keep the records since math is not her strong suit."

Business. Nothing personal. Marie nearly wilted with relief. Or regret? She rubbed her eyes. She must be tired if she was having thoughts like that. "Thank you, Henry. I'll stick around." She hurried away before peering into his brown eyes raised any other odd feelings.

Beth left the moment the last plate came out of the dishwasher, but Deborah stayed close when Henry flopped the ledgers open and showed Marie the expenses and income from the past two months.

Her heart twisted when she witnessed the change in penmanship in the columns, and she couldn't resist running her finger along the lines penned by Aunt Lisbeth's hand.

"All of the monies made have gone directly into the café account at the bank in McPherson," Deborah said, her brown eyes sharp. "It's all there."

Marie glanced again at the ledger and frowned. "Haven't you or Trina kept anything for your labor?"

Deborah pursed her lips. "Of course not. I wouldn't presume to do that for myself."

"But that's hardly fair." Marie flipped a few pages, searching for prior entries concerning the payment of employees. "If you're working, you ought to be paid. Here." She found what she wanted. Pointing at the numbers, she looked at Henry. "This shows an hourly wage plus tips being paid to Trina when she worked with Aunt Lisbeth. We need to figure out what she would have earned over the weeks after Aunt Lisbeth died and get her caught up. We also need to pay Deborah for—"

"I do not require payment for doing a service for a dear friend." Deborah's firm voice brought Marie to a startled halt.

Marie stared at the woman for a moment. Deborah's brown eyes were as determined as they'd been in her youth. Rarely had anyone won an argument with Henry's sister. Recalling some of their girlhood spats, Marie had to swallow an amused grin.

She processed possible means of convincing Deborah to accept payment for her time in the café, but she came up empty until Deborah's words, "*service for a dear friend,*" repeated in her mind. The smile she'd been holding back found its way to her face.

"Deborah, I very much appreciate you giving to Aunt Lisbeth in such a wonderful way. You were a good friend to her, and I thank you. But as you know, I'm going to need you while Beth and I are here. I can't, in good conscience, allow you to continue working without pay. Not for Beth and me."

Deborah flicked a quick glance at Henry, who seemed to be biting down on the insides of his lips.

Marie continued. "Will you please sit down with Henry and discuss a reasonable wage? And we'll put you officially on the payroll, starting today."

For long seconds Deborah stood silently, her gaze boring a hole through Marie, but finally she released a sigh. Running her fingers down the black ribbons of her cap, she gave a nod. "Very well. Starting today."

Marie drew in a deep breath of relief. One battle won.

"I'm going home now. Henry, are you coming?" The pointed question left no alternative for him but to rise to his feet.

"Of course. I'll see you again tomorrow evening, Marie." He headed for the back door.

Marie shot a startled glance at his back.

Deborah made another of her pursed-lip faces. She leaned toward Marie and lowered her voice to a conspiratorial level. "Henry has eaten nearly all of his supper meals at the café for the past twenty years." Her stern gaze flicked in his direction for a moment before returning to Marie. "When the café closed for the evening, he took Lisbeth home." Her stern countenance softened a bit. "I'm sure he misses her. They were very good friends." Then she straightened her spine, her grim expression returning. "But he has accepted her loss, and he isn't seeking a replacement."

Marie felt certain Deborah was attempting to deliver a message of some sort, but tired from her long day, she couldn't decipher it. She merely nodded, acknowledging the words. Deborah removed her apron, slipped on her sweater, and followed Henry out the back door.

When Marie returned to Lisbeth's house, she found Beth at the kitchen table with the lamp burning. A crude map, drawn on notebook paper, lay on the checked tablecloth.

Beth looked up and flashed a smile. "Look here, Mom. I drew this from the one on the post office wall. I can use this when I start my antique hunting tomorrow. I plan to hit every house in town, as well as all the farms around Sommerfeld. Maybe all of them in Harvey County. Who knows?" She suddenly frowned. "You look beat. Why don't you go soak in the tub and then hit the hay?"

Marie smoothed her hand over Beth's head and delivered a kiss on her forehead. "Thanks, honey. I think I'll do that." She took a lamp from the edge of the kitchen counter, lit it, and started for the hallway. Before turning the corner, she peeked back at Beth. "Oh, just a reminder, before you take off on your hunt tomorrow, remember to come by the café just in case

Trina's father doesn't allow her to come work."

"Oh, he'll let her."

Marie propped a hand on her hip. "You're certainly the confident one."

Beth smirked. "I just have the feeling that mom of hers wants to keep her under her thumb, and what better way to do that than have her stuck at the café all day?"

Marie chuckled and headed to the bathroom. How well Beth knew Deborah already! When she was stretched out in Lisbeth's old-fashioned porcelain tub, staring through the lace-covered window to the starry sky, Deborah's parting comment about Henry accepting Lisbeth's loss returned. She frowned. What was Deborah intimating? When understanding dawned, she almost laughed out loud.

Marie had been given a subtle warning not to try to replace Lisbeth in Henry's life. Sinking a little deeper into the scented bubbles, she closed her eyes, smiling. Deborah had no reason to worry. Those Xs Beth made on the calendar each evening would add up fast, she'd be on her way, and no one need even remember she'd passed through. Including Henry.

For some reason, her heart seemed to pinch with the thought.

Twisting her toe on the hot water spigot, she whispered aloud. "It's only because being here is bringing back childhood memories. Henry was a big part of my growing up. It's only natural to think of him maybe more than some others."

She reminded herself of that thought as the

week progressed. On Wednesday she managed to serve Henry his meal without giving him any extra attention. But on Thursday his hand brushed against hers when she placed a newly filled saltshaker on his table, and she felt her face fill with heat. She escaped before he could see her blush and be embarrassed, too. On Friday she pretended she needed to use the bathroom and asked Trina to take his plate. The gregarious teenager acquiesced so innocently, Marie felt a pang of guilt for the deception.

But Saturday evening, even though Deborah carried Henry's steak and potatoes to the dining room, she didn't avoid him. He called her name as she scurried by on her way to the kitchen. Pausing several feet away, she peered at him with raised brows, hoping she gave the illusion of great busyness even though the café was only marginally crowded.

"I wanted to ask you a question." His gaze flicked to the tables on his right and left, communicating his unwillingness to speak loudly enough for any other patrons to overhear.

With a sigh, she approached his table, stopping on the opposite side. "Yes?"

Now that he had her attention, he hesitated, his thick eyebrows knitted. "It's about. . .attending meetinghouse."

Marie took a backward step. "That's a subject best left alone, Henry." She softened the words with a smile, but before he could say anything, she dashed to the kitchen. She made sure she stayed there until he dropped a few bills on the table, rose, and left.

ELEVEN

Marie poured a cup of coffee from Lisbeth's tall aluminum percolator, then doctored it liberally with sweet cream purchased from a local farmer. She sank down at the kitchen table and cradled the warm mug between her palms. Across the house, Beth still slept. She'd probably sleep until noon. Marie shrugged a little deeper into her chenille bathrobe and sipped her coffee, wondering what time it might have been when her daughter had put the cell phone away and finally went to bed. The wee hours of the morning, that's for sure.

She sighed. Beth's venture wasn't turning out as she'd hoped. She had visited two families a day, and despite her most polite demeanor and generous top-dollar offers, no one had agreed to sell her anything for her planned boutique. Marie's heart ached as she remembered her long conversation with Beth last night.

"Mom, I don't understand it. A lot of the stuff I've tried to buy is just out in barns or on back porches—

not even being used except to stack more stuff on or take up space. Why won't they sell it to me and make a little money?"

Marie had tried to explain that the Mennonites, traditionally, weren't interested in gaining earthly wealth, so money wasn't a motivator to them. Beth had demanded to know what was a motivator. At Marie's response that helping a neighbor was of more importance than accumulating wealth, Beth had turned derisive.

"These people are so backward."

Her daughter's statement had brought a rush of defensiveness. "They aren't backward, just different. Frankly, I find it refreshing that there are still people in the world who look out for each other rather than constantly scrambling for the ever-loving dollar."

At that point, Beth's face twisted into a scowl, and she pushed away from the table with a curt, "Well, they sure aren't looking out for *me* by keeping that stuff to themselves. I'm going to call Mitch." Her conversation with her boyfriend had lasted long into the night. Which meant Marie would have a quiet morning to herself.

She raised the cup to her lips and breathed in the rich aroma of the brew. Having grown accustomed, over the past week, to the fuller flavor of coffee brewed in a percolator, she wondered if the drip-machine coffee from home would seem bland. She chuckled softly. Bland. . . Would she have ever thought she would apply that term to anything in Cheyenne?

She rose from the table and crossed to the window,

peering across the stubbly pasture that stretched west of the house. As a little girl, she had stood at this same window with Lisbeth, "watching the wheat grow," as her aunt had put it. A smile of fond remembrance tugged her lips. She could almost feel the tickle of the ribbons from Lisbeth's cap trailing along her cheek as her aunt had leaned forward to whisper in her ear, "Can you see the stalks stretching toward the sun, sweet girl? A wise wheat stalk reaches toward the sun, and a wise person reaches toward the Son."

Marie had dashed into the backyard to dance in circles, her hands reaching upward to catch a sunbeam, laughing out loud while Lisbeth watched from the window, laughing, too. When she'd grown a little older, she'd realized Aunt Lisbeth referred to the Son of God rather than the sun in the sky. The day she'd found the courage to tell Aunt Lisbeth she had finally grasped her meaning, her aunt had tickled her nose with the end of her long braid, making her giggle. "And that proves to me, my darling girl, that you are growing wiser." Tears had winked in the woman's eyes as she'd advised, "Always reach for the Son, Marie. Draw Him closer and closer, and your wisdom will grow more and more."

That afternoon, with Aunt Lisbeth's gentle guidance, Marie had invited Jesus, the Son of God, to enter her heart and forgive her sins. Lisbeth's expression radiated joy as she folded Marie in her arms and whispered, "Welcome to the family of God, my Marie." The look on her aunt's face was permanently etched in Marie's mind.

Something trickled down her cheek, and she brushed her fingers over her face. They came away wet, and Marie gave a start. Why was she crying? The answer came at once. How disappointed Aunt Lisbeth would be to know how far her beloved niece had strayed from the Son.

"I'm sorry, Aunt Lisbeth," she whispered, the pain of her loss striking more harshly than at any time since Henry had delivered the news of her aunt's passing.

A strong desire to see her dear aunt just one more time washed over Marie. Visiting with her in person was impossible, but she could at least visit her final resting place. She set her now-cold cup of coffee on the red-checked tablecloth and hurried to Lisbeth's bedroom, shedding her bathrobe as she went.

Fifteen minutes later she was behind the wheel of her car, dressed in blue jeans and a hooded sweatshirt. But as she turned the key in the ignition, she remembered it was Sunday. The cemetery was next to the meetinghouse. And the meetinghouse would be filled with worshipers. She pressed her forehead to the steering wheel, emitting a low groan. She couldn't go there now. . .or could she? She closed her eyes and forced her mind to picture the layout of the meetinghouse and its surrounding grounds, including the iron-fenced cemetery.

If she didn't use the large driving gate in the corner closest to the back doors of the meetinghouse—if she parked outside the fence and walked through the small gate at the back corner of the cemetery—surely she would be unobtrusive enough to escape notice. No doubt Aunt Lisbeth had been buried in the Koeppler plot, which was in the northwest corner, completely opposite the meetinghouse building.

Maybe she should wait until tomorrow. She wouldn't be working. Maybe tomorrow would be better, she tried to convince herself. But the need to spend time with Aunt Lisbeth became a gnawing ache Marie could not ignore. She twisted the key, bringing the engine to life, and backed down the driveway.

Henry opened his Bible to the book of Ephesians, as directed by Brother Strauss, then lifted his gaze to the minister. Something—a slight movement outside the window—caught his attention. *Probably geese taking flight.* He shifted his eyes without turning his head and peered through the simple glass pane to prove his guess. Instead of birds, a slender human form slipped between headstones at the far side of the cemetery.

Henry's heart lurched. Even though the person wore a hood, which hid the face and hair from view, he knew it had to be Marie. Seeking Lisbeth. He wondered how he could be so sure, and he realized he just knew. Because—even after all this time—he knew Marie.

Although his face remained attentively turned toward the front of the simple sanctuary as if listening to the minister, his mind wandered backward. To another meetinghouse service in another time, when he was a lad of twelve. That was when Marie had first captured his heart.

The Saturday before, she had gone to the creek with the visiting bishop and been baptized in recognition of her acceptance of Jesus. The sight of her on the opposite side of the meetinghouse, with her nutmeg hair smoothed back and her sweet face framed by the white prayer cap and dangling ribbons, had distracted him throughout the entire service. Afterward, he had sidled up to her in the meeting-house yard. Bashfulness had kept his chin low, but somehow he'd managed to tell her how pretty she looked.

Marie's smile had lit the countryside, and although she hadn't thanked him with words for his compliment, her glowing expression had given him all the thanks he needed. After that, no other girl had ever mattered. It was always Marie. Right up until the day he watched her climb into a semi truck and ride away, the white ribbons dancing in the breeze that coursed through the open window.

He swallowed, his eyes once more jerking to the side to peek out. Yes, she was still there, hunkered beside the mound of dirt where Lisbeth had been put to rest. His heart twisted for the pain of loss she must be feeling. He understood it—he felt it, too. Lisbeth had been so special to him. More, even, than any of his own relatives. They had a bond— an affinity—that grew from their sorrow at Marie's departure.

Lisbeth was gone, but now Marie was back. His heart pattered.

His gaze sought and found J. D. Koeppler several pews ahead, in his usual spot. The man sat ramrod straight, his face aimed toward the front of the meetinghouse. A window was at his left. Had his eyes found his daughter, crouching in the cool wind, grieving beside a grave? Henry stifled a snort. Sympathy wouldn't swell in J.D.'s chest. The man's heart had turned to stone over the years.

He hadn't always been so cold. Henry remembered a warm twinkle in the man's eyes when he'd approached Marie's father, at the age of fifteen, and stammered out his desire to court her. J.D. had put his big hand on Henry's shoulder and said, a grin twitching his cheek, "Son, she'd be hard-pressed to find someone finer. But she's just turned thirteen. Can you give her a few years to grow up first?"

Henry had slunk away in embarrassment, but as J.D. had suggested, he'd given Marie a few years. And when she was finally old enough to make a commitment, Jep Quinn's semi had broken down on the highway at the turn that led to Sommerfeld, and within a week she was gone.

Henry sighed. On the bench beside him, his brother Claude poked him with his elbow. Claude's low brows let Henry know he'd been caught daydreaming. He sat up straight and forced his ears to absorb today's sermon. But he couldn't resist giving one more glance out the window.

Marie was gone.

"Where have you been?" Beth met her mother at the back door. She hugged herself and shivered as a gust of wind whisked through the open door. "I woke up and couldn't find you."

"I went to the cemetery." Marie passed through the utility porch to the kitchen and peeled off her sweatshirt while Beth followed, continuing to scold.

"Couldn't you leave me a note or something? I mean, it's unnerving to wake up and be all alone. What were you doing at the cemetery?"

Marie picked up her coffee cup from the table and poured the cold contents down the drain. "Visiting Aunt Lisbeth." A band constricted around her heart. Sitting beside the grave hadn't provided the comfort she had gone seeking. Cup in hand, she headed for the percolator.

"I was hoping we could do some laundry today. I need jeans washed, and we're out of our towels in the bathroom. I don't want to use the ones your aunt left. They smell funny."

Marie clamped her jaw and held back a sharp retort. She poured coffee into her cup, focusing on the swirl of dark liquid.

"I tried some of your coffee, but it tasted bitter to me." Beth leaned against the counter, her shoulders hunched. "So I haven't had any breakfast. And it's cold in here. Can't that furnace put out more heat?"

Marie took a deep breath, seeking patience. "Beth, all you have to do is add coal to it and adjust the damper, and the heat will increase. I've told you that."

Beth tossed her head. "And I've told *you* I'm not going into that basement. It creeps me out."

"Well, I haven't done your laundry since you turned fourteen, and I'm not going to start now," Marie retorted sharply. "The washer is in the basement, so if you need clean clothes, you'll have to go downstairs."

Beth pushed off from the counter, her lips puckering into a startled pout. "Why are you being so grumpy?"

"Why am I—" Marie shook her head, swallowed, and took another calming breath. "I'm not trying to be grumpy, but you have done nothing but grumble since I stepped through the door." What bothered Marie more than Beth's complaints was the fact that her daughter didn't seem to recognize how difficult visiting the cemetery might have been. She needed sympathy, and it wasn't forthcoming.

"I'm not grumbling," Beth protested, a slender hand pressed to her chest.

Marie fixed her daughter with a pointed stare.

The girl blew out a breath that ruffled her bangs. "Okay, maybe I was." She yawned, not bothering to cover her mouth. Running her hands through her tangled hair, she said, "I didn't get much sleep last night."

Neither had Marie, but she didn't share that with Beth. She raised her coffee cup and took a cautious sip of the hot liquid. "And that's my fault because. . . ?"

"I didn't say it was your fault, I just. . ." Beth stared

off to the side for a moment. Finally she brought her gaze around and released a sigh. "I'm frustrated, Mom, and so is Mitch. We put all our hopes into getting our start-up inventory from this town, and no one is cooperating. I know we'll have some stuff if we use all the furniture and quilts and dishes from this house. . ."

Marie's heart skipped a beat.

". . .but we'll need more. And I don't know how to talk people into selling."

Sipping at the steaming coffee, Marie gathered her thoughts. The idea of Lisbeth's things being purchased by strangers made her feel sick to her stomach. But that had been the intention all along—to sell everything and make money. She just hadn't realized how much being in her aunt's home would resurrect childhood memories. Selling Lisbeth's belongings would be like selling a part of herself.

"Mitch is coming up sometime in the next couple weeks, when he can get away."

Marie jerked, pulling her focus back to Beth's words.

"He said maybe if I have cash in hand and I flash it around, people will be more willing to let their stuff go."

Although Marie doubted a fistful of dollars would make much difference, she decided not to discourage Beth right now. Instead, she said lightly, "Well, let's hope it helps. Now. . .about your laundry."

Beth grimaced. "Can't we go to a Laundromat or something?"

Marie put down her coffee cup and folded her arms. "If you want to go to a Laundromat, go ahead. But I think it's a waste of gas and quarters when we have a machine in the basement."

Beth nibbled her lower lip, peering at her mother through a narrowed gaze. Suddenly her eyes widened. "Say. . .what kind of washing machine doesn't use electricity?"

Marie grinned. "Come see." She snatched up a lamp, lit it, and led the way.

Beth tiptoed, holding her arms tightly across her middle as if trying to make herself smaller as she followed Marie down the narrow, open-back stairs. When they reached the dirt floor, Beth glanced at the overhead support beams and shuddered. "I bet there are spiders down here just waiting to drop on my head."

"You're bigger than they are," Marie retorted. She walked past the refrigerator and ducked through an opening in the cinder-block wall that divided the basement in two halves. In the center of the second room, on a sheet of plywood, waited Aunt Lisbeth's 1936 Maytag washing machine.

Beth's eyes bulged. "That's nothing more than a tub on legs!"

"It works," Marie insisted. She tugged Beth by the arm until they stood beside the white porcelain washer. "Look. You turn on the water over there." She pointed, and Beth tiptoed across the floor to the copper line that poked through a hole in the basement's ceiling. She fingered the small iron valve dissecting the pipe.

A rubber hose, clamped to the end of the line, ran across the floor and draped over the edge of the tub. Beth followed the hose back to the washer, leaned over, and peered beneath the tub. "Where does it drain?"

"There's a plug down here." Marie reached inside the tub and pointed out a rubber stopper. "When you pull it, the water goes through this tube and into a drainage hole over there." She pointed to a dark corner of the basement, where the rubber tube disappeared.

Upright again, she reached inside the tub and gave the metal agitator a spin. "After the clothes have agitated, you drain the soapy water, refill the tub for a rinse, and put the clothes through this wringer to remove the excess water. Then you hang them on the clothesline outside." While she explained, she mimed the actions.

Beth's expression grew more disbelieving by the minute. "You've got to be joking."

Marie raised one brow. "I assure you, I am not. I've washed many a load in this old Maytag." She gave the machine a pat. "Aunt Lisbeth hid it down here because she didn't want the neighbors to know how spoiled she was."

Beth choked. "Spoiled?"

Marie nodded, grinning. "See the motor underneath? It's gas powered. You didn't have to crank the agitator yourself."

Beth burst out laughing. Marie couldn't stop

her own smile as she witnessed her daughter's mirth. When Beth was under control, she circled the washer, stepping over the water lines to examine every inch of the ancient machine. Her survey complete, she grinned at her mother.

"Well, I have no intention of using this thing to do my laundry, but I think it will make a great addition to my boutique. I can picture it on someone's sun porch with impatiens spilling out of it." Her eyes sparkled. "Or filled with ice and cans of pop for entertaining." She clapped her hands once. "I'm going to go call Mitch. He won't believe this thing!"

Beth hurried upstairs, but Marie stayed in place, her fingers curled over the cold rim of the cast aluminum tub. Her father's question rang through her mind: *"Haven't you given your daughter any training?"* Beth's coldheartedness concerning the things Marie valued made her wonder if she had failed somehow.

Standing beside the washing machine brought back a rush of pleasant childhood memories. But to Beth, the machine only meant one thing: the almighty dollar.

Twelve

Marie closed the basement door and headed toward the kitchen, but a shadowy figure outside the back door brought her to a halt. Someone stood on the porch, hands cupped beside eyes, peering through the lace curtain. Squinting, Marie stared. Then her jaw dropped.

Dashing to the door, she swung it open. "Joanna?"

A shy smile played at the corners of the woman's lips. "Hello, Marie. May I come in?"

Marie jerked backward a step, gesturing. "Yes, please. It's so good to see you." How Marie longed to throw her arms around her sister. Only a year apart in age, the pair had been inseparable growing up. With their similar hair color—although Joanna's leaned toward brown while Marie's leaned toward red—and identical clefts in the chin of their heart-shaped faces, the two had often been mistaken for twins. Both had loved this, and they'd sewn matching dresses clear into their teens to perpetrate the myth.

Now, looking into Joanna's face, framed by her

white mesh cap and black ribbons, Marie felt as though she were looking into a mirror of what might have been had she remained in Sommerfeld. Instead of reaching for her sister, she took a step back.

Joanna's face clouded. "Would you rather I not be here?"

Marie's hand shot forward, her fingers barely brushing the sleeve of her sister's coat. "Oh no! I just—I'm so surprised." She waved toward the kitchen, releasing a nervous giggle. "Please. Come in. Sit down. Or would you rather go to the front room? There's still coffee in the pot, but I haven't started lunch yet, so—"

Joanna's blue eyes twinkled. "Stop blabbering, Marie. You always were one to blabber when you didn't know what to say."

Marie gawked at Joanna for a second or two, then burst into laughter. Joanna joined her. For a few glorious moments they were teenagers again, elbows linked, sharing a private joke. The laughter faded, and they stood, smiling into each other's matching eyes.

"Well. . ." Marie cleared her throat and pulled out a kitchen chair to sit down. "What brings you here?"

Joanna tugged out a chair, too, and started to sit. At that moment, Beth bounced into the kitchen with an overflowing laundry basket held against her stomach. Joanna jerked upright and stared at her.

Beth came to a halt and stared back. Her gaze bounced between the two women several times; then she released a low whistle. "Wow. This one's got to be related. For a minute, I thought you were Mom in dress-up clothes."

Marie sucked in a sharp breath, but Joanna's tinkling giggle rang. She shook her head, smiling at Marie. "And this one has to be yours. Despite that blond hair, she's got your eyes and chin, as well as your frankness."

Beth raised one eyebrow and fixed her gaze on Marie. "You always told me that whole being-too-frank thing came from Dad's side of the family."

Joanna laughed again. "Did she? Really, Marie. . ." She shook her head, still chuckling. Looking at Beth, she said, "I'm your aunt Joanna. And I could tell you stories about your mom that would make your head spin."

Beth's lips quirked. "Oh yeah?"

"But she won't," Marie inserted.

Beth and Joanna laughed and shared conspiratorial winks.

"Later?" Beth asked.

"Later," Joanna promised.

Marie glowered, but her heart sang at the instant camaraderie of these two women who meant so much to her.

Beth's expression turned sheepish. She set the basket down and dug underneath, removing the quilt that had been on her cot. "Can you tell me how to get nail polish out of fabric?"

Marie jumped up and rushed forward, snatching the quilt from Beth's arms. A bright pink splatter filled the center of the quilt. "Beth! How did this happen?"

She shrugged. "I was doing my toenails, and the bottle spilled. I tried to blot it, but. . ."

Joanna stepped between them, fingering the stain. She shook her head. "I think you'd ruin the fabric if you used something strong enough to remove that stain. This quilt has to be at least forty years old."

Beth groaned. "Oh, that means I won't get a penny for it."

Marie bit back the words that longed for release. This quilt was much more than a dollar sign to her. Why couldn't Beth see the sentimental significance?

"Oh well." Beth rolled the quilt and tossed it aside. "I can always sell it as a 'cutter.' Someone may want to chop it up and make a teddy bear out of it or something." She hefted the basket. "So, where are the car keys? I'm going to hunt up a Laundromat."

Joanna spun, staring at Marie with an open mouth. "Laundry. . .on Sunday?" Then she clapped her hands to her cheeks and moaned. "Oh, I told myself I wouldn't do that." Clamping her hands together and tucking them against her ribcage, she drew a deep breath and smiled at Beth. "There's one on West First in Newton. Just follow Highway 135 North. There's a First Street exit off the highway, so you can't miss it."

"Is there a McDonald's near there?"

Joanna laughed. "Aren't there McDonald's everywhere? Just follow the signs."

Beth grinned. "Thanks!" Turning to Marie, she

raised her eyebrows. "Keys?"

Marie pulled them from her pocket and handed them over. She forced herself to set aside her sorrow over the ruined quilt and focus on the issue at hand. "Do you have money?"

"Yep." Beth headed for the door, her ponytail swinging. "See you later!"

At the slam of the door, Joanna removed her coat, hung it on the back of the chair, and sat down. "She's a pretty girl, Marie."

Did a hint of accusation linger in her tone? Marie picked up the quilt, folded it lovingly, and carried it to the table. After setting the quilt aside, she seated herself. "Yes, she is. She's a challenge at times, but I can't imagine my life without her." She glanced at the quilt, reminding herself that Beth was infinitely more important than squares of fabric pieced together.

Joanna nodded. "I feel the same about my three. My oldest one, Kyra, has the fiery personality I see in your Beth. It's too bad—" She jerked her face away, the black ribbon of her cap crumpling against her shoulder.

"Too bad they didn't know each other growing up?" Marie finished her sister's thought.

Joanna bit down on her lower lip and gazed outward for several seconds before facing Marie again. The hurt in her eyes was unmistakable. "I've missed you so much. Not a day has gone by that I haven't thought of you, wondered how you were, wished I could talk to you. It's been very hard."

Marie tried to swallow the resentment Joanna's

gentle reprimand stirred, but a question found its way out. "Then where were you last week when I pulled into town? Do you know how hard it's been to sit in this house every evening, knowing my family is out there but doesn't care enough to come by?"

Joanna dipped her head. Marie stared at the spot where Joanna's part disappeared beneath the nearly translucent mesh of the cap. Joanna sighed, her head still low. "I wanted to come. But how could I know if I'd be welcome?" Her chin shot up, and tears winked in her eyes. "Twenty years, Marie, and you never wrote or called. How is a person supposed to know what to do?"

Marie's thoughts sniped, *You never called or wrote to me either.* But she held the words back, aware they would do more harm than good. The silence lengthened.

Finally Joanna sighed. "I didn't come here to start an argument. I just wanted to know how you are. To see you again. I—" Joanna lurched from the table and held out her arms.

Marie pushed to her feet and fell into her sister's embrace. They hugged, laughing and crying at once, and Marie felt as though her heart might burst with happiness. Hurts melted away in the warmth of the hug, and when Joanna pulled loose to slip her elbow through Marie's, Marie knew things would be all right between the two of them.

They walked to the front room and perched side by side on the couch. For the next three hours they caught up, sometimes giggling like young girls over remembered silly times, other times vying for who could tell the most outrageous story of parenting. When Marie's stomach growled, it reminded her that lunchtime had come and gone. She pulled back, guilt striking.

"I'm keeping you from your family. They're probably wondering where you are and when they'll be fed."

Joanna shook her head. "They know where I am, and Kyra and Kelly are plenty capable of putting a meal on the table."

Marie grimaced. "Won't Hugo fuss about you spending the afternoon away from home?"

"What are Sundays for except to visit?" Joanna's gently lined eyes sparkled. "But if you offered me a sandwich, I wouldn't decline it."

They returned to the kitchen, where they made sandwiches and then sat at the table to eat. Marie felt a twinge of discomfort when Joanna prayed aloud, asking a blessing for the simple meal. It had been a long time since she'd offered grace before eating. But the easy conversation that followed erased the discomfort.

At nearly five o'clock Beth returned, the clothes folded neatly in the basket. Her face reflected surprise when she spotted Joanna. "You're still here? I figured you'd be long gone by now."

Joanna glanced at the red plastic wall clock and jerked. "Oh my. It is growing late. I should go home." She stood and reached for her jacket. Slipping her arms into the sleeves, she looked at Beth. "I'll have to come back sometime and bring my daughters so we can all get acquainted. Your mother assures me she won't be such a stranger from now on."

Beth shot her mother a quick questioning look, but she recovered quickly and smiled at Joanna. "That would be great. How old are your daughters?"

"Kyra is nineteen and Kelly is thirteen." She smirked. "I also have an eleven-year-old son, Hugo Jr. We call him Gomer. But he isn't one for visiting. Too active." Turning to Marie, she added, "I didn't tell you—Kyra's engagement to Claude Braun's son Jacob was published today at the end of service. They plan a January wedding."

Marie's chest tightened. She and Beth would need to be gone before the wedding. As nonchurch members, they wouldn't be welcome. Being in town, knowing the celebration was going on without them, would be too hard. She nodded. "I wish them well."

Joanna paused, her gaze narrowing, as she examined Marie for a few thoughtful seconds. Then her face relaxed. "Well, I need to go." She gave Marie a quick hug. "But I'll be back, Kyra and Kelly in tow." Pulling away, she cupped Marie's cheek with her hand. "Soon?"

Marie swallowed the lump that formed in her throat. "Very soon."

With another quick smile, Joanna slipped out the back door.

Beth put her hand on her hip. "Careful, Mom."

Marie jerked her gaze to Beth. "What?"

Pointing at the doorway where Joanna had

disappeared, she said, "They're pulling you back. I can see it your eyes. This is *temporary*." She drew out the word, exaggerating each syllable. "Remember?"

Marie nodded, forcing a light chuckle. "Of course I remember." She scooped out the towels from the top of Beth's basket. "I'll go put these away," she said, changing the subject, "and you take care of the rest."

Beth gave her mother a wary look before turning toward the bedrooms. Marie headed for the hallway leading to the bathroom, but as she passed the kitchen window she paused, looking across the landscape behind the house. Aunt Lisbeth's words echoed through her mind. "*A wise person reaches toward the Son.*" For a moment she wondered—was the pull Beth mentioned coming from her family, or from the One she once called Savior?

The telephone jangled on the corner of Henry's desk. He wiped his mouth with a napkin, dropped it beside his plate, and crossed the floor. He lifted the receiver in the middle of the second ring. "Hello?"

"Henry, this is Joanna."

"Don't tell me you're having trouble with the starter in your car again."

Joanna's light laugh sounded, bringing a pang of remembrance. The airy tremble at the end of her laugh sounded so much like Marie's. After Marie had left, he'd considered pursuing Joanna. Fortunately, good sense had reigned. Who could ever replace Marie? His good friend Hugo Dick had asked for

Joanna's hand, and the two enjoyed a happy marriage. While he remained a bachelor.

"No, no, I'm not calling about my car. This is. . . personal."

Henry straightened his shoulders.

"I finally went to see Marie."

His heart began to thud.

"And I'm so glad I did. We spent the whole afternoon together and had a wonderful chat."

Henry smiled. "That's good. And she. . .welcomed you?"

A slight pause. "Yes. I think she was apprehensive at first, but so was I! We had a good time though, and we plan to get together again soon so our girls can get acquainted."

Henry imagined outspoken, wild-haired Beth in her denim pants and shirts three sizes too small next to Joanna's sweet girls with their white caps and modest caped dresses. He shook his head. "I hope that goes well."

His tone must have communicated his doubt, because Joanna laughed. "I suppose it will be interesting, but they're cousins. They need to know each other."

"I agree," Henry said. "I'm glad you're trying to work things out." He paused, wondering if he should keep his next thought to himself, but finally decided to share. "I know Lisbeth would be pleased."

A long sigh came from Joanna's end of the line. "Every time the family was together, Lisbeth mentioned Marie and Beth. Her way, I think, of keeping them alive for us. Dad rarely let her give many details, but I found it comforting to know at least someone was keeping in touch with Marie." Her voice caught. "Being with her today made me realize how much we've missed through this separation. I wish. . ."

Although Joanna let the sentence go unfinished, Henry read the final thought. "Me, too," he said softly.

After a lengthy pause, Joanna's light chuckle sounded. "Well, aren't we a pair, throwing imaginary pennies in a wishing well."

Henry forced a laugh in response.

"I'd better go. I just wanted you to know I followed your advice and went to see my sister. Thanks for pushing me."

He smiled. "That's what friends are for."

"Good-bye, Henry." The line went dead.

Henry hung up the phone and smiled at the receiver. His gaze rose to a framed needlepoint sampler, a gift from Lisbeth. He read the words aloud. " 'But now in Christ Jesus ye who sometimes were far off are made nigh by the blood of Christ.' " He ran his finger along the top edge of the simple wood frame.

"Don't worry, Lisbeth," he said. "I'll keep trying until we bring her home again."

THIRTEEN

Marie examined the tumble of black lumps on the hard-packed ground next to the monstrous furnace. Over the two weeks of their stay in Lisbeth's house, Marie had grown accustomed to shoveling fuel into the belly of the iron beast twice a day, but she hadn't paid close attention to the dent its ravenous appetite had made in the supply.

The Kansas plains could be unpredictable during the winter months. If she didn't replenish the coal supply soon, she and Beth might end up facing some cold days ahead. She hooked the coal hod on its nail and brushed her palms together. She wondered where she could get coal around here. She was certain things had changed tremendously since she'd left with Jep.

Ask Henry, her thoughts immediately prompted. That would be simple since he continued to come to the café for supper every evening. For a moment she allowed a smile to twitch at her lips. Although the conversations with Henry were always brief, both of them aware of Deborah's watchful gaze and listening ear, she had come to enjoy sharing a few moments of chatter with him at the close of each day.

Despite her initial determination to keep a chasm between them, Henry was slowly building a bridge toward friendship. He wouldn't mind if she asked how to get a supply of coal delivered. But she pushed the idea aside. No sense in relying on him any more than necessary. He was already keeping the books at the café and would oversee the distribution of property when the time came. She shouldn't take advantage of his friendship. Besides, she acknowledged with a sigh, leaning on him too much might give him the wrong idea.

Might give her the wrong idea, too.

She trudged up the stairs and went to the kitchen sink to wash the remnants of coal dust from her hands. Outside the kitchen window, the sky looked bleak, the color of an old iron washtub. Rain might spoil Beth's plans for the day. Last night, after she and Beth were in their pajamas and ready for bed, Mitch had arrived to assist Beth in her quest for boutique items. Marie's scalp prickled as her mind replayed the image of her daughter throwing herself into her boyfriend's arms, lifting her face for his kiss.

He slept on the sofa, having collapsed there about a half hour after his arrival. Marie blew out a breath of relief, recalling how Beth had asked for bedding to put together a sleeping spot in the living room for Mitch. Even though Marie hadn't been faithful in church attendance since Beth was a little girl, she had raised her daughter to have morals. Sharing a bed with her boyfriend wasn't something she was willing to do. "Thanks for Beth's appropriate choice," Marie murmured.

She froze. That thought seemed awfully close to a. . .prayer. Had she really *prayed*? She shook her head. No, probably not a true prayer, more an inward statement of relieved gratitude. But it had felt like a prayer. A shiver shook her frame, spurring her to action.

"Breakfast." She tried not to bang things too loudly as she got out a cookie sheet and a knife to slice bread. Humming, she buttered the front and back of each slice. Just as she'd grown to prefer the flavor of percolated coffee, toast made from home-baked bread purchased from the grocer and browned under the broiler before being slathered with Joanna's peach preserves had become her favorite breakfast. Even though Beth continued to grouse about the lack of conveniences, Marie didn't mind the additional steps.

In fact, when she was home again, she planned to put the toaster away and continue to use the broiler. She also intended to keep Aunt Lisbeth's red-speckled percolator separate from the sale items. It was going back to sit on her electric stove and be put to use there.

She opened the oven door to check the bread, smiling as the aroma met her nostrils. The slices were browned to perfection. Just as she pulled the cookie sheet from the oven, Mitch appeared in the kitchen doorway.

"Morning, Marie." Bare-chested, his hair on end, Mitch stretched his mouth in a wide yawn and scratched his toned stomach with both hands. It had been two decades since a male had stood in her kitchen in the morning, sleep-rumpled and relaxed, and Marie found herself blushing profusely at the rush of memories his arrival conjured.

Aware of her gaping robe, which exposed her pink polka-dot flannel pajamas, she turned her back to him, dropped the cookie sheet on the counter, and quickly tied the belt on her robe. Once she was covered more modestly, she faced him. "Good morning, Mitch. Did you sleep well?"

"Pretty well, but that sofa's as hard as a concrete slab." He placed his hands against his lower spine and leaned backward, flexing his shoulders.

Marie turned toward the counter and unscrewed the lid on the jar of preserves. She scooped out a spoonful and plopped it on a piece of toast. "That sofa's been around for a while. I'm sure it's stuffed with sawdust. I'm sorry it wasn't more comfortable."

A low chuckle rumbled, and he cleared his throat. "It's okay. When a person's tired enough, he can sleep just about anywhere." The shuffle of his feet let her know he'd moved farther into the kitchen. His face appeared over her shoulder. "Wow, that toast smells good."

Without looking at him, Marie offered a suggestion. "Go wash the sleep out of your eyes, put on a shirt, then sit down and have some. I made plenty."

His chuckle came again, and the amused undercurrent made Marie's face grow hot. "Thanks." He ambled around the corner toward the bathroom.

Abandoning the toast, Marie dashed to her bedroom and slipped into a pair of jeans and a button-up oxford blouse. Glancing at her glowing face in the small mirror above the dresser, she wondered if he realized the effect he'd had on her. She snorted. Of course he did! What else was that chuckle about?

Well, it wasn't *him* specifically that had her so rattled. She was wise enough to recognize that. It was just having a male, in such a state of dishevelment, so near. Not since Jep's death had a man spent the night under her roof. It could have been anyone standing out there, and she would have experienced the same embarrassed discomfort.

Worry struck. If his presence was this rattling for her, how might Beth respond?

She set her jaw as she lifted her hairbrush and ran it forcefully through her errant curls. If he planned to stick around, he would need to find a hotel in one of the larger towns nearby. Having him in the house day and night might prove to be too tempting for both of the young people. She would mention that to Beth as soon as she woke up.

As she placed the hairbrush back on the dresser, she heard a knock at the back door, followed by Mitch's call: "I'll get it."

She trotted around the corner in time to see Mitch, still shirtless, swing the back door open. Henry stood on the porch.

Henry took a step back when a half-dressed young man opened the door to Lisbeth's utility porch. A flurry of movement behind the man captured his attention, and he peered over the muscular shoulder to see Marie hurrying down the hallway.

She pushed in front of the man. "I've got it, Mitch. Go finish dressing."

The man grinned, scratching his whiskered chin. "Okay, Marie." He lifted his hand in an indolent wave and ambled down the hall, disappearing into the bathroom.

Henry gawked after him, curious about his presence but unwilling to ask.

Marie faced him, her cheeks stained pink. She crossed her arms over her chest and held the door open with her hip. "Good morning. W—would you like some toast?"

Henry shook his head. "No thank you. I've had breakfast."

"Well, at least come in out of the cold." She pushed the door wider.

Aware of the other man inside, he remained on the stoop, holding his jacket closed against the morning breeze. "That's all right. I came to see if you—"

"Marie?" the man's voice intruded. "Can I borrow your toothpaste?"

Marie turned her face toward the bathroom. "Yes. Whatever you need." Her voice sounded tight. She faced Henry again. "I'm sorry. You came to see. . . ?"

"If you need some coal. I'm ordering a ton for my folks' place. I thought maybe you could use some, too."

Her eyes widened. "How could you possibly—"

"—know you need coal?" Henry smiled. "I always got Lisbeth's coal when I got it for my folks. They seem to run out about the same time."

She stared at him for several silent seconds, her brows low, puzzlement in her eyes. Then she shook her head, making her curls bounce. She took in a deep breath. "I was just noticing this morning that I need coal, but I didn't want to bother you. I can get it myself if you'd be kind enough to tell me where."

Henry released a light chuckle. "You'd have a time getting it in that car of yours. I borrow a truck from one of the local farmers and deliver it to my folks. The railroad brings it to town, but the train won't come to your house."

She ducked her head, laughing softly. When she raised her gaze, she looked a little less embarrassed and standoffish. "Thank you, Henry. Once again, your kindness is beyond the expected. Do—do you think you might advise me on how much I'll need to get me through December?"

December. The reminder of her short time here struck again, making Henry's heart race. "You could start with a quarter ton. If you need more, we can always get it later."

She bit down on her bottom lip, her forehead creased in thought. Finally she nodded. "Thank you, Henry. I appreciate your help."

The young man wandered back into the porch. He had slipped on a shirt that was covered in big flowers, but he hadn't bothered with the buttons, leaving it flap open. He stepped beside Marie and draped one arm over her shoulders, holding his free hand toward Henry.

"Hey. I'm Mitch Rogers, Beth's significant other. You must be the Henry Beth told me about."

Henry shook the younger man's hand, disconcerted by his familiarity with Marie. Her cheeks blazed again. He wanted to knock the boy's arm from her shoulder.

"I'm Henry Braun. I'm pleased to meet you." He hoped the Lord would forgive him for his fib.

Marie shifted her shoulders, and Mitch's arm slid away. "Henry is bringing us a load of coal today so I can keep the furnace running."

"Oh yeah?" Mitch leaned against the doorjamb, as if providing chaperonage. "Good. We can use the heat. Pretty chilly in here in the mornings."

Henry thought the man would stay warmer if he'd button up his shirt. He backed up, reaching for the stair railing. "I'll have that coal here late this afternoon, Marie. I'll just dump it through the basement window, like always."

"That sounds fine."

He felt reluctant to leave, yet had no excuse to stay. "I'll see you later." He turned and jogged to his waiting car, hoping his face wasn't as red as the heat behind his cheeks indicated.

Driving toward his shop, he wondered about his

strange reaction. Why should he care if some young man put his arm around Marie? It wasn't any of his concern. Marie had been taking care of herself ever since Beth was a tiny baby. She could continue to do so. Yet he couldn't deny the protectiveness he felt toward her.

Pulling behind his shop, he killed the motor and sat in the car for a few minutes, gathering his thoughts. "I promised Lisbeth to do all I could to bring her home. But home meant Sommerfeld, not my heart," he reminded himself sternly. "I can help her as a Christian brother concerned for her well-being, but I have to stop being jealous."

Jealous. The word made him set his jaw. He had no right to feel jealous toward anyone who showed attention to Marie. And he knew just how to get over that feeling.

Slamming out of his car, he headed to the back door of his shop and punched the key into the lock. "I'll just get busy," he said as he swung the door open and flipped on the lights. Unfortunately, no matter how busy he kept himself, the image of Mitch's arm draped over Marie's shoulders would not leave him alone.

"So you've been to each of these farms and everyone said no?"

Beth nodded at Mitch, irritation rising again at the memory of all those polite yet firm refusals. "And there's some neat stuff there, too." She sighed, brushing aside the remaining crumbs on the tabletop. "But there are plenty more places to go. We'll just have to hope for the best."

Mitch shook his head, his dark eyes gleaming. "First we'll go back to each of these farms. Give them a second chance." Slipping his hand into his back pocket, he removed his wallet. He flopped it open and grinned, rifling his thumb over the stack of twenty-dollar bills. "Ammunition, dear Lissie. We'll capture 'em yet."

Mom interrupted. "Don't make pests of yourselves. If the people don't want to sell, they don't have to. It's their right to keep their own belongings."

Beth turned in her chair and scowled at her mother, who stood at the sink, drying the last of the lunch dishes. Mom had been uptight all morning, fussing about Mitch being here and how it wasn't appropriate to have him in the house. Now it seemed she didn't want them to buy things for the boutique either. Didn't she understand how a successful store would benefit all of them? "What's your problem today?"

Mom blinked in surprise. "I don't have a problem. I'm just saying, don't get pushy. If they don't want to sell, they don't have to."

Mitch hooked his elbow on the back of the chair and grinned. "Aw, c'mon, Marie, I'm not going to threaten anybody. But the opportunities are too good here. Beth told me about some long bench with a lid that had a feather tick inside it. You'd never find anything like that in the city."

Mom nodded. "A sleeping bench. They were fairly common when I was growing up." She leaned against the counter, and a slight smile graced her lips. "My mom kept one in the basement, and she'd sleep down there during the summer when it got too hot in the house."

Mitch nudged Beth's shoulder. "See there? Another one available. Where do your grandparents live? We can ask about theirs, too."

Mom's smile turned into a grimace. "Don't bother. They won't sell." She reached for another plate.

Beth huffed. She flipped her hand toward her mother. "That's the attitude around here, Mitch. 'They won't sell.' " Irritation mingled with hopelessness. Sighing, she raised her shoulders in a defeated shrug. "We might as well just catalog everything in this house and plan on it being our starting inventory. Maybe we can use some of the money you got to hit some auctions and buy stuff that way."

Mitch's gaze narrowed, his eyes snapping. "Absolutely not. I took my vacation to come out here and build our inventory. That's exactly what we're going to do." He took Beth's hand and raised it to his lips. His chin whiskers pricked her skin. Rubbing his fingers over her knuckles, he leaned forward and whispered, "I'm a salesman, remember? Together we'll convince 'em, Lissie. Trust me."

Beth giggled, her earlier despondence melting away under his fervent gaze. She bounced to her feet. "Let's go to the café and get on the Internet. We can scope out some of the stuff I've already seen and get an idea of secondary market value."

Mitch rose more slowly. His lazy amble was only one of the things that drew Beth to him. His laid-back attitude was in direct contrast to her whirlwind emotions, and she loved how they balanced each other. They'd no doubt be very successful together in business. . .and in love. Her heart pounded with the thought.

She leaned into him, snuggling against his chest and releasing a sigh of contentment when his arms closed around her. Still nestled, she peeked at her mother. "We're going to the café, Mom. Be back by suppertime, okay?"

Mom gave a nod, but she didn't push any words past her tightly clamped lips.

Fourteen

Hi, Aunt Marie." Joanna's daughter, Kyra, slid into the corner booth and took the menu Marie offered.

Marie's heart fluttered, just as it had the first time one of Joanna's children used the title. The feeling of acceptance the simple word *aunt* delivered made her want to close her eyes and savor it. "Hi, honey. What brings you out this afternoon? Didn't you like what your mom was fixing for supper?"

Kyra laughed, the trickling tone very much like Joanna's. "No, it isn't that at all." She laid the menu on the table and folded her hands on top of it. "I really came to see Beth, but she isn't here. Again. I haven't been able to track her down all week."

Marie frowned. Beth had spent the entire week with Mitch, rarely appearing in the café except to grab something to eat and leave again. Mitch had indicated his vacation was nearing its end, and Marie admitted she'd be relieved to see him go. Beth's dissatisfaction with Sommerfeld had increased tenfold during her boyfriend's stay. The last few Xs on the calendar had been penned with force.

"She's been pretty occupied with Mitch." Marie managed to smile.

Kyra tipped her head, her cap ribbons shifting with the movement. "Has she had much success in buying items?"

Marie shook her head. "Not much, I'm afraid. A few things, but not nearly what she'd hoped. But in true Quinn fashion, she isn't willing to concede defeat. She intends to visit every house in Harvey County before she's finished."

Kyra laughed again. "She is determined!"

"More like stubborn," Marie said on a sigh.

"You know, I really admire her," Kyra said thoughtfully. "She sees what she wants, and she's willing to go after it. A lot of people, when faced with the kind of negative responses she's gotten, would just give up. But Beth continues to move forward because it means so much to her."

Marie wasn't sure Kyra fully understood Beth's motivation—achieving financial security at any cost—but she appreciated her niece's kind response. "Maybe you're right."

"I know I am." Kyra giggled, peeking around at the nearly empty café before leaning forward and whispering, "I had to be determined when it came to my relationship with Jacob. He's as bashful as his uncle Henry, and he would never have made a move if I hadn't let him know I was interested." She shook her head, her blue eyes sparkling. "But determination pays off." Pausing, she licked her lips. "You and Beth will be here for the wedding, won't you?"

Marie's heart sank. Despite having spent time with Joanna and her family over the past couple of weeks, no other relatives had approached to welcome Marie back. She was fairly certain she would not be welcome at a family event, but she hated to hurt Kyra's feelings. She spoke cautiously. "I'm not sure right now, honey. We'll probably go back to Cheyenne right after Christmas."

Kyra nodded, a sweet smile tipping up her lips. "I understand. Well. . .if it works for you to be there, I'd sure like that."

Marie's heart melted. "Oh, I would, too." She took in a deep breath, changing the subject. "You said you were looking for Beth. What did you need?"

Kyra sat up straight, eagerness showing in her bearing. "A bunch of us are driving to Newton tomorrow night for a skating party. I wondered if she and Mitch would like to join us. Several of her cousins are going, along with our friends, and we thought it would be a good way for her to get to know us better."

Marie slid into the opposite side of the booth. "Oh Kyra, it's so nice of you to want to include her, but. . ." Beth spending an evening with the Mennonite young people? While Mitch was in town? Marie couldn't envision it.

"We won't be out late," Kyra added. "With service on Sunday, we need to be home by ten at the latest. We all plan to meet at Uncle Art's business and carpool, and we always eat at McDonald's before we go to the skating rink, so we'll leave at five o'clock."

Marie sat silently, uncertain how to avoid hurting Kyra's feelings.

Kyra leaned back, linking her fingers together. "Just tell her, okay? If she and Mitch are there, they can ride over with Jacob and me. If they're not, I'll know they didn't want to go."

"I can't believe I'm doing this." Beth stood in the hallway, hands on hips, a scowl marring her pretty face. "Skating. . .in a skirt!"

Marie glanced over Beth's outfit—meshy-looking pink sweater, flaring peasant-style skirt, and brown T-strap flats. Six inches of bare leg showed between skirt and shoes. "You'll need socks."

"They're in my purse. There's no way I'm wearing them in public until I have the skates on my feet." She shook her head, her ponytail swaying. "I'm going to feel like such a misfit."

Marie recognized the insecurity beneath Beth's adamant statement. She stepped forward, cupped her daughter's cheeks, and gave her a kiss on the forehead. "You'll be fine."

Beth grasped her mother's wrists and gave them a squeeze. "I wish Mitch were coming."

"Why isn't he?"

The girl scowled. "He said he needed to get all his stuff packed to head back to Cheyenne tomorrow morning. But I think he just doesn't want to hang out with Kyra and Jacob and the rest. He feels funny around them."

Marie nodded. "I suppose that makes sense."

Resting her weight on one leg, Beth tipped her head and sighed. "Tell me again why I'm doing this?"

Marie imitated Beth's stance. "Number one, because it will do you good to get out with people your own age. And number two, because you'll get to know some of your cousins. . .at least a little bit. They are family, you know."

A lengthy, melodramatic sigh followed Marie's comments, but Beth made no disparaging remark. "Okay. Maybe if the young people get to know me, they'll tell their folks to sell stuff to me after all. I guess that would make this all worthwhile."

The reference to money-making made Marie clench her jaw.

"I just hope I stay on my feet, or everyone will see what I have on underneath." With a smirk, Beth lifted the hem of her skirt to reveal knee-length Spandex biking shorts.

Marie burst out laughing.

"I know, I know," Beth groused, "but I didn't have anything else. I'd stick out even worse if I wore my jeans."

"You could borrow my denim skirt. At least it won't flare out."

Beth shook her head. "Huh-uh. It's not my style. Besides"—she grinned impishly—"when I whirl around the floor, this one will be bee-yoo-ti-ful to watch." Rising on one toe, she spun in a circle, the

KIM VOGEL SAWYER

batik-patterned fabric becoming a blur of color.

Tears stung behind Marie's eyes as another picture formed in her memory—Beth on the first day of kindergarten in a pink polka-dot dress, twirling to make her skirt flare, a huge smile on her sweet face.

"All right then." Marie gave her daughter a hug, holding on tight. For some reason, letting Beth go was as bittersweet as it had been on that first school day so long ago. "Have a good time."

"I'll do my best." Beth headed for the door, her arm around Marie's waist. "What are you going to do while I'm out?"

"Empty Aunt Lisbeth's closet and bureau so I can put my own clothes away. I've been putting it off, but I can't handle living out of boxes any longer."

"Okay. Well—" They reached the back door and Beth grabbed the doorknob. "See you around ten."

Marie held the door open and watched Beth skip down the porch steps. When she reached the bottom, she lifted her hand in a brief wave, then rounded the corner to the car. Marie waited until the car had pulled out of the driveway before closing the door and heading to Lisbeth's bedroom.

She sat on the bed for a long moment, an odd loneliness filling her. The need to talk to someone, to share her concerns about Beth, struck hard. It wasn't a new feeling—she'd experienced it often during her years of raising a daughter alone. But it was one to which she'd never grown accustomed.

Over the years, the need to share her life with someone had often welled up. Sally had pushed her to date, to explore relationships, but something always held her back. Fear. Fear of choosing someone who wouldn't be able to love Beth, or who might even mistreat her. She read reports weekly in the newspaper about men abusing their stepchildren. Marie couldn't bear the thought of bringing someone home who would prove detrimental to Beth's well-being. So she'd always forced the loneliness aside, focusing instead on the relationship with her daughter.

But now Beth was grown, fumbling out into the world on shaky wings. It wouldn't be long before those wings would grow strong enough for her to fly, and Marie would be alone. What would she do then for companionship? But sitting here thinking wasn't getting her clothes put away.

Sighing, she pushed to her feet and crossed to the closet. She opened the single door and peered into the shadowy depths. Only about a dozen dresses hung there, all made from the same pattern. Although the dresses worn by Joanna and Deborah and many other women in the community were made from patterned fabric, all of Aunt Lisbeth's were solid colors—mostly deeper shades of blue, brown, or green.

Marie pulled one out and held it at arm's length, taking in the rounded neckline and attached modesty cape. Running her finger along the edge of the cape, she mentally compared the dress to the things in her clothes box. How her wardrobe had changed since she left Sommerfeld.

She laid the dress on the bed, then stacked the others on top of it, slipping the hangers free. When she had her own clothing hung up, she turned back to the stack of dresses and began folding them to put in the now-empty box. Before placing the last one in, she paused. Almost without thought, she slipped off her shirt and pulled the dress over her head.

A smile formed on her lips. She remembered Aunt Lisbeth as being very petite and slender, but she must have gained weight as she aged—the dress hung loosely on Marie's frame. She smoothed her fingers along the cape, her eyes closed, recalling how Mom had often scolded her for running her fingers up and down the cape edge of her dresses and leaving difficult-to-clean smudges in the fabric.

Turning to the small mirror above Aunt Lisbeth's dresser, she examined her reflection. A laugh blasted. She was glad there was no full-length mirror available to see the complete effect. The Mennonite dress's simple neckline combined with her untamed curls looked ridiculous.

But if her hair were smoothed down and a cap in place. . .

She hurriedly removed the dress and put her shirt back on. But as she picked up the dress to fold it and put it away, she found she couldn't do it. For some reason, sealing that dress in the box would be like sealing away her past. For good.

She shook her head. What was wrong with her? She dropped the dress on the bed and padded out to the living room, where she curled up in Aunt Lisbeth's rocker, one foot tucked up on the seat. Rocking gently, she looked out the window at the deep evening shadows and let her mind drift across the community. Several blocks over, Joanna probably had the ironing board out, pressing crisp creases into the pants her husband and son would wear to the meetinghouse tomorrow. She smiled, remembering the hubbub of getting things ready for Sunday when she was a little girl.

Caught in the middle of seven siblings, she had to listen to oldest sister Abigail's bossing and ignore her younger brothers' teasing. Her job had always been to make sure everyone's shoes were shined. She wondered if Mom still used a cold biscuit on Dad's shoes on Saturday nights or if they'd finally resorted to shoe polish and a buff cloth.

The sense of unity and belonging that came from the family piling into the buggy together on Sunday morning and rolling over the country roads, meeting other buggies and other families, was something she hadn't experienced since she was a teenager. Loneliness had been alien to her as a child. There was always someone—whether a brother or sister or friend—close at hand. The close-knit community had met every need for companionship. She would have never imagined feeling this alone.

Pain stabbed at her as she thought about all she'd lost when Jep died. She clutched her stomach as she remembered the horror of learning that his semi had gone off an embankment just weeks before Beth's birth. With his death, her dreams of family also died. From that point forward, it had only been her and the baby—no husband, no brothers or sisters for Beth.

And with her father's refusal to allow her to return home, not even cousins and aunts and uncles and grandparents. Just a young mother and her little girl.

Marie shot out of the rocking chair. She didn't want to revisit those pain-filled days. She paced through the dining room to the kitchen, seeking some task to fill her hands so her mind would stop reminiscing. Everything was put neatly away, so no work waited. There was no television with which to numb her senses. A glance at the clock told her it was too early to go to bed. Besides, she wanted to be awake when Beth came home.

Restlessness drove her to the bedroom, where Aunt Lisbeth's dress waited, mocking her with the differences between her childhood and her adulthood. She yanked up the dress, folded it into a bulky square, and shoved it into the box with the others. After sealing the box, she pulled on a jacket and stormed to the back door. A long walk should clear her mind. She'd walk until the memories faded away.

Even if it means I walk all the way back to Cheyenne.

Henry held a napkin around his peanut butter sandwich and ambled to the front-room window. While he ate, he watched two squirrels play a game of tag, their bushy tails fluffed out behind them. If he still had his old dog, Skippy, those squirrels would have a third playmate. Skippy had always enjoyed chasing the furry pests up into a tree. His barks would drown out the squirrels' scolding chirps.

He missed that old dog. He'd been a good companion. Between Skippy and Lisbeth, there'd always been someone to talk to in the evenings. Now? He sighed. Only squirrels.

He started to turn from the window, but a movement caught his eye.

Leaning forward, he focused on the street. A woman charged down the road, hands deep in the pockets of a jacket, hood shielding her profile from view. But the blue jeans identified her. Marie. No other woman in Sommerfeld would wear jeans.

He ducked away from the window, concerned she might turn her head and spot him watching.

Back in his kitchen, he leaned against the counter and finished his sandwich, the image of Marie's low-chinned pose making his heart thud. He wondered if she were heading out to the cemetery again. She was moving in that direction. She'd looked forlorn. Lonely. Henry understood that feeling.

He wadded up the napkin and threw it away before returning to the front room. Leaning into the corner of the couch, he closed his eyes and replayed evenings in Lisbeth's front room, seated beside her, peeking at an open letter in her lap. Lisbeth had shared every one of Marie's letters with him.

Marie hadn't been a prolific writer—sometimes entire months passed without word. But each time a letter arrived, Lisbeth would save it until Henry drove her home from the café, then she would read it out loud.

Snippets of letters came back to him—Beth's learning to walk, the loss of her first baby tooth and her delight at the quarter the tooth fairy left behind, starting new jobs, mourning the loss of Jep's mother to cancer, Beth's graduations from junior high, high school, and college.

A lifetime of memories were contained within Marie's letters, and Henry had lived each one of them vicariously through the words on the page.

He'd always held his breath when Lisbeth started reading, afraid she would announce that Marie had found another man to share her life. But no mention had ever been made of dating—her focus was always on providing for her daughter. The little girl who meant everything to her had grown into a young woman, who meant so much to her that Marie was willing to come back to a place she didn't want to be.

From the slump of her shoulders as she'd paced by his house, he knew being here was a heavy burden. In the nearly three weeks she'd been here, he hadn't witnessed many people reaching out to her, other than her sister Joanna. How hard it must be for her to go to the café every day and not be accepted.

He longed to relieve some of the sorrow she carried. As much as his heart twisted with the admission, he still loved her. It seemed odd, this long-held feeling for someone he hadn't seen on a daily basis for more than two decades. Yet his love for her had stayed alive, thanks to Lisbeth's willingness to share the letters. A part of him wanted to tell her that someone besides Joanna loved her. But he wouldn't do it.

On the shelf in his closet, a small box bore mute testimony to his love for her. For a moment he considered going in and opening the box, peeking at the white Bible he'd purchased as a way of proposing to her without having to rely on speech to communicate. How he hated his penchant for growing tongue-tied! But he'd known the little white Bible, traditionally carried in place of a wedding bouquet, would let her know what his heart felt.

He had tried to speak of his love that day long ago when he realized she intended to leave with Jep Quinn. He'd touched her arm and whispered, "I'll wait for you, Marie." How he had hoped she would look into his eyes and realize how much he loved her—and that he would take her back the moment she chose to return. And even though he still felt the same, he was older now. Wiser. He remembered too well the searing pain of watching that semi roll away, carrying the woman he loved.

A heart could only bear that kind of pain once in a lifetime. So he'd keep his feelings to himself this time. Apparently his love hadn't been enough to hold her in Sommerfeld twenty-three years ago. He wouldn't risk it again. This time, when she drove away, he wouldn't be watching.

FIFTEEN

Beth waved good-bye to Kyra and the others before sliding into the car and starting the engine. She released a huge breath of relief. The evening was over, and she'd survived. Actually, she mused, once she got over the initial embarrassment, it hadn't been so bad. Awkward, yes—especially in McDonald's, where people kept staring at the oddly dressed Mennonites—but not awful.

Beth angled the vehicle onto First Street, shaking her head. How did Kyra stand all that gawking every time she ventured out? It wasn't as if Beth wasn't accustomed to people looking at her. She realized she was attractive, and she dressed in a way that showcased her attributes, essentially inviting second glances. But tonight, the way people gaped and whispered behind their hands. . . Those stares weren't out of admiration, but morbid curiosity. She hadn't liked it at all.

She made the turn onto Cottonwood, and the headlights illuminated a dark-clothed pedestrian.

Beth recognized the gray hoodie—Mom. She came to a stop and rolled down the window. "What are you doing wandering the streets this late?"

Mom popped the door open and slid into the seat, even though the house was only a few yards ahead. "I went for a walk and ended up at the cemetery."

"At night?" Beth stared at her mother.

Mom leaned her head against the headrest. "Whew! I'm worn out. That was more of a hike than I expected at the end of a day."

Beth shook her head and pulled forward, turning into the driveway of the house. "Honestly, Mom! Walking to a cemetery at night? You would never have done that at home."

Her mother laughed softly. "Of course not. The cemetery is miles away. Everything here is within walking distance." She angled her head to smile at Beth. "How was the skating?"

Beth popped the car into PARK, jerked off the ignition, and scowled. "The skating part was fine, believe it or not. I had fun once I figured out how to turn corners without waving my arms all over the place and looking like an idiot. But how did you stand all those people staring at you? I felt like part of a circus freak show!"

Mom sighed, shifting sideways in the seat to face Beth. "You get used to it. Or you learn to ignore it."

"Well, I hated it. If I were a Mennonite, I'd change the dress code."

Mom burst out laughing.

"It's not funny!"

Mom's chortles continued. "Oh honey, I'm not laughing at you. But if you could have seen your face. . ."

Despite herself, a smile twitched at Beth's cheek. It was good to hear Mom laugh, to see her happy. Being here had been tough on her—Beth had seen evidence of that in how she often stared off into space or stood alone in the corner of the café's kitchen, her head low. But as soon as their three months' stay here was done and she had the money in hand, she'd make it all worthwhile for her mom.

Reaching across the console, she gave her mother's hand a loving squeeze. "Come on. Let's go put another X on the calendar—celebrate another day closer to being able to go home."

Marie rolled over, teased awake by the song of a cardinal from the spirea bushes outside the window. She lay, eyes closed, listening to the cheerful tune, and suddenly a hymn replaced the bird's song. "*Faith of our fathers, living still. . .*"

Her eyes popped open as the hymn filled her heart, seeming to echo through her soul. A strange tug brought her out of bed, to the window, to peer across the landscape of stubbly fields to the barely visible gray line of highway. Last night Beth had been eager to follow that highway back to Cheyenne. But, oddly, the X on the calendar had filled Marie with an unexplainable sadness.

"Faith of our fathers, holy faith. . ."

Last night's sadness returned, wrapping around her heart like a band. Her gaze fell to the box tucked in the corner—the one holding Aunt Lisbeth's clothes, the outer trappings that told of her inward beliefs. Beliefs Marie had held so long ago.

"I want your faith, Aunt Lisbeth," she whispered aloud, finally acknowledging the root of the tug on her heart. But how to regain it? With a pang, Marie realized she didn't know the answer to that question. Sinking onto the edge of the bed, she covered her face with her hands as loneliness smacked again—a loneliness that had haunted her for too many years.

In the past, she'd managed to push past the loneliness with busyness. Being a single mother, she'd poured herself into her daughter. As the only breadwinner, she'd poured herself into her work. But here, with Beth pursuing her own dreams, and hours of freedom away from the café, she had no escape. It engulfed her, increasing her longing for something—someone—to fill the void.

"Aunt Lisbeth, I wish you were here to advise me." She uttered the words on a note of anguish. And immediately an answer came: *Look to the Son.*

Of course. Aunt Lisbeth had always said the answer to any problem lay in God's handbook, the Bible. Marie knew where her Bible was—on the bookshelf back in her apartment in Cheyenne, no doubt covered with a layer of dust from lack of use. But surely Aunt Lisbeth's was here somewhere. Marie sat up, her gaze bouncing from the bureau to the chest in the corner to her aunt's desk to the closet and finally to the stand beside the bed.

Her hands reached toward the drawer in the little bedside stand. Holding her breath, she eased the drawer open, and her heart leaped with relief. There it waited, its faded black cover with the gold letters—*Holy Bible*—inviting Marie's entrance.

She slipped it from the drawer, cradling it between both palms, and carried it to the front room. She tugged Aunt Lisbeth's rocker until it faced the east window, then sat. For a moment she hesitated— where should she begin? *"Faith of our fathers, holy faith. . ."*

With a deep breath, she rested the book's spine against her lap and let it fall open. Psalm Twenty-three, all underlined in blue ink, came into view. Marie leaned over the Bible and read.

Dimly aware of her surroundings—the shifting shadow across the hardwood floor, the creaking of Beth's cot, the occasional sounds of vehicles outside the house—she moved from Psalms to Isaiah to John, thumbing in search of places where her aunt had underlined passages or written notes in the margins. Then she sought favorite verses from her childhood, reading entire chapters, absorbing, renewing, accepting.

When someone called her name, she jerked, half surprised that the voice was feminine and not a deep, masculine, heavenly timbre. Looking up, she spotted Beth in the wide doorway between the front room and the dining room. Her daughter's brow furrowed as her gaze landed on the book.

"What are you doing?"

"Reading." Marie's fingers twitched, eager to seek more passages. "If you're hungry, there's cereal and milk." She hoped Beth understood the message: *Please take care of your own needs right now so I can take care of mine.*

"Yeah, okay. Want a bowl?"

"No thanks. I'm fine."

Beth scratched her scalp with both hands, tousling her hair. "You okay?"

Marie smiled. "I'm fine, honey. And getting better by the minute. Enjoy your morning."

"I'm going to run a bath, then." Beth sent an odd look over her shoulder as she headed for the bathroom.

Marie returned to her reading. She continued until the banging of pots and pans in the kitchen disturbed her focus enough that she had to set the Bible aside and investigate. Beth, a towel wrapped turban-style around her head, gave her mother a scowl. "Are you finally done?"

Marie ignored the sarcastic bite in Beth's tone. "For now." She glanced at pans on the stove. "What are you doing?"

Beth shrugged and pulled a fork from a drawer. "Fixing lunch. You obviously weren't going to do it. I asked you twice."

Marie stared at her daughter. "You did?"

"Yes."

Marie lifted lids and discovered canned corn, potatoes, and pork chops. She turned to Beth in surprise. "Why so much food?"

Beth's jaw dropped. "You invited Joanna and her family for lunch today." She flapped her hand toward the living room. "Then you sat out there and didn't bother to fix anything. They'll be here in less than half an hour. I haven't even gotten dressed because I've been in here peeling potatoes." Looking pointedly at Marie's pajamas, she added, "What's the matter with you this morning?"

Marie reached out to give Beth a hug. The girl remained stiff and unresponsive. "There's nothing wrong with me, honey. In fact, I think I'm more right than I've been in quite a while. But we can talk about that later. I've got to take a bath."

"A bath?" Beth put her hands on her hips. "What about all this?" She gestured toward the stove.

"You're doing great." Marie blew Beth a kiss as she scampered around the corner. "Just watch the pork chops—don't want them to get too brown."

The water spattering against the porcelain tub covered Beth's grumbles.

⁂

Over the next two weeks, Marie started and ended each day with time in Aunt Lisbeth's Bible. Prayer grew from the Bible reading, and by the end of the second week Marie found herself whispering little prayers over the course of the day, conversation with her heavenly Father springing naturally from an overflowing heart.

She wanted to share with Beth the changes taking

place inside her, but her daughter resisted speaking of spiritual issues. Beth's attitude seemed to grow more surly by the day, complaining about Mitch's departure and the slow progress she'd made in securing items for her planned boutique. The highlight of her day was drawing a big, black X in the box on the calendar.

Joanna, however, had squealed with delight when Marie told her she was finding her way back to her childhood faith. "Oh Marie! How? When?" Joanna wrapped her in a hug that stole her breath. "Oh, never mind—I don't need the details. It's enough just to see the sparkle in your eyes." Pulling back, she had cupped Marie's face and beamed with tears glittering in her eyes. "Oh Marie. . .welcome home."

"Welcome home." As much as Marie had celebrated hearing those words from Joanna, she still held a deep longing to hear them from the lips of her father. When she'd mentioned that to Joanna, her sister's face had clouded.

"Marie, don't put your faith on Dad's shoulders. He'll only let you down."

Marie's mind replayed Joanna's warning as she loaded the last of the dirty dishes into the dishwasher at the café. Tiredness from the busy Saturday made her shoulders ache, but it couldn't compare with the ache that stabbed her heart every time she recalled her father's condemning tone and harsh expression. She knew she would never feel as though she had truly come home until she made peace with her father. But how?

The back screen door squeaked. Her focus on

emptying the bin of dirty dishes, she didn't look up. "Hey Beth."

"It's me, Henry."

Marie jerked upright and spun toward the door. Automatically, she smoothed her hand over her hair. The curls had grown, becoming less manageable over her weeks in Sommerfeld. She'd pulled her hair into a ponytail at the crown of her head, but errant strands sprang free in every direction. She wasn't sure why it bothered her to have Henry see her in a state of unkemptness. She only knew discomfort struck with his presence.

She went back to transferring plates from the bin to the dishwasher, jabbering to cover the erratic beat of her heart. "Deborah and Trina aren't here. I told them I could finish up and they should go home. W—what brings you back? Deborah said you'd finished the bookwork for the week."

"A storm is brewing. There's sheet lightning in the east."

Marie glanced at him. His dark-eyed gaze followed her every move. She swallowed and turned back to the plates. "A lightning storm in November?"

He shrugged. "It's unusual but not unheard of. Kansas is unpredictable."

So are you. "I—I haven't heard any thunder."

He took a forward step, bringing himself into her line of vision. "It's not close enough yet. But the wind is picking up. It won't be long before we'll hear it."

That still didn't explain why he was here. "Thank you for telling me. Guess I'll hurry home then."

"I could drive you."

The quiet statement sent Marie's heart into her throat. She didn't look at him. "I can walk."

"I know you can. I've seen you walking all over the place."

The gently teasing undercurrent forced Marie's gaze around. His smile invited her to respond with one of her own.

"These storms can come up fast, and I don't want you caught in it. I'll be happy to drive you."

Marie stood, hands curled around a plate, peering into Henry's eyes. The realization that he'd observed her restless strolls, that he'd returned out of concern for her safety, brought a rush of gratefulness. . .and something else she couldn't define. "I appreciate that, Henry. Thank you." She focused on the dishes, stacking the last few as quickly as possible into the tray. "Beth went into Newton earlier. I have no idea if she's back yet."

Henry leaned against the far end of the rinsing trough. "She isn't."

Marie chuckled as she pushed the tray into the dishwasher, slid the door closed, and flipped the switch. The pound of water against the metal walls of the washer drowned out the sound of her laughter.

"What's so funny?" Henry raised his voice above the noisy machine.

Marie removed her apron, shaking her head. "I'd forgotten there were no secrets in Sommerfeld. I should have just asked you if Beth had returned."

Henry grinned. "Speaking of no secrets. . ." He

hesitated, his grin fading and his neck blotching with red.

Marie's hands froze in the process of rolling the apron into a ball. She waited, the pulsing beat of the dishwasher matching the pound of her heart. She had to strain to catch his next words.

"Joanna tells me you're praying and reading the Bible every day." He swallowed, the bob of his Adam's apple capturing her attention. "I'm happy for you, Marie. Lisbeth would be, too."

Her gaze bounced up to meet his, and the twinkle of tears in the corners of his eyes made her heart lurch. Unable to reply, she merely nodded.

He blinked quickly, and the shimmer disappeared. He held his hand toward the door. "Are you ready?"

She nodded, scooped up the basket of dirty linens, and scurried toward the door while Henry turned out the lights. The cool air, heavy with the essence of rain, filled her nostrils. The first gentle rumble of thunder in the distance echoed in her ears. Henry's trembling fingers on her back ignited her senses.

"Come on, Marie. Let's get you safely home."

Sixteen

Marie stood in front of Lisbeth's closet, remembering her reaction to the whisper touch of Henry's fingers on her back as he'd guided her to his waiting car so he could transport her safely home last night. *Just loneliness*, she told herself. Like her flustered reaction when Mitch stepped into the kitchen. She would have had the same response with anyone. It had been a long time since she'd been shown that kind of consideration.

It wasn't Henry. It was loneliness.

She told herself this again as she dressed for service. Her heart pounded as she considered the possible ramifications of her showing up this morning. She knew Joanna would be thrilled. So would Henry. But everyone else? She hoped no one—her father, in particular—would make a scene that would embarrass her sister or Henry. But it was time for her to worship formally again.

Beth didn't understand. When she had returned from Newton in the midst of a pouring rainstorm,

Marie had told her she planned to start attending church. Beth had argued, pointing out all the things Marie herself feared. "You're just going to get yourself hurt," she shouted, her voice booming more loudly than the thunder that shook the house. When Marie remained determined to go, Beth had stomped off to bed.

Well, Marie decided as she buttoned her blouse beneath her chin and tucked the tails into her skirt, *Beth might be right.* She could get hurt. But she knew she would hurt more, in her heart, if she ignored the tug of the Holy Spirit to return to the fold. Even if people rejected her, she had to at least try.

In the bathroom, she pulled her hair into a ponytail and formed a makeshift bun. Using bobby pins, she anchored the strands that were too short to reach the tail. She had found Lisbeth's caps in a box on the shelf of the closet and had even considered putting one on, but in the end she decided against it. She wasn't a meetinghouse member, and she wasn't sure she would seek membership again. Right now, she only wanted to attend, to listen, to learn, to rediscover a portion of what she'd left behind when she drove away with Jep.

One step at a time.

She peeked in at Beth. Her daughter slept soundly, her hair spread across her pillow. The familiar swell of mother-love rose in her breast, and she tiptoed across the room to smooth the tangled blond locks and place a kiss on Beth's forehead.

Beth stirred, her face crunching. Her eyes slid

opened, and she blinked several times, her bleary gaze on Marie's face. "Mom?" her voice croaked.

"I'm sorry. I didn't mean to wake you."

Beth scowled at her mother. "You're going, aren't you?"

Marie nodded.

"But it's still raining, isn't it?"

The patter on the roof gave the answer. Marie smiled. "I won't melt. I'm not made of sugar." How often had she told Beth she needn't fear the rain because only sugar melted in the rain. Her own mother had told her the same thing.

Beth rolled over. "Well, have fun."

Her daughter's tone stung a bit, but Marie smoothed her hair again and focused instead on the calling of her heart. "I'll be back by noon; then I'll fix us some lunch."

Beth didn't reply. Marie tiptoed out, pulling the door closed. She took a jacket from the hooks by the back door and held it over her head as she hop-skipped around puddles on the way to the car.

When she reached the meetinghouse parking lot, she felt a lurch of discomfort. How obvious her bright red car looked among the plain black ones lining the side of the meetinghouse.

"No more obvious than my uncovered head," she reminded herself. Reaching under the seat, she located an umbrella. She heaved a sigh of relief when she discovered it was her own solid blue one rather than Beth's bright orange, daisy-covered one. Much less conspicuous.

Headlights cut through the curtain of rain as another car pulled up next to hers. Marie squinted through the foggy glass and saw a familiar face—Joanna's. Heart leaping with gratitude for the perfect timing, she popped her door open and thrust out the umbrella. Joanna stepped from her car and joined Marie under the plastic cover.

"You ready?"

Marie took in a fortifying breath. "As ready as I'll ever be."

Joanna's husband and children jumped from their vehicle and dashed toward the white clapboard meetinghouse. Hugo and Gomer entered the door at the right corner in the front of the building, and Kyra and Kelly ran side by side to the door at the back. Joanna and Marie followed the girls, their elbows linked, sidestepping around puddles.

A musty smell from the coats dripping on hooks assaulted Marie's nose as she entered the cloakroom. Several women stood in the room, quietly chatting. When Marie entered, the talk immediately stopped, leaving an uncomfortable silence. Marie put her coat on a hook and then turned to face Joanna.

Joanna offered an encouraging smile. "Let's go find our seats."

A shiver shook Marie's frame. She no longer had a seat. After she'd left with Jep, the leaders had voted on her excommunication. What would happen when she entered the worship room? Would people point fingers and send her away, as her father had done?

Joanna took Marie's arm. "Come on." Her voice was gentle, understanding.

Swallowing, Marie stayed close to Joanna as they stepped past the quiet women who watched their progress. A flurry of voices sounded behind them the moment they left the cloakroom. "That was Marie! Yes, Marie Koeppler—remember?" Marie ignored the hushed remarks.

When she and her sister entered the simple square worship room, Marie let her gaze sweep the area. Memories rushed back as she found the preachers' bench along the side wall behind the unstained wood pulpit. Two rows of benches faced the pulpit. Several men and boys, dressed in black suits and white shirts, sat on the right-hand side. A hat rack, suspended from the ceiling, hung over the last row of men's benches. The hats, wet from the rain, dripped onto the heads of the men seated beneath them.

Joanna tugged on Marie's arm, leading her to a center bench on the left-hand side. Joanna slid in first, followed by Marie; then Kyra and Kelly sat on Marie's other side, surrounding her with their comforting presence. A quick glance confirmed her parents had not yet arrived. She aimed her gaze at her lap, her heart pounding, fearful of what might happen when her father came through the front door and spotted her uncovered head.

She knew, even without looking, the instant he arrived. A hush fell over the room, followed by an air of expectancy. Her scalp prickled, and she wondered if her father's large hand would grab the back of her neck and pull her from the seat. Her heart pounded with the thud of footsteps on the wooden floorboards. Then the creak of a bench and a sigh as collective breaths were released.

Marie peeked sideways to see the swish of a dark blue dress moving down the side aisle. Allowing her gaze to drift upward, she focused on the profile of the woman who moved into an open spot two benches closer to the front. Her heart skipped a beat and tears stung her eyes. *Momma*. Her throat convulsed with the desire to rush forward, to cry out the name she hadn't uttered in more than twenty years, to embrace the woman who once held her to her breast.

Joanna's hand clamped over Marie's fist in her lap, and Marie jerked her head to peer into her sister's eyes. Joanna's eyes also glittered. Marie's gaze moved past Joanna to the other side of the church, to the man who had raised her. His face was aimed forward, his jaw firm, his eyes steely.

Marie swallowed. He didn't want her here. She read that clearly in his stiff bearing and clamped jaw. But he stayed silent on his bench. Throughout the entire service—the entry of the ministers, the hymn singing, the prayer and scripture reading, the sermon, the closing hymn and announcements—her father remained silent on his bench, never so much as flicking a glance in her direction.

When the benediction was complete, he stormed to the hat rack, snatched his hat from its hook, and charged out the door. His wife followed.

Marie's heart leaped with hope when, just before

slipping through the cloakroom door, her mother paused and looked over her shoulder, meeting Marie's gaze. A tender longing lingered in the brief, silent exchange. Then she disappeared from view.

Joanna squeezed Marie's hand as three men stepped to the end of their bench. Marie swallowed the tears that choked her throat and turned to face the men. She held her breath, waiting for them to tell her she should not return. But to her surprise, the tallest one offered a hesitant smile.

"Marie?" He clutched his hands against his stomach, his blue eyes searching hers. "Do you remember me?"

She frowned, looking into lined eyes. Suddenly recognition dawned. "Art?"

He nodded, his smile growing. He gestured to the two younger men standing behind him. "And Conrad and Leo, too."

Marie met each of her brothers' gazes in turn. Still holding Joanna's hand, she stammered, "Oh my. You—you're all grown up, you little pests."

Her face filled with heat as she realized what she'd just said, but all three men laughed, earning a stern look from the residing preacher.

Art touched her arm. He kept his voice low. "Where can we go and visit?" His gaze swept across the other family members standing in an awkward circle.

"My house," Marie blurted. *My house? Since when is it* my *house?* She remembered too late that Beth was there, maybe still in her pajamas, not expecting company.

Joanna shook her head as Hugo and Gomer joined the little circle. "My house is bigger, and I have a turkey in the oven. Let's all go there today, hmm?"

Marie's eyes filled with tears. Obviously Joanna had planned—in advance—a welcome-back-to-the-family celebration for her. Knowing her parents wouldn't be there made the situation bittersweet, yet how wonderful to experience the warmth of her sister and brothers' acceptance.

"Thank you. I'll need to go home first and—" She intended to say, "Tell Beth where I'll be." But Art offered a suggestion.

"You could pick up your daughter. We'd like to get to know her, too."

Tears of gratitude spilled down Marie's cheeks. Swallowing, she offered an eager nod. "I'll be there soon."

She turned to retrieve her jacket from the cloakroom but froze when she heard her sister's words: "Henry, if you don't have lunch plans, please come to our house. We have plenty."

Her heart pounding, she waited for his response.

"I usually have lunch with Deborah's family on Sundays. They're expecting me. But thank you for the invitation. Maybe another time?"

Joanna's laughter rang. "Sure. There'll be plenty of other times."

Marie experienced a brief roller-coaster ride of emotion—relief, followed by disappointment, followed by elation. Before she could examine the odd feelings, she dashed to the cloakroom, grabbed her jacket, and ran through the drizzling mist to her car.

Henry slapped his hat on his pant leg, shaking off the raindrops, before knocking on Deborah's front door. Normally he entered through the back, but on Sundays his sister insisted on formality. Trina opened the door to him and took his hat with a twinkling grin. He chucked her under the chin to thank her, smiling when she giggled.

Trina scampered to the hall tree, hung up his hat, then headed toward the back of the house. "C'mon, Uncle Henry. Mama's just about got everything on the table."

Henry smiled and followed. Of all his nieces and nephews, Trina was his favorite. Her infectious giggle and freckled nose had always been impossible to resist. There were times when sympathy swelled for her—he believed her parents were too strict, their expectations unreasonable. But he was cautious enough to keep that opinion to himself. No need to incite rebellion in the teenager's heart. He also carefully refrained from giving her preferential treatment to avoid conflict with her cousins. But he couldn't deny she possessed a special piece of his heart. If he had a daughter, he'd want her to be like Trina. Suddenly an image of Beth Quinn in her faded blue jeans and tight shirt flashed in his memory. He scowled. There was no comparison between Beth and Trina. And hadn't he decided to come to his sister's house today so he wouldn't be faced with Marie Koeppler Quinn and her daughter? There was no sense in thinking about either of them.

Still, as he sat at Troy and Deborah's table, eating his sister's good cooking and participating in the conversation, his mind kept flitting down a few blocks, to where half of the Koeppler family had gathered. He chewed Deborah's baked ham and wondered if Marie and Beth were enjoying Joanna's turkey. He listened to Troy's opinion on the proper irrigation of winter wheat and wondered what kind of reminiscing was taking place around Joanna's dining room table. He watched Trina and her brother Tony engage in a quick exchange of elbow pokes and wondered if Beth was feeling at ease with Kyra and her other cousins.

By the time Deborah served dessert, Henry knew he wouldn't be able to relax that evening unless he could find out how the reunion between Marie and her brothers had gone. He excused himself as soon as he could, experiencing a prick of guilt at Trina's hurt look when he refused a game of Wahoo, their usual Sunday afternoon activity. He gave his niece a one-handed hug and promised, "Next Sunday we'll play two rounds, okay?"

Trina nodded, releasing a sigh. "I'll just play with Tony." She shot her brother a pointed look. "Unless he cheats. Then I'm putting it away."

Henry shook his finger at the thirteen-year-old. "No cheating, Tony. Playing fair in games leads to playing fair in life."

The boy sent him an innocent look. "I don't cheat. . .much."

Henry stifled the chuckle that rose in his throat. Affecting a stern look, he said, "Any is too much. Understand?"

Tony shrugged, offering a sheepish grin. "Okay." He punched Trina in the arm. "I get the blue marbles."

Both scurried off. Henry called good-bye to his sister and brother-in-law, then headed for his car. The rain had stopped, but the sky still looked overcast and dark, much like a late winter evening. A glance at his wristwatch told him it was still early afternoon. He snorted. He'd been foolish to leave his sister's place so soon. Surely the Koepplers were all still visiting, getting reacquainted. He should have stayed and played Wahoo with his niece and nephew. Should he go back in?

No, he wouldn't be able to focus on the game anyway. He put the car in gear and drove slowly through the rain-drenched streets, his tires slipping in the softened earth. His windows fogged, and he cracked one open, allowing in the fresh scent of after-rain. Passing Hugo and Joanna's house, he cranked his head around, searching for Marie's car. It wasn't there.

With a frown, his heart pattering in concern, he faced forward again. Why would she have left so early? Maybe the reunion hadn't gone well after all. Worry struck hard, and he curled his fingers around the steering wheel and increased his speed slightly, eager to reach his home and telephone Hugo.

He cleaned his feet on the doormat and headed to his telephone without removing his hat. He dialed with a shaking finger and waited through four rings before a female voice answered. "Hello?"

"Is this Kyra?"

"No, it's Kelly."

She would do. "This is Henry Braun. I just wondered. . ." Suddenly he felt foolish asking the teenager about Marie. He blurted, "Is your father or mother there?"

"Just a moment, please."

After a scuffle, accompanied by the mumble of voices, he heard Joanna's voice. "Hello, Henry. What can I do for you?"

The telephone tight against his chin, he whispered, "Did Marie leave already?"

"No, she's still here." Joanna kept her voice low, too—as if they shared a secret. "She and the boys are having a wonderful time visiting."

Henry frowned. "I drove by, and when I didn't see her car, I became concerned."

"Ah." Joanna didn't question why he was driving past her house when it was out of the way between his home and Deborah's. "Beth left with the car about an hour ago. Said she had some things to do this afternoon. But she's coming back around seven to pick up her mother."

"Oh." A relieved breath whooshed from his lungs. "I hope all went well."

"Very well." Joanna's tone held an undercurrent of joy.

"Good." Henry swallowed, suddenly wishing he could be at Joanna's, be a part of the circle accepting Marie home. "Well, I'll let you go then."

"All right. Good-bye, Henry."

He placed the receiver in its cradle, then stood, his hand still cupping the black plastic, his gaze on Lisbeth's sampler. He smiled. Marie had been welcomed home, first by her sister and now by three of her brothers. Surely it was only a matter of time before her parents and remaining siblings accepted her as a member of the family again. Just as Lisbeth had hoped and prayed.

Unless. . . His smile faded. Unless Beth created problems. Why hadn't the girl stayed, become acquainted with her uncles and aunts and cousins? Beth meant so much to Marie. The rebellious young woman could pull her away again.

SEVENTEEN

Marie refilled a customer's coffee mug, offering a smile and a cheery, "Can I do anything else for you?"

The man glanced at his wife, then shook his head. "No thanks. Just the check, please."

"Coming right up." Marie nearly skipped to the back to tally the tab. Her heart continued to sing despite the gloomy weather outside the café. The wonderful afternoon two days ago with Art, Joanna, Leo, Conrad, and their families—talking, laughing, hugging, bonding—still lingered, offering a peace and acceptance that resulted in an explosion of joy. *Thank You, Lord, for this step toward reconciling with my family.* She couldn't stifle the smile on her face, even when patrons didn't respond to it.

They would respond someday, she assured herself. If her family could welcome her back, the community would, too, given time. And if they didn't? She shrugged as she wrote the final dollar amount at the bottom of the ticket. She would be fine. She had her

God, her daughter, and her sister and brothers again. That was more than she'd ever hoped to have. More than enough.

She returned to the table and slipped the square of paper next to the man's elbow. "Have a good day, and come see us again."

"We will," the man responded. "And maybe when we come back, you will have solved your mystery."

Marie tipped her head. "Mystery?"

The couple exchanged a quick look. "The whole town is buzzing," the man said. "We even got wind of it in Lehigh."

Marie moved closer to the table, her curiosity piqued. "What's the buzz?"

The woman leaned forward, her eyes snapping with eagerness. "This past Sunday, two families returned from afternoon visits to discover their homes had been burglarized."

Marie jerked back. "In Sommerfeld?"

The man shrugged, his thick eyebrows pulling down. "To be honest, I'm surprised it hasn't happened before. You don't have any police force on duty here, and you're right off the highway. That's an open invitation to criminals."

Marie looked back and forth from the man to the woman. "Were the homes vandalized, as well?"

"Oh no," the woman said. "No damage was done."

Marie blew out a short breath. "That's a relief."

The man's expression turned thoughtful. "From what I heard, there was no disruption of property at all, and only one or two items were taken from each residence. It's almost like the thief knew exactly what he wanted and where to find it."

At the man's words, a warning bell clanged in Marie's head. She forced a quavery smile. "Let's hope it was just a fluke. I'd hate to think of the town being targeted by thieves."

"I'm sure it was just a one-time thing," the man said, pushing himself from the table. "It's too bad though. After all these years of peaceful living, your little community has to be impacted by the world's evil."

Marie stood beside the table while the man and his wife shrugged into their jackets, picked up the tab, and headed to the cash register. Burglaries. In Sommerfeld. That explained the subdued behavior of many customers this morning.

The sounds of the café drifted into the distance as she replayed the man's comment about the thief knowing what he wanted and where to find it. An unpleasant idea formed in her head, washing away the happiness of the morning.

As soon as the couple left, Marie charged across the floor to Trina, who was closing the cash drawer. The girl released a gasp when Marie touched her arm.

"Trina, do you know anything about the burglaries that took place Sunday?"

The girl's gaze flitted to the side, and she nibbled her lower lip.

Marie gave Trina's arm a gentle squeeze. "Please, honey. I really want to know."

Trina's wide-eyed gaze met Marie's. "All I know

is what I've heard in passing. Maybe you should ask Mama."

Marie looked toward the kitchen doorway. Even though the other woman had loosened up a bit over their time of working together, Deborah had been exceptionally tight-lipped today, reminding Marie of her first days in the café. Her heart pounded, fear taking hold. Did Deborah suspect what Marie was now thinking?

After giving Trina's arm a light pat, Marie entered the kitchen.

Deborah sat on a stool near the dishwasher, her head back and eyes closed. Marie cleared her throat, and the woman opened her eyes and shifted her gaze. When she spotted Marie, she pursed her lips. "Did you need something?"

Marie moved in front of Deborah. "Yes. I need you to tell me what happened in town Sunday afternoon."

Deborah's eyes narrowed. "I don't like to gossip."

Marie sucked in a deep breath. "I'm not asking you to. But I need to know what happened."

Deborah sighed. "Marie." She shook her head. For a moment she appeared to falter, her forehead creasing with a pained expression. But then she thrust out her lower jaw in an expression of stubbornness. "I can't say. I don't have facts, only hearsay, and I won't repeat it." She charged across the floor to the stove and banged pots around.

Marie stood for a moment, staring at Deborah's back. Her heart pounded so hard she feared it would leave her chest.

Pulling her apron over her head, she called, "The breakfast rush is over. I'm taking a break. I'll be back in half an hour or so."

Deborah nodded without turning around.

Marie left the café and followed the sidewalk to Henry's shop. A cool breeze nipped at her bare legs, and her feet slipped on the rain-slick bricks, but she kept a steady pace.

The overhead garage door hung half open, and she heard muffled clanging from the depths of the metal building that housed Henry's mechanic shop. She ducked through the opening and blinked as her eyes adjusted to the bright fluorescent lights that hung on chains from the ceiling. A truck stood in the middle of the concrete floor, and two legs stuck out from beneath it.

Marie walked to the legs, her wet shoes squeaking. "Henry?"

His legs jerked. Then his feet rose slightly, and his body glided out from beneath the truck on a flat, rolling platform. Once he was clear of the vehicle, he sat up, gaping at her. A smudge of grease adorned his left cheek, and he held a wrench. "What brings you here?"

Marie crouched down, bringing her eyes level with his. "Henry, will you tell me about the burglaries that happened Sunday?"

He grimaced, rubbing his hand over his face. The action smeared the grease almost to his jaw. Had the situation been less serious, she might have teased him about it.

"I don't know a lot," he said slowly, placing the wrench on the floor beside him with a light *clank*.

"Please." Marie detested the tremble in her voice. "Tell me. I need to know."

He met her gaze, and she saw sympathy in his dark eyes. "Apparently, while the Albrechts and Goerings were visiting neighbors Sunday afternoon, someone broke into their houses and took some things."

Marie frowned. Her mouth went dry. "Antiques?"

He fiddled with the wrench, his head low. "Yes."

She swallowed hard. "Do you know what?"

His sigh sounded pained. "A Russian trunk from the Goerings and a mantel clock from the Albrechts."

Marie's heart caught.

His gaze still aimed downward, he added, "They might not be the only ones missing things."

"What do you mean?"

"After the news came out, people started checking their barns and sheds. Some found things missing they didn't notice right away because they weren't items they used every day."

Marie lurched to her feet.

Henry pressed one hand to the concrete and stood. He held his dirty hand toward her. "Now don't jump to conclusions."

Whirling on him, Marie's temper flared. "I don't have to. The whole town will jump to conclusions for me. You know they'll blame Beth."

His silence confirmed her statement.

She laughed. "All morning, people were giving

201

me funny looks, whispering behind their hands. I thought it was because I'd dared to show up at the meetinghouse, but now it makes sense. They're all thinking my daughter is a thief!"

"Marie—"

She spun away from his reaching hand and tender look. "Just because I raised her in the world doesn't mean I raised her poorly. I taught her right from wrong."

"Of course you did."

His calm reply deflated her anger. Did he truly believe her? Did she truly believe it herself? Tears stung her eyes. "But no one else will believe it, will they?"

Once again, Henry fell quiet.

Marie shook her head. "I'd better let you work. Thanks for telling me." She heard him call her name as she dashed toward the door, but she didn't turn around. As she hurried down the sidewalk, her heart thumped out a fear-filled message: *Not Beth, not Beth, not Beth.*

Marie bypassed the turn to the café and went directly to Lisbeth's. She walked around to the back. The car wasn't there, which meant Beth was still hunting. Or stealing. *Stop that!* Maybe they hadn't attended church regularly after Jep's mother died, and they hadn't prayed together the way her parents had with her, but she had taught Beth morals. Beth would not steal. She wouldn't!

Marie repeated those words in her mind as she moved from room to room in the small house, peeking in closets and under the cot in Beth's room. She found nothing that didn't belong there, unless she counted the two mismatched socks hiding beneath the cot. Given Beth's irrational revulsion for the basement, she didn't bother to check there. As she stood in the middle of the dining room, realization struck.

There wasn't any place in the house to hide things, but there was a shed behind the Café. At one time it had sheltered Lisbeth's buggy, but the buggy had been sold years ago. Deborah had said it stood empty, too run-down to be of any real use. It would be a perfect place to hide things.

Marie took the shortcut between the houses that led to the alley behind Lisbeth's café. Despite the cool temperature, she broke out in a sweat. By the time she reached the double doors that opened out onto the alley, she found herself taking great heaving breaths. She examined the ground in front of the shed, looking for evidence of recent activity, but the rains had swept the area clean.

Her heart pounding, she clasped the board that lay across metal hooks, sealing the doors closed. She hefted the weathered board aside and slipped her fingers through the hole that served as a handle in the right-hand door. Her chest boomed with each heartbeat as she tugged the door. The metal hinges resisted her efforts, and she grunted, giving a mighty yank that swung the door wide. An unpleasant odor greeted her nostrils—mildew and mouse. She covered her nose with her hand and forced herself to step inside.

Only thin slivers of murky light sneaked between cracks in the planked walls. She squinted, forcing her eyes to adjust to the shadows. When she could finally focus, her legs nearly gave way.

Except for a pile of mouse-chewed burlap sacks and two rusty tin cans, the shed was empty.

She stepped back into the alley and slammed the door shut, sagging against it, her chest heaving with breaths of relief. Eventually her quivering limbs returned to normal, allowing her to stand upright. She dropped the board in place, berating herself. Of course Beth was innocent. How could she have thought otherwise, even for one moment? Guilt struck hard. She wouldn't let Beth know of her momentary fears.

Tonight, when they were alone, she would find out where Beth had gone Sunday afternoon. Armed with that information, she would be ready to defend her daughter to anyone who dared suggest she had something to do with the burglaries.

She headed for the café, sucking in big gulps of the clean air, ridding herself of the worry that had driven her across town in search of the truth. As the customer from Lehigh had said, with no police force in town, it was inevitable that something like this would happen. Beth had nothing to do with it.

Marie entered the café, her head held high.

That evening, when she and Beth sat at the kitchen table enjoying glasses of milk and leftover apple pie from the café, Marie leaned back in the chair and let out a sigh. "I suppose you've heard the scuttlebutt around town."

Beth raised one eyebrow, a bite of pie halfway to her mouth. "I haven't been in town the past few days. But the people have sure been acting whacky. I actually had a door slammed in my face this morning." She put the bite into her mouth.

"I hear there have been some burglaries." Marie watched Beth's face.

Beth went on eating. "Oh yeah?"

"Antiques from houses, and items from barns and sheds."

The fork paused in its path, then lowered to her plate. "Oh, great."

Marie nodded. "That's what I thought this morning when I found out."

Beth pushed her plate away. "I suppose as the newcomers we're being held accountable."

Marie shrugged. "It does probably look suspicious— first you going door-to-door, soliciting antiques and unusual items. Then those same items being taken."

Beth pressed her palms to the table, ready to jump up.

Marie put her hand on her daughter's arm. "But we can eliminate the suspicions very easily."

Beth sank back into the chair, a scowl marring her face. "How? Let them invade our privacy and search the house? They won't find anything."

"I know." Marie slid the half-eaten slice of pie back in front of Beth and picked up her own fork. "All we have to do is account for our whereabouts. If we can prove where we were on Sunday when the thefts took place, no one should be able to point fingers."

Beth sat back in her chair and crossed her arms. "Why should I do that? Isn't my word good enough?"

"Honey—"

"No!" Beth held up both hands, as if deflecting a blow. "I'm not *accounting* for anything. I didn't do it, and I'll tell that to anyone who asks. That's going to have to be good enough."

Shaking her head, Marie fixed her daughter with an imploring look. "Beth, I understand how you feel, but unless you set the community's mind at ease, things could get very uncomfortable here. . . for both of us."

"I don't care." Beth pointed to the calendar and gave an arrogant toss of her head. "See all those Xs? That means my days here are limited. These people can think what they want to. It doesn't matter to me."

Marie's hand trembled as she put down her fork. "Will you at least tell *me* where you were?"

"Where I was is my business. No one else's." Beth rose, her eyebrows high, her head held at a haughty angle. "You're just going to have to trust me, Mom. I know what I'm doing." She stormed from the room. The slam of her door signaled the end of the conversation.

EIGHTEEN

Henry sat at his usual table in Lisbeth's Café, an untouched plate of scrambled eggs and bacon in front of him. He was the only Sommerfeld resident in the café. Every other customer was an out-of-towner. Each morning over the past two weeks, he'd noticed fewer and fewer townspeople coming into the café, but this was the first time absolutely no Sommerfeld residents started their day with one of Deborah's fresh-baked cinnamon rolls.

As the month marched toward the Thanksgiving holiday, the tension in town increased. Talk had started about foregoing Sunday afternoon visits so everyone could go home and watch their properties. Henry wasn't in favor of this—the tradition of Sunday visits was something that went back through generations, and he feared if it stopped for a short time, it might permanently drop away. These kinds of changes had led to congregation splits in the past.

Although he'd been very young, he still remembered the upheaval of the last split, when the decision was made to allow church members to have electricity and drive automobiles. Some of those who were in fierce opposition to making use of the worldly conveniences joined a community in southeast Kansas. His own parents and Lisbeth, like a few other families in the community, hadn't adopted the changes, but had left it to individual conscience rather than condemning those who elected to make use of the technologies.

But now, with burglaries continuing to take place every week, the murmurs were rising, the cry for protection heard from several corners of the community. Henry feared what might happen if the thief was not caught soon.

Marie bustled past, plates in hand. She flicked a glance in his direction but didn't smile. His heart ached. She looked haggard, the lines around her eyes pronounced, the bounce gone from her step. Although she had continued to attend service at the meetinghouse, which thrilled him, he wondered when she would finally grow weary of the members holding themselves aloof and stop coming.

She headed back into the kitchen, and he stared at the doorway for long minutes, wishing Lisbeth were there. Lisbeth, in her wisdom, might have ideas on how to bring everyone together, to eliminate the fears and find the truth.

Truth. Henry lowered his gaze to the tabletop. What was the truth? Marie had been adamant when she'd come to his shop two weeks ago seeking answers. He wanted to think as she did, that her daughter had nothing to do with the disappearance of those belongings. Yet part of him couldn't help but wonder about the coincidence. Beth had asked about purchasing certain items, the owners declined, and the items disappeared.

The town had already tried and convicted Beth. He knew that's why people were staying away from the café—they didn't want to support a person they viewed as immoral. *Lisbeth, this isn't what you had in mind when you established the conditions of your will, was it?* How could Marie even think about staying in Sommerfeld permanently with everyone thinking ill of her and her daughter? He pushed his plate away, his appetite ruined by his thoughts.

Dear Lord, why did this have to happen now, when Marie was turning back to You and her faith?

Marie came around the corner with a bin on her hip. Normally Trina bussed tables, but Deborah had been making her stay home the past few days. She gave the excuse that, with the dwindling clientele, she wasn't needed, but Henry suspected it had more to do with trying to keep her from having any contact with Beth and Marie.

Another heartache.

Marie paused beside his table, frowning at the untouched plate. "Was something wrong with the food?"

Henry shook his head. "No. Just not hungry."

She sighed, glancing at the nearly empty room. "That seems to be going around."

Henry peeked over his shoulder. The few

customers appeared to be eating, not needing attention. He pointed to the chair across from him. "Want to sit down for a minute?"

She tipped her head, and the hint of a smile curved her lips. "On one condition—you don't mention the word *thief*."

The sadness in her eyes stabbed his heart. He smiled and nodded toward the chair. "Agreed."

She sat, plunking the bin on the corner of the table. She looked at him, quiet and waiting, and he found himself tongue-tied. With her hair pulled back, the errant curls held in place by a kerchief tied around her head, and her blue-eyed gaze pinned expectantly on his face, she had the same effect on him that she'd had at fifteen. The silence grew lengthy, uncomfortable. She squirmed.

"What are your plans for Thanksgiving?" he blurted before she could get up and move away.

Marie blinked, her long lashes sweeping up and down. She took in a breath and gave a graceful shrug. "Joanna has asked me to join her family, but I'm not sure I will."

Henry scowled. She shouldn't be alone. "Why not?"

"Well. . ." She linked her fingers together and rested them on the edge of the table, then seemed to examine her thumbs. "If Joanna has her own dinner, that means she won't be with my parents. The only reason she's doing this is because she knows Beth and I aren't welcome at the farm. I don't want her to separate herself from the family because of me."

The sadness in her tone tugged at Henry's heart.

Here she was, in the community, so close to her family, and yet so far from them. He wished he could build a bridge that would bring them together. He reached across the table and placed his hand over hers. Her gaze bounced up, meeting his.

He felt heat building in his cheeks, but he didn't avert his gaze. "Joanna wouldn't do it if she didn't want to."

"I know, but. . ." She paused, shifting her gaze to the side for a moment, as if gathering her thoughts. "I don't want people to have to choose sides." She looked at him again, one eyebrow quirked. "There's no sense in stirring up trouble when our time here is so short."

Henry jerked his hand back, then regretted his hasty action when he saw her expression cloud. He cleared his throat. "Regardless of the length of your stay, any reconciliations will be beneficial to your family, don't you think?"

Another hesitant shrug communicated her apprehensions. "One can hope, I suppose. I'd like to think that, after Beth and I return to Cheyenne, I'll stay in touch with my family. But it will be up to them."

Henry nodded, and silence fell between them. Once more, he wished for Lisbeth's presence. She would have been an excellent mediator between Marie and her family, he was sure. His skills in that department were lacking—he didn't have an inkling how to bring things to right.

"Well," Marie said, but she was cut short by the call of one of the customers requesting a refill on coffee. Henry watched her bounce to her feet and dash to the table that held the coffeepots and carry one to the table. From there, she made the rounds, avoiding his table.

He knew what his breakfast cost without needing a check. Shifting his weight to one hip, he tugged his billfold from his back pocket, removed a five-dollar bill, and slid it under the edge of his plate.

Out on the sidewalk, he drew in great breaths of the cool air, attempting to clear his cluttered mind. Turning toward his shop, he processed his thoughts.

Henry knew Marie's family was more important to her than the community, but less important than Beth. If the girl decided to make Sommerfeld her home, Marie would no doubt settle in as well. If that happened, surely her entire family would eventually come to accept her.

Turning the key in the lock of his door, Henry released a snort. Beth wouldn't stay. Not after the way everyone had pointed fingers. If she were guilty, she would have to take her stolen goods and go. He flipped on the light switch, then sank onto a metal stool beside his work counter. The situation seemed hopeless.

No, nothing was ever hopeless. He knew that. Ducking his head, he closed his eyes, a prayer rising in his chest. *She's back, Lord, and she's seeking You. Please let this mess be fixed to the betterment of all.* He recognized the underlying selfishness of his request, knowing much of his motivation was his long-held love for her. He wanted her here, with him. But he also wanted her happy. He knew she couldn't be happy until all of the relationships were restored.

Slapping his knees, he rose and reached for his toolbox. Sitting here worrying about Marie wouldn't get Lucas Schrag's oil leak repaired. He'd have to leave Marie in God's hands.

※

Beth put another piece of gravy-drenched turkey in her mouth, chewed, and swallowed. She might as well have been eating sawdust. Despite the lace tablecloth and candles, the array of foods and polished silverware, despite Joanna's tremendous effort to make this first Thanksgiving together in more than twenty years a festive event, it was a flop.

Tension hung so heavy it was palpable, making it hard to swallow. A glimmer of tears shone in Mom's eyes, and at times in Joanna's, too. Beth felt a stab of sympathy, but there wasn't much room for sympathy with the amount of anger she held.

Her uncle Leo and his wife and kids had come to Joanna's for this meal, but neither Art nor Conrad were there. They'd chosen to go the farm, to have Thanksgiving with Beth's grandparents. From the whispers she'd overheard in the kitchen, an aunt and uncle she had yet to meet, who lived in neighboring communities, were also at the farmhouse. They'd been invited to come by Joanna's to see Mom but had refused.

Little wonder Mom battled tears. Beth understood

her mother's heartache, but she also resented it. Hadn't Mom figured out by now these people weren't worth tears? The two of them had always made it just fine on their own. When Grandma Quinn passed away and Grandpa moved to Florida, Mom had wondered how they'd get by alone, but they'd managed. To Beth, that proved they didn't need anybody except each other.

They especially didn't need this town full of righteous blame finders.

She'd observed the way customers reacted to Mom in the café. From her spot in the corner, hunched over her computer, she'd seethed with frustration when Mom's friendly overtures were ignored. And now that Mom was going to that church, it was even worse! Beth's solution was to spend less time at the café and more time away from the town. But Mom was stuck. Beth stifled a frustrated snort. She wished she'd never come to Sommerfeld. It was all a huge mistake.

On her left, her cousin Kyra asked quietly, "Would you pass the pickled beets, please?"

Beth handed them over, her gaze meeting Kyra's briefly. Beth couldn't help but feel a prick of guilt for lumping Kyra and her family in with the rest of the community. Joanna and her husband and children hadn't pushed Mom or her aside. Beth appreciated that, but it wasn't enough. Mom needed all or nothing. There was no way she'd ever have it all, so. . .

Beth shoved her chair back and stood. Every

person seated around the table stopped in midbite and stared at her. "I'm sorry, but I'm not feeling well. Will you excuse me, please?" Without waiting for a response, she charged through the kitchen to the back door. As she expected, Mom came around the corner a moment later, her brow creased in worry.

"Honey, are you okay?"

Beth shook her head. "No. And neither are you." Taking her mother's hand, she implored, "Let's go back to the house."

Mom's face puckered in concern. "Are you feeling that bad?"

Beth huffed. "I'm not sick, Mom, unless you count sick of this town and these people. We should never have come. I'm sorry I dragged you here. I—" She shook her head and gave her mother's hand a tug. "Let's just go."

"In the middle of dinner?" Mom slipped her hand free. "Sweetheart, Joanna went to a lot of trouble for us. She and Leo and their families chose to be here for us. I can't leave."

"Yes, you can."

"No, honey, I can't." Mom lowered her voice to a whisper, but her tone was firm. "I will not walk away from a dinner that was set up just so we could spend some time with family this holiday."

Beth stared at her mother, ire rising higher by the minute. Couldn't Mom see that staying only created more problems? More heartache? She had to get her mom out of here. She grabbed her jacket off the hook and jammed her arms into the sleeves.

"Well, I've had enough family for one day. I'm leaving."

Mom wrung her hands. For a moment Beth hesitated. She hated to see her mother so torn. But this family had cut her off a long time ago. And they would abandon her again when it came time to leave. Having the money from the café and house would enable Beth to repay her mom in some way for all the sacrifices she'd made over the years. But surely the gift wouldn't be worth the heartache she was experiencing now. It was better to make the break now, before her mother got in too deep.

Mom touched her arm. "Will you be okay at home by yourself?"

Home? Since when was Lisbeth's house *home*? Beth's heart twisted. She forced a sarcastic tone. "I'll be fine. All by myself on Thanksgiving."

Mom shook her head, her eyes sad. "Honey, it's your choice to leave. You can stay here with us."

Beth turned away, her chin quivering. "Us" used to mean her and Mom. She closed her eyes for a moment, gaining control of her emotions. When she felt she could speak without her voice breaking, she looked at her mother. "Enjoy yourself. I'll call Mitch. I know he'll have time for me today."

She slammed through the door, thrusting her hands deep into her pockets. She and her mother had walked to Joanna's—she followed the same route back to Lisbeth's.

As she passed houses, she couldn't help but peek through plate glass windows to the groups gathered inside. The scenes she witnessed—smiling, laughing groups—provided a stark contrast to the isolation she felt as she walked under leafless trees across brown yards. Back in Cheyenne, even with only Mom for family, she'd never felt as alone as she did right now, in this community where grandparents and aunts and uncles and countless cousins resided.

Hunching into her jacket, she forced her gaze straight ahead and moved as quickly as she could over the uneven ground. How she wished Lisbeth hadn't sent Henry Braun with that message. How she wished Mitch hadn't talked her into heeding the request. How she wished. . . She sighed. Wishing was a waste of time. Nothing would ever be the same.

When she reached Lisbeth's, she went into the house and grabbed the car keys from the corner of the kitchen counter. No way was she staying here by herself. Not when there were things she could be doing. Things that would benefit her—and Mom—once her time in Sommerfeld was over.

"I'm doing this for you, Mom," she muttered, "and you'll understand it all when I finally get you out of here." Beth started the engine, backed out of the drive, and headed for the gravel road that led out of town.

NINETEEN

Marie handed a dripping plate to Joanna, then plunged her hands back into the warm, sudsy water. With a chuckle, she said, "I never thought I would actually enjoy washing dishes after having an automatic dishwasher for so many years."

Joanna laughed. "If someone's sharing the chore, it can be almost pleasant. We used to have some good conversations over the dishpan, didn't we?"

Marie sent her sister a smirk. "Yes, when Abigail wasn't listening in so she could run and tattle if we said something we shouldn't."

"As if we ever said anything we shouldn't have." Joanna winked and bumped Marie's arm with her elbow.

Marie giggled, relishing the kinship she'd renewed with her sister. She gave Joanna a sideways glance and dared to share a piece of her heart. "One of my biggest regrets with Beth is she never had the pleasure of brothers or sisters. You and I had such fun growing up, and she never experienced that."

"She never had any fun?"

Joanna's feigned expression of shock made Marie laugh, but she shook her head. "You know what I mean. She missed out on a lot."

Joanna put down her dish towel and gave Marie a quick hug. "I'm sure she never realized she was missing anything. It's obvious she adores you."

Marie quirked her brow.

Joanna shook her finger under Marie's nose. "Now stop that. What you're going through with Beth right now is growing pains, pure and simple. It happens. But she loves you as much as you love her. Nothing will ever change that." She took another plate and swished it dry with the embroidered tea towel.

Pain stabbed anew as Marie considered the shattered relationship between herself and her parents. Her hands stilled in the water as she remembered how many precious things had been destroyed by her decision to leave with Jep.

Joanna's mind must have drifted in the same directions as Marie's, because she dropped her gaze, her forehead creasing. "Sometimes, I suppose, relationships do change. But—" She met Marie's gaze, her tone turning fervent. "Things can always be put to right again with a little effort."

Considering her father's behavior thus far, Marie wasn't sure she agreed with Joanna, but she decided not to argue. No sense in upsetting her sister any more than Beth's untimely departure three hours ago had. Lifting out a bowl, she forced a smile. "Effort. . . and time. . .and prayer."

Joanna hugged the bowl to her chest, creating a wet circle on her apron bib. Her eyes filled with tears. "Oh Marie, it thrills me to hear you say that. Do you know how much Lisbeth and Henry and I have prayed over the years for you to allow God back into your life? And now I see it happening. I'm so thankful!" Her voice broke.

Marie felt the sting of tears herself. She imagined her sister, her aunt, and Henry kneeling in prayer. . . for her. . .and felt humbled by their steadfast concern. She would have expected Aunt Lisbeth and Joanna to maintain their desire to bring her back to faith—they were family. But Henry? Wonder filled her heart. The man she'd jilted had spent twenty years praying for her faith. How did one say thank you for that kind of dedication?

"And I believe," Joanna went on, sniffling, "that our prayers will bring Dad around, too. If he bends, everyone else in the family will follow suit, from Abigail down to Conrad. So don't lose heart, okay?"

Marie didn't have to force this smile. She tipped her head to touch Joanna's forehead, the little sign of affection she had used often as they were growing up. "I won't." Straightening, she added, "But I hope—"

A rap at the front door interrupted her words. Joanna's eyes flew wide. "See! I bet that's Abigail, Ben, and Conrad with their families, here to spend a little time with you."

Marie's heart pounded, and she licked her lips as her breathing increased. She mentally prepared a greeting for her older brother and sister as she followed

Joanna to the front room, wiping her hands on the apron. Kyra, Kelly, and Gomer came from their bedrooms at the same time, and they were all gathered together when Hugo pulled the front door open.

To Marie's disappointment, two men from town stood on the porch, hats in their hands, their expressions somber. Hugo invited them in, and Joanna bustled forward.

"Kurt, Robert, how good to see you this evening. I have some pumpkin pie and whipped cream left over if you'd like a piece."

The men exchanged glances, and the taller of the pair shook his head. "That's kind of you, Joanna, but we didn't come for socializing."

Hugo crossed his arms, his brows pinching together. "Oh?"

Marie's scalp prickled when both men fixed their gazes on her.

The second man said, "There's been some trouble in town today, and we thought you needed to know about it."

An arm slipped around Marie's waist. Marie jerked her gaze and found Kyra close. She gave the young woman a quick smile of thanks before looking back at the men.

"What trouble?" Hugo asked.

"Leonard Dick returned to his home after spending the afternoon at his daughter's place. His front door stood open. The sleeping bench from his second bedroom was gone."

Marie's knees buckled, and she would have gone

down if Kyra hadn't supported her. Joanna guided her to the sofa, where she sank onto the cushion, her ears ringing, her heart pounding furiously. Beth had mentioned a sleeping bench when speaking of the items she hoped to buy. But she wouldn't. . .would she?

"We're telling everyone in town to be careful," the taller man said. "Be sure your doors are locked, and maybe put the things you value under cover so they can't be seen by peeking in windows."

"Thank you, Kurt. We'll do that." Hugo's voice sounded strained.

The man shifted his feet in a nervous dance. Marie focused on his hands, which twisted the brim of his hat. "Some of the men in town are going to set up a community watch day and night. If you want to be involved—"

"I sure do," Hugo inserted.

"We're getting together at eight this evening at the meetinghouse. We'll see you there."

The men left. Hugo closed the door, then turned his grim expression on Marie. "It sure would have been better if Beth had stayed here with us today."

Joanna gasped. "Hugo! You don't think—"

"I don't want to." Hugo pushed his hands into his pockets and hunched his shoulders. "But everyone else in town was with family, celebrating the holiday."

Marie rose on shaky legs. "She went home. I know she did. She'll be there, waiting for me. You'll see."

Hugo looked at Joanna, who beseeched him with her eyes. Turning back to Marie, he said, "It's getting dark. I'll drive you."

Marie knew it was a desire to satisfy himself to Beth's whereabouts that brought about the offer, but she nodded mutely. She hugged her sister, nieces, and nephew, then followed Hugo to his car.

Lights shone in every house—more lights than Marie had seen before. People stood in yards in small clusters, talking. They stared as Hugo drove slowly down the shadowy streets. *Please be there, Beth. Please, let's be able to prove them wrong.*

When Hugo pulled into Lisbeth's yard, Marie noticed windows glowing in the front bedroom—Beth's room. Her tense posture sagged with the rush of relief that swept through her. Hugo drove to the back of the house, where Marie's car waited a few feet from the back porch, in the same spot she had left it yesterday when she returned from the café.

Her chest flooded with elation. "See? The car's here, and Beth is here."

Hugo walked her to the porch, but instead of stepping onto the wooden platform, he moved to Marie's car and placed both palms on the red hood. He jerked his gaze toward Marie. The look on his face made her break out in a cold sweat.

"It's warm."

✦

"I'm telling you, we need to go to that house, knock on the door, and demand to look around." Jay Albrecht stood with crossed arms at the end of his bench, his dark eyebrows pulled down in a ferocious scowl. Albrecht had assigned himself as leader of the meeting. Having had his grandfather's mantel clock taken, he was the angriest of all the thief's victims.

Henry noticed several men nod in agreement of Albrecht's bold suggestion. Every male over the age of twenty-one appeared to be in attendance at this community meeting, including all four of Marie's brothers, two adult nephews, and her father, who sat in a silent row on the preachers' bench behind the empty podium.

"And if we found things, what then?" The question came from the back of the room, offered by Allen Wedel. The Wedel place had lost several enamel buckets and a hand plow.

"That would be proof," Albrecht declared in a booming voice. "We could then take the Quinns to the police."

The thought of Marie and Beth being hauled to the police station in one of the larger nearby towns made Henry feel as though someone had kicked him the stomach. He wanted to speak out in their defense, but his tongue seemed glued to the roof of his mouth.

Henry's nephew Jacob rose and faced Albrecht. "Even if we did find the missing items, we wouldn't be able to prove the Quinns stole them. Not unless they were seen taking them."

Albrecht snorted. "Why would they have them if they weren't responsible for the stealing?"

Jacob shrugged. "Maybe someone else took the things and hid them there."

A snicker went across the room. Doug Ortmann asked, "For what purpose?"

"To make it look as though the Quinns were responsible."

Albrecht waved his hand. "Bah! No one else has a reason to take those things. We all know why those women are here—to get whatever they can lay their hands on. And that's exactly what they've been doing!"

The murmur of concurrence made Henry's stomach churn.

Hugo Dick stood and joined Jacob. "I don't agree, Jay. Maybe the daughter came to get what she could, but I don't think we can say that about the mother."

"Then why do you think she's here?" Albrecht's tone turned derisive.

Hugo glanced at Henry. "As an answer to prayer."

Henry looked at his feet, certain his face was glowing red.

"My wife, Joanna, her aunt Lisbeth Koeppler, and Henry Braun here have all prayed for years that Marie would return to this community. That she would be able to restore lost relationships. I think Marie came for that reason."

Mumbled voices rose and fell. Henry couldn't resist the urge to look at Marie's family. All faces were stoic, their gazes downcast except for J.D., who stared straight ahead with his arms folded tightly across his chest.

"Don't be ridiculous." Albrecht's scowl deepened, his angry glare fierce. "You know as well as I do that nothing like this has ever happened in our community. But these two women arrive, and immediately there's trouble."

Ortmann turned in his seat to face Jacob and Hugo. "I agree with Jay. I believe that girl wants our things badly enough to take them."

"No one saw Beth take anything," Jacob said, raising his voice to be heard over the rumbles that rolled across the room. "No one has even seen the goods." His gaze swept the room, silencing the murmurs. "I thought we came here to organize a community watch to prevent future burglaries, not form a trial and jury."

"You're being sassy, boy," Albrecht growled.

Henry's ire raised with Albrecht's condemnation. With a silent prayer for strength, he pushed to his feet and put his arm around his nephew. "Jacob has a right to speak his opinion, just as you do, Jay." He spoke calmly. "And in this case, he's right. We're not accomplishing anything here with all this faultfinding. Let's organize our watch and wait to see what happens."

"And if the thief never shows again? What then?" Ortmann demanded.

"Then we've been successful," Jacob said.

Albrecht threw his arms outward. "But we don't get our things back!"

"Maybe not." Henry looked around the room. "But I think we need to look at our motivations here." His gaze flitted toward Albrecht. "Some folks here seem bent on revenge. But the Bible says vengeance belongs to the Lord."

An uneasy silence fell over the gathered men. Albrecht's face turned scarlet. He sat down abruptly, his mouth set in a grim line.

"Who brought paper?" Jacob asked.

Henry patted his shirt pocket. "I have a small pad and a pen."

Jacob smiled at him. "Good. Uncle Henry, would you please write down the names of all the men in attendance?"

Henry flipped open the pad and jotted down the names. He looked up, pen poised. "Jay?" He waited until Albrecht lifted his head. "Would you like to schedule everyone's time for watching?"

The man's gaze narrowed, and for a moment Henry feared he would storm out of the room. But he gave a brusque nod. "Four-hour shifts?"

Several nods and mumbles came from the group.

Albrecht fired out time slots and called for volunteers. Henry carefully recorded the information. In the midst of the planning, he heard a shuffle along the side bench.

J. D. Koeppler stood, his sons and grandsons following suit. The entire Koeppler family filed out of the meetinghouse without volunteering for a shift. Henry watched them go, his heart heavy. None of them had said a word in support of Marie throughout the entire meeting.

But then something else occurred to him. Neither had any of them condemned her.

TWENTY

"This is nice." Beth cupped her hands around her coffee mug and smiled across the table at her mother. "With all the hours you've been spending at the café, we don't get much time together anymore. I'm glad we decided to leave the place closed all weekend."

Marie's throat tightened at her daughter's words. She, too, had missed time with Beth. Lately, even when they were together, the tension made it difficult to enjoy Beth's company. Last night, when Hugo discovered the car's engine was warm—evidence that it had been driven recently—Marie approached Beth, intending to ask where she'd gone. But her daughter's defiant attitude made her change her mind. Maybe a part of her feared knowing the answers to the questions that pressed her mind.

But this morning she saw no sign of yesterday's defiance. Beth seemed relaxed, open, more like the girl she'd been back in Cheyenne. Marie's heart rose with hope that what Joanna had said was true—Beth was merely experiencing growing pains and their relationship wouldn't be irreparably damaged by their time in Sommerfeld.

"What should we do today?" Marie gave a cautious sip at her mug.

"How about packing our bags and taking a quick trip?" Beth's eyes danced. "If we left here in the next hour, we could be in Kansas City by midafternoon."

Beth's enthusiasm gave Marie's heart a lift. "What would we do there?"

Beth shrugged. "Rent a room in a nice hotel, sit in a hot tub, watch television. . .something *normal*. Since the café won't open again until Tuesday, we could stay clear through Monday. It'd be like a minivacation."

"But I have service Sunday." Marie was struck by two simultaneous emotions—surprise that attending service had become so important to her, and regret that her daughter's enthusiasm immediately deflated.

Beth shook her head, her hair spilling across her shoulders. "Mom, I don't get you. You'd blow an entire weekend away from here just to go to that little church?"

Marie lowered her head. She wished Beth understood the changes taking place in her heart. But she couldn't quite comprehend it herself, let alone explain it to someone else. All she knew for sure was she didn't want to miss service at the meetinghouse. Reaching her hand across the table, she touched Beth's rigid arm.

"Honey, I don't mean to disappoint you."

Beth jumped up and moved stiffly to the stove, where she poured another cup of coffee. Leaning against the counter, she fixed her mother with a unwavering glare. "The last thing I expected when we came here was for our family to fall apart."

A pang pierced Marie's heart. For many years "family" had meant the two of them. But now it was so much more. Even if the rest of Marie's family never came around, surely Beth would benefit from having Joanna and some of her cousins in her life. How could she help her see that?

"You aren't the same mother I've had for twenty years. You dress different—I can't remember the last time you wore a pair of jeans. You talk different—bringing God and prayers into nearly every conversation. And you act different—all quiet and accepting instead of standing up for yourself. I don't feel like I even know you anymore!"

Marie tipped her head, narrowing her gaze as she reflected on Beth's statement. "I suppose I have made some changes since we arrived. Being here has helped me remember the teachings of my childhood and how important they were to me. They've become important to me again. I hope the changes aren't bad ones." She spoke slowly, thinking carefully as she formed words. "But I've seen you change, too. You've become resentful, snappy, and. . .sneaky."

Beth jerked upright, her brow creasing sharply.

Marie knew she'd struck a nerve. She proceeded with caution. "What do you do while I'm at the café all day?" Although she kept her tone soft and noncombatant, Beth's face blazed pink.

"Here we go again. Crazy Beth is robbing everybody blind."

"If it isn't true, why not prove them wrong? What are you trying to hide?"

Beth shifted her gaze to the side, the muscles in her jaw twitching. Although Marie waited for several moments, Beth didn't answer.

Marie released a sigh. "It's okay. You don't have to tell me."

Beth swung back, flinging one arm wide. "See? That's exactly what I mean! Back home, if I tried to keep something from you, you'd bug me until I caved in."

"You want me to bug you?"

"No."

"Then what do you want?"

Beth stared, her body angled forward as if poised for a fight. "I want us to go back to how we were before. You and me against the world. Maybe it wasn't perfect, but it was secure."

Marie shook her head. "Sweetheart, I love you, and I always will. You're my daughter—my precious gift." Her throat went tight as love filled her so completely she ached. "But I don't think we'll ever be the way we were before. I've found something here that I lacked for too many years. And I know I'll never be able to let it go again."

Beth poked out her lips, her expression sour. "You're talking about God, aren't you?"

Marie wasn't sure which feeling took precedence at that moment—elation that Beth had recognized the light of God in her mother's bearing, or sorrow that she spoke of it with such disdain. "Yes, I am."

Beth marched to the sink and dumped the coffee. Dark spatters rose with the force of her swing. "And I suppose you'll choose Him over me, just like you've chosen your family over me."

Marie bolted from her chair and rushed across the floor to envelop Beth in her arms. Even though her daughter stood stiffly, keeping her arms at her sides, Marie held her close, stroking her hair with a trembling hand. "Sweetheart, I'm not choosing anything over you. Nothing will change how much I love you. But I can't give God up for you. I hope you understand that."

Beth allowed the embrace for a few more seconds before she pulled back. The hurt in her eyes stabbed Marie. "No, Mom, I don't understand. And frankly, I don't want to." She moved to the doorway leading to the hall and then paused, her shoulders tense. "Since you don't want to go away this weekend, I guess I'll go on my own. I could benefit from some normalcy. Maybe I'll call Mitch, see if he wants to fly in and meet me."

Marie clamped her jaw, refusing to respond. There was no point—Beth already knew how Marie felt about her spending time with Mitch. Instead, she posed a practical question. "How will you pay for your minivacation?"

"Maybe I'll take some of the money out of the

account in McPherson. . .unless you have a problem with that."

Marie sighed. "That account will be yours soon anyway. I won't oppose it."

Peeking over her shoulder, Beth sent Marie a brief questioning look. When Marie met her gaze, remaining silent, Beth released a huff and disappeared around the corner.

Marie sat back at the table and buried her face in her hands. *God,* her heart cried, *I won't choose Beth over You. But please don't let me lose her. She means so much to me. . . .*

Henry glanced at the overcast sky as he slid into his vehicle. He released a shiver. The temperature had dropped overnight. The gray sky and the snap of the air gave the promise of snow. He smiled. From the time he was a boy, he had anticipated the first snow of the season. Often it came right after Thanksgiving, which always brought a rush of eagerness for Christmas.

Pulling his car onto the fog-shrouded road, he let his thoughts drift ahead to Christmas. It would be different this year, without Lisbeth. Fondness brought a smile as he remembered past years and the traditions he'd shared with his dear friend. He would miss her homemade noodles and spicy mince pies. He would miss shopping for fabric for her quilts. How she teased him about choosing such unattractive patterns! He could still see her crinkly smile, hear her teasing comment, "What do men know?" The comment always brought a laugh, never indignation.

Mostly he would miss *her*—their time together.

He supposed it seemed odd to others, how close he had been to Lisbeth. But there was no denying how much he had come to love the old woman. And he was sure she loved him like the son she never had.

His tires crunched on the hard ground as he rolled slowly toward the church, the empty seat beside him serving as another reminder of Lisbeth's absence. Even when she'd still had her buggy, he had driven her to the meetinghouse on days of inclement weather. If she were alive, he'd have her company today.

Through the murky morning light, he glimpsed a figure hunching forward into the wind and moving in the same direction as he. He squinted, and his heart lurched. Marie? Bringing his car to a stop beside her, he reached across the seat to pop open the passenger door.

"Marie!" He heard the concern in his tone but did nothing to squelch it. "What are you doing walking in this cold? Get in!"

She made no argument, but slipped into the seat and yanked the door closed behind her. "Brr!" She hugged herself as she smiled at him. Her nose was cherry red, her eyes watery. She still looked wonderful. "Thank you. I didn't realize how cold it was. The wind bites this morning."

"Yes, it does. You should have more sense than to walk." He shifted the car into gear, his heart thudding at his own audacity. Had he scolded her?

But she laughed. "It had nothing to do with sense. My feet were my only transportation today. I don't have a car."

He shot her a sharp look before turning his attention back to the road. "Is something wrong with the engine?"

"No. Beth went away for the weekend, and she needed the car." He detected a hint of sadness beneath her statement. "So if I wanted to attend service, I had to walk."

"Well," he blustered, "the next time you need a ride, let me know. You shouldn't be out when it's this chilly. You could get sick."

He sensed her pleasure by the upturning of her lips although she kept her gaze aimed ahead. "I appreciate that, Henry, but I wouldn't want to put you out."

"I always took Lisbeth to service." He glanced at her. "I was just thinking how the seat seemed empty without her. It's nice. . .to have someone there." He was rewarded by her smile. He drew a breath and made a brave offer. "I can pick you up every Sunday if you like. That way if Beth wants the car. . ."

Marie looked at him, her face pursed into a thoughtful expression. When she spoke, her voice was soft, hesitant, yet he also detected gratitude. "I appreciate that, Henry. Thank you."

"You're welcome." He pulled into the churchyard and parked close to the women's entrance rather than his normal place at the front of the church. She got out before he could rush around and open the car door for her. Disappointment struck, but he pushed it aside. "I'll give you a ride back to your house afterward, so come out here after service."

She flashed him another quick smile before ducking into the hood of her furry coat and dashing for the door. Henry had a difficult time focusing on the singing and sermon, knowing he would have time with Marie that afternoon. Brief time, certainly, since the drive to Lisbeth's was less than a mile, but any time was a treat.

His heart pattered hopefully as he recalled her decision to attend service despite having to brave the cold morning. Her desire to return to her faith must be strong. He offered a silent prayer for the work that had started in her soul to continue, as Lisbeth had hoped, and bring her completely back to the fold.

His gaze flitted to the back of J. D. Koeppler's head. The man's thick, steel gray hair stuck up in the back, exposing a tiny bit of his freckled pink scalp. He stared at that spot of skin, wishing he could peel back the layers of J.D.'s heart and get to the soft center. How the man had hardened himself over the years.

Lisbeth once said the pain of Marie's departure had given J.D. a heart callus. At the time, Henry had been dealing with his own pain and hadn't wasted any sympathy on J.D. Now, however, he had to wonder how much the man was hurting by being so near to his daughter yet holding himself at a distance. Or had his heart grown so hard that he didn't experience any discomfort? Henry couldn't tell by looking.

He turned his head slightly and located Marie's mother. He was certain Erma would embrace Marie if given the opportunity. He'd witnessed her sidelong glances, the longing in her eyes each time she looked at her daughter. But if J.D. didn't bend, Erma wouldn't make any overtures. She honored her husband in every way, even at the expense of her own heartache.

Henry admired Joanna for making a stand against her family and welcoming Marie back into her life. She knew the woman paid a price, being ostracized by her parents and siblings, but Joanna followed her own heart. She and Marie were a lot alike. Marie had followed her heart twenty years ago. . .right out of Sommerfeld.

But would she do it again? Henry's chest grew tight as the question formed in his mind. He didn't dare speculate on the answer to that question.

The congregation shifted, slipping to kneel at the benches for the final prayer. Henry knelt, too, and when he folded his hands and closed his eyes, he repeated the prayer that had been a part of him since he was a young man of twenty-two. *Bring her back to us, Father.* He knew he meant not only spiritually but also physically.

When the service ended, Henry reached for his hat from the overhead rack. Someone caught his arm, and he turned to find Doug Ortmann beside him. The man crooked his finger, indicating for Henry to follow him to the corner. Once separate from the crowd, Doug spoke in a hushed tone.

"Have you heard, Henry? There haven't been any thefts since Thanksgiving Day."

Henry nodded. Apparently the watch system was working. Of course, no one watched during service—the men had agreed service was too important for any of the members to miss. "I'm thinking the thief knows people are actively seeking him. He's probably moved on."

Doug nodded. "I hope so. I didn't like thinking Marie. . ." He shook his head, sadness in his eyes. "She's a cousin, you know."

Henry clamped his hand over the man's shoulder. "I know. It's been hard on many people, the speculation and worries."

Doug nodded. "But if no more thefts take place, things will settle down, won't they?"

Henry took in a big breath. "I pray so, Doug."

"Me, too." The man smiled. "My family's waiting. I'd better go."

The man's blithe words cut Henry. What must it be like to have family waiting? Then his heart lifted—today he had someone waiting. Marie. He hurried his steps to his car.

TWENTY-ONE

Marie slipped her hood over her head and crossed her arms, tucking her hands in her armpits, while she waited beside Henry's car for his return. She watched the men's door, standing on one foot then the other in an attempt to keep warm. When she spotted him she bounced forward two steps and met him in front of the hood.

"Henry, Joanna invited me over for lunch, so I'm going to ride with Hugo. I just wanted to let you know."

His smile immediately faded. "Oh. All right." He shrugged, his lips forming the semblance of a grin that didn't reach his eyes. "Of course, that makes sense for you to ride with them."

The depth of his disappointment seemed disproportionate to the situation. Guilt wiggled through Marie's heart when she recalled his comment about the empty seat in his vehicle serving as a reminder of Lisbeth's absence. Maybe she should let him transport her. But no, she wasn't Lisbeth, and serving as a replacement wouldn't be healthy for Henry. Or her.

She risked grazing his sleeve with her fingertips in lieu of the squeeze she wanted to deliver. "I do appreciate your willingness to give me a ride." She licked her lips, her heart suddenly racing. "I would appreciate a lift next Sunday morning if the offer still stands."

"Sure it does. The wintry weather seems to have arrived. No need for you to get frostbite."

The hint of teasing in his tone made Marie smile. "Thank you." She sidled toward Hugo's waiting car. "I'll see you Tuesday, right?"

For a moment he looked baffled, then his expression cleared. "Oh! At the café. Yes, sure. You know you will."

She gave a quick wave, then jogged the final few feet to Hugo's car. Sliding into the backseat with Kyra, Kelly, and Gomer, she released a giggle. "Whew! Maybe I should have let Henry take me. This is a tight fit!"

Gomer scooted forward and draped his arms over the back of the front seat, giving the girls more space. "How's that?"

Marie tousled his short hair with her fingers. Although the Kansas seat-belt laws prohibited Gomer's position, Marie knew no police officer was likely to swing through Sommerfeld and ticket Hugo for not having his son belted in. "Thanks, kiddo."

He grinned.

Kelly tapped Marie on the arm as the car backed

out of the churchyard. "Aunt Marie, are you and Mr. Braun courting?"

"Kelly!" Joanna gasped and abruptly shifted to stare into the backseat.

Kelly pressed herself farther into the seat, her gaze bouncing between Marie and her mother. "What did I say?"

Kyra bumped her sister's arm. "It's a nosy question, Kel."

Kelly folded her arms, her lower lip puckered. "I wasn't trying to be nosy. I just wondered."

Marie swallowed. "W—what would give you that idea, honey?"

The girl shrugged. "I don't know. You used to court. Mom said so."

Joanna spun to face the front. The back of her neck, visible between her coat collar and her hairline, turned bright pink.

"And sometimes," Kelly continued, "people who courted when they were young get back together when they're old."

Marie nearly giggled at being referred to as "old," but she suspected Kelly would take offense.

Hugo, his hands clamped over the steering wheel, glanced into the backseat. His forehead creased into a scowl. "Have you been reading romance books again?"

Kelly blushed crimson and ducked her head.

Kyra burst out laughing. "Kel!"

"I don't see anything funny." Kelly's tone turned defensive.

Huge sent his daughter a glowering look. "I don't see anything funny either. Those books give you wrong ideas. No more of them, Kelly."

The girl kept her head low. "Yes, Dad."

Kyra continued to chuckle.

Kelly socked her in the arm. "Stop laughing!"

Kyra brought herself under control as Hugo pulled into the driveway. Gomer clambered over Marie's legs and shot out of the car. Marie followed more slowly, slipping her hand through Kelly's elbow so they could walk together behind the rest of the family.

On the porch, after everyone else had gone inside, Marie gave Kelly a one-armed hug. "Honey, I'm not upset with you."

Kelly's blue eyes shimmered as she peered into Marie's face. "Are you sure? I didn't mean anything bad when I asked. I just. . ." She lowered her gaze.

Marie cupped her chin and lifted her face. "Tell me what you're thinking."

Kelly shrugged. "I just think it would be neat if you and Mr. Braun got together. Then you could stay here and not go back to Cheyenne."

A teasing grin twitched at Marie's cheek. "What, I can't stay here alone?"

Kelly released a self-conscious giggle, hunching her shoulders. "Well. . .I suppose you could." Tipping her head to peer at Marie out of the corners of her eyes, she said, "But wouldn't it be more exciting if you had a beau?"

Marie pinched the end of her niece's nose. "You

have been reading romance novels."

The girl giggled, her eyes sparkling. "Don't tell Daddy, but my friend Abbie Muller gave me one about this couple who dated all through high school. They were going to get married, but they split up when the girl got swept off her feet by a traveling salesman. But the salesman died, and the girl came back to town, and she and her high-school boyfriend got together again." Kelly released a deep sigh. "It was a really good story."

Marie shook her head.

"It reminded me of you and Mr. Braun," Kelly went on eagerly. "The couple in the story was really happy they got back together. Don't you think you'd be happy with Mr. Braun?"

Marie smoothed a wisp of hair behind Kelly's ear. "Honey, life never works out like storybooks. It's a good idea in theory, but. . ."

Kelly tipped her head to the side. "But what?"

"In storybooks, people often don't think about what God wants for them." Marie smiled, her heart lifting at the realization of how important God's will had become in the past few weeks. She hadn't even considered whether leaving with Jep was what God wanted for her back then—she'd just gone. Now she didn't want to proceed on anything without His blessing. "I need to do what God would have me do, not what sounds romantic. Do you understand?"

Kelly nodded, but Marie could see by the loss of sparkle in the girl's eyes that she was disappointed. Flinging her arm around Kelly's shoulders, Marie aimed her toward the door. "I tell you what. If God lets me know He has romance in mind for me, you'll be the first one to hear about it, okay?"

The thirteen-year-old's face lit with pleasure. "Okay!"

That evening, in Lisbeth's bedroom, snuggled beneath one of her aunt's quilts, with a lantern illuminating the pages of Lisbeth's Bible in her lap, Marie reflected on her conversation with Kelly. As much as she hated to admit it, she felt haunted by the girl's innocent question: *"Don't you think you'd be happy with Mr. Braun?"*

She had many memories of Henry, and none of them were unpleasant except the one from the day she left Sommerfeld with Jep. The image of his stricken face, tears glittering in the corners of his dark eyes, brought a stab of guilt as sharp as the one she'd felt that day. Even though she hadn't looked back, she knew Henry stood beside the road until the semi was out of sight. She knew he had mourned her leaving. Even if Lisbeth hadn't shared Henry's heartbreak in her letters, Marie would have known.

But she had loved Jep. They'd been happy. He'd teased her about being his little Mennonite girl, but he'd never been put off by her cap and simple dresses. He hadn't even insisted she adjust her attire after they recited vows in front of a justice of the peace. Jep had been raised in the Baptist church but slipped away due to his job as a truck driver. All the traveling pulled him away from regular church attendance, but Marie had insisted on finding a church to visit every Sunday when she began traveling with him.

She smiled, her heart swelling with gratitude as she remembered Jep holding her close, whispering, "Marie, honey, you've been so good for me. I feel like Jesus is my friend again. Thanks for getting me back on track." She had been so happy with him, so certain God meant for them to be together.

But their time together had been short-lived—not quite two years. She hugged the Bible to her chest, pain stabbing with the memory of the day the police officer knocked on the apartment door and told her Jep was gone. He'd fallen asleep at the wheel, the man had said, and rolled the semi over an embankment. He'd been killed instantly, so he hadn't suffered. Marie hadn't found much comfort in that fact at the time.

In the numb days following Jep's funeral, his parents had been wonderful, supportive, assuring her they would help her with the baby, who would never have the opportunity to know the father who had celebrated her conception. But Marie had wanted her own mama. So as soon as she could travel—when Beth was a mere two weeks old—she had climbed on a bus and returned to Sommerfeld.

Only to be sent away by her father.

So she had left, disgraced and aching, and moved in with Jep's parents, relying on their help. The day she moved under their roof she discarded the outer coverings that told of her Mennonite faith.

Marie touched her tangled hair, recalling how odd it had felt those first days without her cap in place.

A sudden desire struck. Almost against her will, she set the Bible aside and slipped from the bed. Padding on bare feet to the closet, her heart pounding, Marie sought the old, familiar covering. Lisbeth's caps rested in a box on the closet shelf. She removed the box, set it on the bed, and lifted out one cap. Her hands trembled as she fingered the white ribbon—white, because Lisbeth had never married. Her cap would require black ribbons.

Her breath caught. Did she truly want a cap again?

She licked her lips, her mouth dry, and crossed to the bureau and the round mirror that hung above it. Placing the cap on the bureau top, she smoothed her unruly hair from her face and examined her image. When she lowered her hands, the strands flew in disordered curls around her cheeks. The lantern light brought out the gold and red highlights. Henry had always admired the red in her hair.

Shaking her head, she pushed thoughts of Henry away. This had nothing to do with him. Picking up the cap, she held her breath and slipped it over her curls. With quivering fingers, she tucked the errant curls beneath the sides of the cap. Her reflection blinked back at her, her face pale, her eyes wide. The white ribbons trailed down her neck. Time melted away, and Marie looked into the face of her youth. A tear slid down her cheek.

Closing her eyes, she dropped to her knees beside the bed. "Oh my Father God, I've missed You. I'm so glad to have You back in my life. I know when I leave here, You will go with me. I can worship You away from Sommerfeld. But I don't know what to do." For long moments she remained beside the bed, hands folded beneath her chin, her knuckles digging into her flesh, her heart crying out for guidance.

When she got to her feet again, she had no sure answers, but she knew one thing. If she were to stay in Sommerfeld, she wanted to be part of her childhood congregation once more. Her decision to leave with Jep had resulted in excommunication. But her fellowship could be restored if given approval by the bishop.

She experienced a sense of loss as she tugged the cap free and returned it to the box. One ribbon hung along the cardboard side, and she lifted it, twisting it around her finger. A smile formed as she envisioned God twisting Himself around her heart. "All right," she whispered. "I'll try to regain my membership. If they refuse me, then I'll leave. . .again. But this time—" Her heart caught, tears filling her eyes. "This time I won't leave You behind."

"Are you sure?" Henry leaned his elbows on the table, bringing himself closer to his brother-in-law. He and Troy shared a corner booth in the café. Henry was pleased to see business returning since the town had enjoyed a full week without thefts. The café didn't bustle with Sommerfeld residents, but members of the community filled three tables. It was a step in the right direction. And if what Troy said was true, there was an even bigger reason for celebration.

"She told Deborah about it herself." Troy lifted his mug and sipped the steaming brew, his eyebrows high. "And Deacon Reiss told me this morning that the bishop is coming on Sunday to visit with her."

Henry slumped in his seat, his spine suddenly unable to hold him erect. After all the years and countless prayers, it seemed Marie was returning to the church. And if she did, she would no doubt remain in Sommerfeld. "Well, I'll be."

Troy set his mug down and frowned across the table. "Now, Henry, Deborah asked me to tell you about it, but she also wanted me to tell you something else."

Henry angled his head.

"Don't get your hopes up. Just because she wants to come back to the church doesn't mean. . ." Troy turned his gaze away.

Henry nodded. Troy didn't need to finish the sentence. Marie's return to the church didn't necessarily mean she would return to him. She'd made her choice long ago, and based on what he'd overheard the day he'd brought her father to the café, her love for Jep Quinn had gone deep. There might not be room for another love.

Releasing a little huff of laughter, he shifted forward again. "Tell Deborah not to worry." He waited until Troy met his gaze. "God has brought Marie back to faith, and that's a real answer to prayer. It's what Lisbeth wanted. I can be happy with that."

Troy nodded and went back to sipping his coffee,

pulling in noisy slurps. It was clear he was pleased to be finished with the conversation.

Henry leaned into the padded seat, his thoughts racing. What he'd told Troy was truthful—he could be happy for Marie if she managed to regain fellowship with the congregation. But he also knew it would be difficult to be happy for himself if Marie were to remain in Sommerfeld and not be a part of his life.

TWENTY-TWO

Beth closed the cover on her laptop, sighed, and massaged her neck with both hands. When would this tension ease up so she could relax? Her weekend away, although enjoyable—especially after Mitch arrived, even though he looked ridiculous sporting a new, short haircut—hadn't accomplished what she'd hoped.

Her gaze flitted to Mom, who lifted two plates from the serving counter and headed toward the dining room. Tears stung behind Beth's eyes. Instead of her time away making Mom see how important it was for them to stick together, it had pushed her in the direction of the church. This past Sunday she had even talked to the head honcho about becoming a member again!

In four more weeks, she would be able to officially claim the inheritance, sell the house and café, gather up Lisbeth's antiques, and return to Cheyenne to open her boutique with Mitch. He'd located a shop area they could rent in one of the older buildings on

Capitol Avenue. It would be pricey, but he was certain they'd be able to make it work. The thought of having a successful decorator boutique thrilled her on many levels. But—her throat tightened—Mom might not be going with her. And if Mom didn't come, how could Beth possibly do all the things she'd planned in order to repay her?

How could her mother betray her this way? All her growing-up years, Mom had been there—the one stable, unwavering, unshakeable relationship in a world where others came and went. But now her mother was slipping away, choosing others over the child she had claimed meant everything to her.

Beth felt as though her dreams were crumbling at her feet.

Trina turned from the dishwasher and flashed Beth a bright smile. "All done researching?"

Beth lowered her hands. She didn't feel like talking to anyone, but Trina was hard to resist. The girl was incurably cheerful. Despite her controlling mother, bleak surroundings, and dismal wardrobe, she always wore a smile. Kind of like Mom these days.

"I wasn't researching." She swiveled on the stool and watched Trina load plates. "I was making sure the café and house were listed on the Realtor's website."

Trina's expression clouded. "So you're really doing it, huh?"

Beth flipped her hands outward. "That's what I came to do. I follow through on my plans." *Unlike someone else I know.*

Trina went on stacking, her hands moving rhythmically between the bin and the washer tray. The little ribbons from her cap swayed with the steady movement. What would Mom look like if she started wearing one of those caps?

"Well, I'm glad you're getting to do what you want to, but. . ." Trina paused for a moment, pulling in her lower lip and furrowing her brow. "Are you sure you want to sell everything?"

"Why wouldn't I?" Beth propped her elbows on her knees. Out of the corner of her eye, she saw her mother hand Deborah an order ticket. Mom said something Beth couldn't hear from this distance, and Deborah smiled in return, resulting in Mom's low-throated chuckle.

Her heart caught at how at ease her mother appeared. And how left out that ease made her feel. She fit her thumbnails together and stared at them, her chest tight. Speaking loud enough for everyone in the kitchen to hear, she said, "I'm absolutely sure. In fact, I'm counting the hours until I'm outta here."

Trina gave a quick nod, then focused on the dishes, clearing out the bin and sending the tray through the washer. She flipped a switch, and the roar of running water almost covered her comment. "I'll miss working here. Daddy probably won't let me work anywhere else. He trusted Miss Koeppler to keep an eye on me."

Trina bustled off, pushing the metal cart in front of her, and Beth sat upright, realizing something for the first time. Selling the café didn't only affect her—it affected Trina and Deborah, too. Did they rely on the income? Trina certainly relied on the opportunity to mingle with people. She'd never met a more gregarious kid than Henry's niece. She had no idea why it suddenly bothered her to think of Trina and Deborah being ousted, but she couldn't deny a pang of guilt.

Maybe she could tell the new owners the Muller mom-and-daughter team was part of the bargain. She snorted at the thought. Why should she care about grumpy Deborah and her happy offspring? They were nothing to her. Just as this town was nothing to her.

Pushing from the stool, she headed for the back door. Cool air slapped her face when she stepped into the alley, and she sucked in a sharp breath. It wasn't as if she had never experienced a cold winter—she was raised in Cheyenne, after all—but for some reason the Kansas cold seemed to penetrate deeper.

Or maybe she just had less tolerance for anything related to Kansas.

Deciding not to dig too deeply along those lines, she climbed into the car. She jammed the key into the ignition and started the engine. This bad mood wasn't her fault. It was Mom's. *Mom and all her changing.* Beth's hand stilled on the gearshift as a realization struck. Despite the lack of creature comforts, the continued rejection by the majority of her family, and the undeniably long days of working in the café, Mom seemed more content than Beth could ever remember.

Slapping the gearshift into position, Beth shook

her head and pushed on the gas. Maybe Mom *thought* she was content, reliving all her childhood stuff, but just wait until Beth had money in hand and finally told her everything she'd been doing to ensure their brighter future. That would win her back. That's when real contentment would begin.

The first smile of the day found its way to Beth's face as she aimed the car toward the highway. Her future awaited.

Henry licked the tip of the pencil before recording the total at the bottom of the column in the ledger. He ran his gaze down the line of numbers, mentally adding. Convinced the calculator had figured correctly, he underlined the total and closed the ledger. He lifted his head to find Marie watching him.

Heat flooded his chest. He forced a wobbly smile. "You're still here."

"I'm waiting for Beth." She perched on a stool at the end of the counter, near the back door. Over her blouse she wore a hip-length, thickly knit sweater that had belonged to Lisbeth. The collar was folded under on one side, and his fingers twitched with the desire to straighten it for her. But if he touched the collar, her nutmeg curls would certainly brush his knuckles, and he might end up doing more than fixing her collar.

He looked back at the ledger. "She knows you're finished here?"

Marie sighed. "I'm sure she does. The café closes

every day at eight o'clock, and I'm always ready to leave by eight forty-five." She glanced at the clock hanging above the stove. "I suppose she's not terribly late. It's not quite nine yet."

"But you've had a long day."

Marie laughed lightly, her blue eyes tired. "I've had a long *week*."

Henry wondered what meaning hid beneath her blithe statement. He rose. "I'll take you home. If the lights are off here, Beth will know you've gone on."

Slipping from the stool, Marie covered a yawn with slender fingers. "Thank you. I'll take you up on that offer."

After he shrugged into his jacket and joined her at the door, she turned off the lights. They were immediately plunged into darkness, giving an intimacy to the setting. Henry fumbled for the doorknob, heaving a breath of relief when he located it.

Swinging the door open, he said, "Go ahead. But be careful—the ground is uneven."

Marie preceded him, and he followed slightly behind and to her left, his hand poised to steady her in case she tripped. But she moved with her typical grace through the shadows to his vehicle. She reached for the door handle, but he caught it first, opening it for her. The interior lights lit the underside of her jaw, bringing out the little cleft in her chin and highlighting a few wisps of hair that had slipped free of their bobby pins.

He swallowed and gestured silently for her to slide into the car. She did so, first sitting and then drawing in her legs in a fluid movement. He slammed the door a little harder than necessary, his heart in his throat. Maybe it hadn't been such a good idea to give her a ride home. On Sundays, with the sun lighting the landscape and worship on his mind, it was easier to distance himself. But under the stars, with shadows showcasing the delicate curve of her jaw and deepening the color of her eyes, old feelings ignited.

Walking around the car, he sucked in big gulps of cold air, trying to cool his racing thoughts. Behind the wheel, he flashed her a quick smile. "Okay, let's get you home."

They rode in silence through the still streets. He wanted to ask her how her meeting with the bishop had gone, if she'd heard anything from the deacons who would determine her future position within the congregation. He wanted to tell her he'd been praying that she would be granted membership. But fearful of her answers—would he be able to hide his disappointment if the response was their refusal?—he kept his mouth closed.

His gaze bounced along the houses, noting how many places hadn't bothered with porch lights this evening. The town finally seemed to be settling down from its scare with the thief. The watchers would continue through December, just to be safe, but Henry believed the worst was over. They could all relax.

He pulled behind Lisbeth's house, as he had so many times over the years of transporting Lisbeth. Marie craned her neck as they rounded the back corner, and he heard her breath release in a sigh as he stopped beside the porch. Something in her pose made his heart turn over. The engine still idling, he faced her. "Is something the matter?"

She glanced at him. Her eyes appeared black with the absence of light. "I just hoped Beth might be here. She—she's been gone so much lately."

The sadness in her tone pierced Henry's heart. He forced a chuckle. "Well, she's young. Stretching her wings."

"I suppose." Marie remained in the seat, her hands in her lap, her head tipped thoughtfully. "But her wing-stretching was different before we came here. It didn't concern me the way it does now."

Henry put the car into Park but left the engine running. The gentle hum provided a soothing lullaby. The dash lights illuminated the interior enough to highlight her features but little more. The cover of night gave him the courage to speak openly. "Tell me why."

Her head jerked backward as if she were surprised. She blinked several times, her lips sucked in, and for a moment he expected her to grab the door handle and let herself out. But instead, she shifted slightly in the seat, angling her body to face him, and licked her lips.

"I think I messed up when I raised Beth. I was so hurt by Dad sending me away, I turned my back on the way he raised me. I didn't make knowing God a priority for Beth." She shook her head, grimacing. "I took her to Sunday school when she was little—we went with Jep's parents. But when Beth was six, her grandmother died, and the next year, her grandfather moved to Florida. After that, I had to work more hours since I didn't have their financial support, and. . .well, church just went by the wayside."

Henry nodded. He already knew all this—Marie had shared with Lisbeth in letters, and Lisbeth had shared with him. But he stayed silent and let her talk.

"Beth's always been a good girl though. Respectful to me. Respectful to others. I did teach her that." She turned her head, her gaze out the window. "Since we've been here though, I've seen so much resentment in her. I'm not sure where it's coming from, and I don't like it. But I can't seem to talk to her anymore."

Looking directly at Henry, she offered a sad smile. "We were always lucky that way—we could always talk. More than other moms and daughters. I really miss that."

"You'll get it back," Henry said, unable to keep himself from giving some small encouragement. She seemed so forlorn. "Beth is balking at the restrictions here, that's all. She isn't accustomed to this simpler lifestyle."

"But that's just it." Marie's frustration came through clearly in her tone. "It's more than the lifestyle that's bothering her. I think she's gone so much because she's trying to avoid what I've found here—a relationship with God. It frightens her, and that's the last thing I'd want her to feel."

"The unknown is always frightening." Henry wove his fingers together to keep from reaching for her hand.

The longing to give her comfort became difficult to resist. "The more Beth sees evidence of God's touch on your heart, sees how it brings you joy, the more open she'll be to it."

"Are you sure?"

The uncertainty in her quavering voice pained Henry. He gave in to the impulse and placed his hand over hers. "Yes, I'm sure. How did you come to accept it? By witnessing it in the lives around you—in the lives of those you loved who loved Him."

Marie made no effort to extract her hand from his clasp. Instead, she turned her hand palm up and slipped her fingers around his hand. Henry felt certain she was unaware of the action, but the simple touch filled him with heat.

"Of course." Her whispered voice barely carried over the engine's gentle rumble. "How could I have been so foolish as to forget?" Her fingers trembled within his grasp. "Lisbeth always lived her faith quietly, yet it was evident. If I try to emulate her, surely the reality will eventually reach Beth's heart, opening her to receiving God's love." A smile broke across her face. "Thank you, Henry. I feel much less worried now."

He forced even breathing, bringing his racing heart under control. "You're welcome."

They sat, their hands joined, for several seconds before Marie spoke again. "Do you realize you're the first man I've ever talked to about Beth?"

He didn't know how to respond. One word squeaked out. "Oh?"

Her nod rearranged the wisps of coiling hair. "Since Jep's father moved away, there hasn't been a man in our lives."

Henry thought his heart might pound out of his chest.

"I've thought. . .so many times. . .how Beth and I could both benefit from a man's point of view. Admittedly, I—I always hoped my father. . ."

Her stammered words, and her convulsing fingers, nearly melted Henry. But his throat was too tight to speak. So he increased the pressure on her hand, letting her know he cared. She returned the contact, curling her fingers more securely around his, giving a silent *Thank-you*.

Henry remembered a conversation he'd had with Lisbeth about J.D.'s stubborn refusal to read any of Marie's letters. Lisbeth's theory had been that J.D. knew he was wrong for sending his daughter away, and by ignoring her, he could ignore his guilt. His self-righteous grumping, she had concluded, was just a cover-up for the unhappiness underneath. Could Marie benefit if he shared Lisbeth's wisdom now?

"Your father. . ." Henry's voice cracked. He cleared his throat and started again. "Your father lost a great deal by his hasty actions. He lost you, and he lost Beth. He isn't a foolish man—he recognizes his mistake. But his pride. . . Lisbeth prayed, and I keep praying, that he will swallow his pride and choose to reach out to you."

A tear rolled silently down Marie's cheek, dripped from her chin, and landed on Henry's hand.

Without thinking, he lifted his fingers and brushed the moisture away. She caught his wrist, pressing his fingers against her cheek for a moment. Then, with a jerk, she released him. Even in the faint light, he saw the color in her face deepen.

Turning from him, she grabbed the door handle. "I'd better go in."

"Let me walk you."

"No." She swung her feet out and looked over her shoulder. "I'm fine." Stepping from the car, she stood for a moment in the triangle of soft light. She leaned forward slightly to meet his gaze. "Thank you again, Henry." She slammed the door and moved quickly around the front of the vehicle.

He watched her shadow gain substance as she ran through the paths of white created by the headlights, Lisbeth's sweater flapping. He watched her clamber up the porch steps, snatch open the door, and disappear inside. Then he watched the window until a pale glow indicated she'd managed to light a lantern.

He could go now. She was safe.

When he reached for the gearshift, he realized his hand was shaking. He released a snort of self-deprecation. Marie might be safe, but he most certainly was not.

TWENTY-THREE

"Henry, it's only right that you come for lunch today." Joanna's blue eyes sparkled as she looked at Henry. "After all your years of faithful prayer, you need to join us in celebrating Marie's return to our fellowship."

Henry's heart certainly celebrated. Deacon Reiss had announced at the close of service that morning the decision to accept Marie Quinn as a member of the Sommerfeld congregation. Art, Conrad, Leo, and their families all intended to meet at Joanna's in honor of Marie's official return. He wanted to be there, yet he hesitated. He would be the only nonfamily member. If Lisbeth were there, too, it would be fine, given their unique friendship, but. . .

Snowflakes danced by, reminding him they were standing out in the cold while Joanna waited for an answer. He looked into her eyes, their hue the same as Marie's, and he gave a nod. "I'll be there. Thank you."

Her smile lit her face. Touching his sleeve, she

said, "Good. Don't dally—we want as much of the afternoon as possible to make merry!" She turned and scurried to her car, where Hugo waited with the engine running. In moments, Hugo's vehicle left the churchyard. Marie waved from the backseat, her smiling face pressed to the glass. He answered with a smile and wave of his own, then turned toward his car.

Across the churchyard, he spotted J. D. Koeppler assisting his wife into their buggy. Like a handful of other older members, the Koepplers hadn't adopted the use of more modern transportation. Their ride home would be chilly today.

As Henry reached for his door handle, something in his soul compelled him to cross the hard ground to Koeppler's buggy. He reached it just as J.D. picked up the reins.

The man gave a start when Henry touched his arm, and he turned a stern scowl down on Henry. "What do you want?"

The growl was certainly intended to put Henry off, but he didn't back away. Giving the man's arm a gentle squeeze, he said, "Are you coming to Hugo and Joanna's?"

Erma leaned forward slightly, her gaze flittering between J.D. and Henry. There was no denying the longing in her eyes. But J.D. didn't look at his wife— he looked firmly ahead, his jaw thrust forward. His mouth barely moved as he grated out his response. "I have nothing to celebrate."

Henry jerked his hand back. Although he had witnessed J.D.'s stubbornness frequently over the years, his adamant denial of what had taken place inside the meetinghouse today still took Henry by surprise. "Mr. Koeppler, the lost has been found. The prodigal has returned. There is much to celebrate."

But J.D.'s gray brows pulled down, giving him a fierce look. "I don't buy into her games. She and her daughter only came when the opportunity to carry away the spoils was presented to them. They have no interest in relationships, only riches."

Erma dropped her gaze to her lap, and Henry was certain he saw tears glint in her eyes.

J.D. went on. "Kyra told us how they count down on a calendar, marking off the days until they can be away from us again. The lost is not found, Henry, but merely biding her time until she can discard us once more. I will not celebrate that." Clicking his tongue, he encouraged the horse to pull away from the hitching rail.

Henry stood silently as the buggy rolled backward several yards. With a tug of the reins and a call to "Giddap," J.D. directed the dappled gray beast to pull the buggy toward the road.

Henry watched it go, his heart heavy. J.D. was wrong in his assumptions about Marie. Yes, Beth had come for riches, but Marie was here for relationships. Henry was certain of that. His conversation with her last night in the car spoke clearly of her inner battle of balancing the important relationships in her life. She wanted her family—*all* of her family.

His sigh hung in the crisp air. Shaking his head, he moved toward his car once more. Perhaps J.D.

wouldn't celebrate, but Henry would. He, with Marie's brothers and sister, would make merry and praise God for Marie's decision to return to Sommerfeld.

As he pulled away from the churchyard, his gaze found Lisbeth's simple headstone. What would Lisbeth say to J.D. if she were still alive? Even though Henry had spent time nearly every day for the past twenty years with the dear woman, he was unable to determine the answer to that question.

⁂

Although Marie relished the long afternoon with Henry, her siblings, and their families, she would have been lying if she said she didn't regret the absence of some important people. Beth's and her parents' lack of attendance cast a pall over the celebratory mood, and she suspected she wasn't the only one to feel it.

Many times she'd seen a glimpse of something in Henry's or Joanna's eyes that expressed a hint of sadness. In those moments, their gazes had locked, and she felt a silent kinship of understanding. She knew, even without saying the words, they wished as deeply as she did for the circle to be complete, for the entire family to meet and rejoice together.

By midafternoon, the young people, who ranged in age from four to twenty-one, gathered in various bedrooms for quiet activities or naps, leaving the adults alone to chat. Hugo carried in chairs from the dining room, creating a misshapen circle of seats in the front room. Marie found herself in the center of the sofa between Joanna and Art's wife, Doris. Henry sat on a ladder-back chair across from her. Having him directly in her line of vision proved distracting, and she played with the buttons on her blouse to avoid gazing into his warm brown eyes.

Doris gave Marie's knee a pat. "So, what are your plans now, Marie? Will you stay permanently?"

Marie looked at Doris, aware of Henry's attentive gaze from across the circle. "Now that I'm part of the congregation again, I would like to stay. But there are many things to work out. I'll need a place to live and a way to take care of myself."

Art leaned forward, placing his elbows on his widespread knees. "Seems to me you've already got that covered with the café and Lisbeth's house."

Marie smiled at her brother. "No. Those are Beth's, not mine."

"She wouldn't let you have them?"

Art's frown brought a rush of defensiveness. "It's not a matter of her letting me. I wouldn't ask. She's depending on the proceeds from the sale of that property to start her own business. I won't take that away from her."

"Well," Doris suggested, her brow puckered thoughtfully, "maybe you could buy the properties?"

Marie allowed a light laugh to escape. "If I had money to buy a café and a house, I would have offered to help Beth fund her business without coming here." Her words created a stir around the room, and she realized how ungrateful she sounded. She held up her hand. "Please don't misunderstand. I don't regret coming. But if it hadn't been for Lisbeth's unusual will"—her gaze met Henry's, and she felt her lips twitch in a smile—"there would have been no motivation for me to return to Sommerfeld. I would never have found the courage to do it had it not been a means of helping Beth."

Henry looked away, a hint of something—pain? regret?—flashing in his eyes. Before she could explore his reaction, Art spoke again.

"I understand." He sighed, shaking his head. "You know, the new owners of the café, whoever they might be, will still need workers. So even if it sells, you'd probably have the opportunity for a job. But a place to live. . .that's a little harder."

Conrad crossed his legs and looked at his wife. "When Sonja and I got married, we wanted to find a place to rent. But there was nothing available. If old Mr. Brandt hadn't passed away, we wouldn't have had a house. There's just not much turnover in Sommerfeld."

"Maybe. . ." Joanna's pensive tone captured Marie's attention. But before she completed her thought, she shook her head and emitted a rueful chuckle. "No, that wouldn't work."

Hugo prodded, "What?"

Joanna's gaze bounced around the room, as if gathering courage, before returning to Marie. "I was just thinking. . .there's so much room at the farm now that all of us are on our own. With just Mom and Dad rattling around out there, I know they have space for Marie."

A negative murmur made its way around the circle.

"See?" Joanna threw her hands outward, her expression regretful. "I told you it wouldn't work."

"It would work," Art inserted, "if Dad weren't so obstinate. I think Mom would be okay with the idea."

Leo nodded. "I know she would. She told Phyllis at Thanksgiving how hard it was to know Marie was in town yet not at the house for the holiday."

Marie stared at Leo's wife. "She really said that?" Her heart lifted with hope, then plummeted. "But she'd never cross Dad. He's the head of the home."

"And she's right to honor him." Henry spoke, surprising Marie. He'd been largely silent through most of their time together. Everyone looked at him, and he squirmed in his seat. His Adam's apple bobbed before he spoke again. "God can't honor her if she doesn't honor her husband—you all know that. I'm not saying J.D. is right in what he's doing, but Erma is right in what she's doing. Asking her to cross J.D. wouldn't be. . ." He shrugged, red mottling his cheeks. "It wouldn't be right."

Another mumble sounded, each husband and wife conferring quietly. Marie stared across the room at Henry, who stared back, a silent apology in his eyes. Marie felt her heart double its tempo. She understood the meaning behind his words. He wanted J.D. to accept her as much as she did, yet he didn't want any more conflict while they waited for her father to bend. The same feeling of kinship that had swept over her at other times in Henry's presence returned, rising higher and causing her pulse to pound.

"Marie—"

Reluctantly, she turned her attention back her older brother.

"Doris and I have a room you could use."

Marie's breath came out in a sigh, tears stinging her eyes. "Oh Art, I appreciate that so much." She glanced at Henry. "But you know, what Henry just said about Mom needing to honor Dad. . ." She let her gaze sweep the room, briefly touching each of her siblings. "I think all of us need to honor him, too. I am thrilled to be here today, but I know your choosing to be with me instead of with the folks creates conflict between you and them. My moving in with any of you would only expand that conflict. I don't want to be responsible for creating any more trouble than I already have."

"So what will you do?" Joanna asked, tears in her eyes.

Marie took her sister's hand, looking at their intertwined fingers. "I don't know. But I know who does know, and we can petition Him in prayer. If I'm meant to stay in Sommerfeld permanently, He will provide whatever is needed. And if those needs aren't met. . ." The next words had to be forced past a knot in her throat. "Then I know it's His will for me to go back to Cheyenne."

Marie lifted her gaze to look around the room at each person. "But this time, I'll make sure God is a permanent part of my life. I won't cast Him aside again." Smiling through the tears that blurred her vision, she added, "I can be Mennonite in Cheyenne.

And I will visit. Often. I won't separate myself from any of you again."

A lengthy silence followed, in which each person appeared introspective, their gazes aimed unseeingly at various spots in the room. Except for Henry, whose gaze remained pinned to Marie's face. She returned his unwavering gaze, hoping he read in her steady contact that she meant the promise for him, too.

Eventually, the silence was broken by a thump and a startled wail from one of the bedrooms.

"That's got to be Sharolyn," Phyllis said, bouncing to her feet and heading for the hallway.

Conversations broke out again, the topics less serious. Phyllis returned, carrying her daughter, who tumbled into Leo's arms and snuggled her tear-streaked face against his shoulder. Marie settled back on the sofa and absorbed the typical, boisterous, clamoring scene, a lump of gratitude in her throat for having the opportunity to be part of this large family once more. At the same time, she offered yet another prayer for the circle to extend to include Beth, Abigail, Ben. . . and her parents. She missed them with an intensity that created an ache deep inside. Looking at Sharolyn in Leo's arms provided a reminder of the long-lost relationship between herself and her father, as well as Beth's lifelong absence of a father.

The clock on the mantel chimed five times, signaling the approach of suppertime. Joanna slapped her hands to her knees, pushing herself to her feet. "Well, I guess I'd better pull out some lunch meat and—"

A knock at the door interrupted her words. Hugo started to rise, but she waved her hand at him. "Stay put. I'm up."

She opened the door, and a slightly younger, more slender version of Art stepped over the threshold. Marie leaped to her feet, her arms automatically reaching for the brother who, two years her senior, had alternately teased and protected her while growing up. "Ben!"

But Ben remained rooted on the little braided rug inside the door, his unsmiling gaze sweeping around the room.

Art rose haltingly. "Is something wrong?"

Ben's jaw thrust out, reminding Marie of her father's stern posture. When he spoke, his voice thundered with accusation, bringing another reminder of J.D. into the room. "My house was broken into this morning."

Gasps filled the air. Marie's legs trembled, and she sat back down, her eyes dry but unblinking. A hand descended on her shoulder—Joanna's. She clutched it, grateful for her sister's comforting presence.

"The thief is still in Sommerfeld?" Leo's disbelieving query hung in the room.

Ben nodded stiffly. "Apparently so. And he strikes at the only time the watch isn't active. That tells me this thief is knowledgeable of the town's activities." His glare turned on Marie. He took one step toward her. "Only one person in this town knows all the goings-on but avoids the meetinghouse. You know, too, don't you?"

Marie gaped at her brother, her jaw flapping uselessly. She knew. Lord help her, she knew.

Twenty-four

Marie drew in a deep breath as Henry turned into the driveway of Lisbeth's home. Her car waited at the back of the house, indicating Beth was there. She released the breath slowly through her nose, praying for strength.

Her gaze on the car, she gave a start when a hand closed over hers. Turning her head sharply, she found Henry fixing her with a concerned look.

"Would you like me to go in with you. . .to support you?"

Marie's heart turned over. Henry had been such a good friend in her younger days. It amazed her that, after the number of years that had slipped by and all the changes, he could still offer his friendship so easily. A part of her wanted him to come in with her, to stand beside her, to face Beth with her. But the greater part knew she couldn't depend on him that way.

With a sigh, she said, "I appreciate your offer, Henry, but it's better I go alone." She gave the hand holding hers a quick squeeze, then pulled away. A chill struck with the removal of his warm touch. Before she changed her mind, she opened the car door and stepped out, then hurried to the back porch. She stepped into the house without looking back at Henry.

Beth sat at the kitchen table, a newspaper spread in front of her. At Marie's entrance, she looked up, and her face broke into a huge smile. "I've been waiting for you! I can't wait to show you something."

Marie's heart pounded. "Honey, I need to talk to you."

Beth jumped up, her blue eyes dancing. "Can't it wait? I think you're going to be surprised."

Removing her coat with trembling hands, Marie debated the best thing to do. She draped the coat over the back of a chair and looked once more into Beth's eyes. Suddenly she couldn't ask the question that pressed at her mind. She forced her lips into a smile. "What surprise?"

Beth grabbed her mother's hand and led her down the hallway to her bedroom, chattering as they went. "I originally planned to save this for Christmas, but I can't wait. I hope it's okay if you get a present two weeks early."

It had been weeks since Marie had seen Beth so cheerful. She offered a silent prayer for guidance, then managed to answer in a teasing tone, "I'll take a present anytime. What is it?"

With a giggle, Beth pulled her through the door and pointed at the cot where a teddy bear sat, its arm outstretched as if reaching for a hug. Tears filled

Marie's eyes, blurring her vision, but she recognized the fabric used to create the bear. Lisbeth's appliquéd heart quilt.

On shaky legs, she moved to the cot and lifted the bear. She turned to face Beth, who beamed from the doorway.

"Are you surprised?" Before Marie could answer, she bubbled, "I'm sorry to have been so secretive, but I really wanted to surprise you. I've been spending a lot of time in Newton with an older lady who is teaching me different crafts. I saw her advertisement in the paper, and I thought having some unique craft items in addition to the one-of-a-kind antiques for the boutique would draw in more customers. So I've learned how to turn cutter quilts into stuffed animals or wall hangings, and I've even learned to make stained glass windows. It's been fun!"

Beth crossed to Marie's side and touched the wide ribbon tied around the bear's neck. "Mrs. Davidson actually did most of the sewing on this one, because I wanted it to be absolutely perfect." Her expression turned uncertain. "You're not upset, are you, that I cut it up? After I dumped that nail polish on it, there wasn't any other way to salvage it."

Marie set the bear on the cot and enfolded Beth in her arms. The quilt became secondary as the full magnitude of Beth's admission sent a wave of relief through her. Beth wasn't the thief. She had been working on the furtherance of her business, but not the way the town had surmised. Marie berated herself for believing the worst of her daughter. How grateful she was that she hadn't accused Beth when she'd arrived home!

Still in her mother's embrace, Beth released a light laugh. "Does this hug mean it's okay I chopped up the quilt?"

Marie pulled back and cupped Beth's cheeks. "It's beautiful, Beth. Thank you." Picking up the bear again, she gave it a hug, smiling over its head. "I think Lisbeth would be pleased, too."

"Oh good!" Beth hurried toward the closet and pulled the door open. Pushing her clothes aside, she said, "There was enough of the quilt left to make two smaller ones, too." Turning to face her mother, she held twin versions half the size of the one Marie had been given. "I'd like to keep one, and if it's okay with you, I'd like to give the other one to Trina since she worked so closely with Lisbeth at the café."

Once again, tears gathered. Marie nodded and forced words past the knot in her throat. "I think that's a wonderful idea."

With the two bears in her arms, Beth sat on the cot and tipped her head. Blond hair spilled across her shoulders, the strands shimmering in the light of the lantern that glowed on the dresser top. "Now, what did you want to talk to me about?"

Marie swallowed, shaking her head. "Nothing. It's not important now." Leaning forward, she gave Beth a kiss on the forehead. "Thank you for my gift, honey. I'll treasure it."

Marie left Beth's room, carrying her bear. In her own bedroom, she set the animal on the bed, resting it against the pillows. She sat and fingered one ear. A question remained unanswered. If Beth wasn't the thief, who was?

✦

Beth crept into her mother's room Monday morning and touched her shoulder. "Mom?"

Her mother stirred, scrunching her face and blinking rapidly. She turned blearily in Beth's direction, rubbed her eyes with both fists, and finally sat up. "What is it, honey?"

Beth smiled at the croaky tone. Maybe she should have brought in a cup of tea to clear the sleep from Mom's throat. "I'm going in to Newton to finish a stained glass project. I wondered if you'd like to come along and meet Mrs. Davidson."

Mom pushed the covers down and swung her feet from the bed. Seated on the edge of the mattress, she peered groggily at Beth. "I'd like that." She yawned and ran her hands through her hair, making it even more mussed. "And maybe I can do a little fabric shopping while we're in town."

Beth crossed her arms and smirked. "You gonna make teddy bears, too, and compete with me?"

Mom's soft laughter sounded. "No. But I need to pull out Lisbeth's machine and make some dresses. I think I can remember how to sew."

Taking a step back, Beth frowned. "Dresses? What for?"

Her mother pulled in her lower lip, a sure sign of nervousness. Beth's heart rate increased.

Mom patted the mattress beside her. "Sit down for a minute, honey. I need to talk to you."

With some trepidation, Beth approached the bed and perched on the edge of the mattress. "About what?"

"You know I talked to the bishop about rejoining the church."

"Yeah."

Mom sucked a breath through her nose, as if she needed strength. "Well, yesterday the announcement was made that I've been accepted back into fellowship."

Beth's jaw dropped. "So you're staying here? For good?" The apology in Mom's eyes pulled at Beth. She jumped up and moved several feet away before whirling on her mother. "You aren't coming back to Cheyenne with me?"

Mom stood, reaching her hand toward Beth. "It's not for sure yet. I'd need a place to live and a way to support myself here. Both of those are big needs, and I'm not sure how they'll be met. But if I'm meant to stay, I know God will provide."

A band of pressure seemed to wrap around Beth's heart at her mother's words. How could she choose the town over her own daughter? She took a backward step, shaking her head slowly. "I wish we'd never come here."

Mom leaned her head back, her eyes closed. Beth knew she battled tears. She ping-ponged between wanting to rush forward and hug her mother or rush out of the house and not return. Finally Mom lowered her head and looked at her.

"Honey, I'm glad we came here. It hasn't been an

easy time for either of us. But being here has restored something I've missed for many years. Now that I'm back in fellowship with God, I feel. . .whole again. I can't regret that."

Her mother's quiet, sincere tone made Beth ache with a longing to understand what Mom meant by being "whole." Yet she rebelled at the insinuation that her mother had lacked something all her years away from Sommerfeld.

"Are you telling me you haven't been happy since you left here? That my dad and me—" Beth couldn't continue. She clenched her fists, pressing them to the sides of her head. "I can't listen to this anymore. I've got to—" She raced toward the back door.

Mom's pounding steps came behind her. "Beth, wait!"

Beth grabbed the door handle, wrenched it violently, and threw the door open. It banged against the wall and bounced back. Beth charged through the storm door, allowing it to slam on her mother, who followed closely on her heels. Mom stood on the porch, stretching out her hand in a silent bid for her return, but Beth ignored her. She revved the engine and squealed out of the drive.

Escape. . . Escape Sommerfeld. Escape Mom. Escape the odd longing that rose up from her breast and tried to choke her breath away. *Just. . .escape.*

The remainder of the week passed in a dizzying blur of tumultuous emotion. Marie's elation at being welcomed back into the fellowship of believers battled with despair at Beth's reaction; her delight at being a part of the lives of Joanna and three of her brothers warred with the pain of continued distance from Abigail, Ben, and her parents; relief at the knowledge of Beth's innocence concerning the thefts couldn't quite eradicate the concern that somewhere in Sommerfeld the thief still existed, casting a spirit of unease over the entire community.

She leaned against the counter and caught one black ribbon that dangled from her cap, twisting the satin strip around her finger. After only a few days, the cap felt as natural as it had in her youth. Even the dresses—a far cry from the clothing to which she'd become accustomed since Jep's death—offered a sense of coming home. Aware that the articles of clothing were merely exterior trappings, she still experienced a sense of security in the donning of the simple symbols of her restored faith and fellowship.

Deborah turned from the stove, wiping her hands on her apron, and gave a slight start when she spotted Marie. She shook her head, her ribbons waving, before heading into the storeroom.

Marie stifled a giggle. She'd grown accustomed to the double takes. It seemed the community was having a harder time adjusting to her cap and dress than she was.

With the exception of Henry.

Her heart skipped a beat as she remembered his reaction the first time she came around the corner from the kitchen, attired in the caped dress and mesh cap of their sect, to take his order. His eyes had grown wide, filled with tears, and then his face had broken into a smile that sent her heart winging somewhere in the clouds. His joy—so evident—had brought a sting of tears to her eyes.

He had swallowed, brushed his hands over his eyes, and said in a voice thick with emotion, "Lisbeth would be so pleased."

Tears stung again now, remembering. Regret smacked hard. She should have returned sooner. Should have spent time with her aunt. Resolutely, she pushed the regret aside. She couldn't change the past—she could only change the future. And from this day forward, her heart and her will would be in alignment with God. It would be her aunt's legacy, one she would do her utmost to pass on to Beth.

Beth. . . Marie closed her eyes and prayed again for her daughter. The open rebellion pained her heart. *Father, I give her to You,* she said, repeating words that had become almost a mantra in the past few days.

The jingle of the bell that hung over the dining room entry door captured Marie's attention. Customers. She headed to the dining room, snatching up a handful of menus on the way.

The remainder of the day stayed busy. Saturdays always brought in the highway traffic, and Marie had little time to herself throughout the afternoon and evening. As was his custom, Henry ate his supper at the café, then stayed to tally the receipts and balance the books.

Deborah and Trina took care of the kitchen

cleanup while Marie placed the orders for next week's supplies and Henry finished the bookwork. They all completed their tasks about the same time, and as he always did, Henry offered to take Marie home. She accepted, but on this evening they spoke little. Marie pondered the odd silence and decided her reticence had to do with the change in her standing in the community.

No longer could she be considered an "outsider." She was now an accepted part of the fellowship. Tomorrow she would attend the meetinghouse for the first time in more than twenty years as an official member. Why that seemed to impact her relationship with Henry, she couldn't be sure. She only knew it felt different— as if a barrier had been removed. But a barrier from what?

Her heart thumped. She knew from what.

She risked a glance in his direction. The muscles along his jaw looked tense, as if he gritted his teeth. It increased the tremble in her tummy. Could Henry be thinking the same thing as she— that her acceptance in the fellowship would mean a community acceptance of their relationship moving beyond friendship?

Jerking her gaze out the window, she tried to eliminate those thoughts. Yet they niggled, increasing her discomfort as they rode silently through the star-laden evening.

When he pulled into the drive behind Marie's car, Henry put his vehicle into PARK and faced her. Her heart pounded at the uncertainty reflected in his eyes.

"Do you—do you need me to drive you tomorrow?"

"No, thank you." Marie swallowed, regret and relief bouncing back and forth and wreaking havoc in her soul. "I'll have my car. Beth was running a slight fever this morning, so I doubt she'll be going anywhere tomorrow."

Concern etched his brow. "Is she all right? Do you need to take her to the hospital?"

Marie's heart welled at his kindness. "No, I'm sure it isn't serious. Just a cold that got out of hand. It's that time of year."

He nodded, his expression thoughtful. "Well, then, you take care of yourself." The dash lights gave his face a rosy glow. At least, she blamed the color on the dash lights. "I'll see you tomorrow, at our meetinghouse."

She couldn't deny the rush of pleasure that came with his words. *Our meetinghouse*. Hers now, too. She gave a quick nod. "Yes. Tomorrow. Thank you for the ride, Henry." Hand on the door handle, she turned back and added, "And for your friendship. It's meant a lot to me."

His lips tipped upward, the left side climbing a fraction of an inch higher than the right. It gave him a boyish appearance that sent Marie's heart fluttering. "You're welcome."

With another nod, she bounced out of the car and hurried inside. After checking on Beth and insisting she drink some more juice, she readied herself for bed. Sleep tarried, her thoughts cluttered with the odd emotions Henry had stirred.

When morning came, his face—the sweet, lopsided smile of last evening—lingered in her memory and teased her as she prepared for service.

Her hands trembled as she slipped her cap into place, and she gave herself a stern command to gain control. She would miss the point of the sermon if she spent her morning daydreaming about Henry Braun! A quick check on Beth showed her fever had broken during the night, but she had no desire to get up, so Marie gave her a kiss and headed for the car with the promise she would come straight back after service rather than going to Joanna's.

Her thoughts on the service, she almost didn't stop for the brown van that crossed her path on Main Street, heading north. The driver, his black, flat-brimmed hat pulled low, glared in her direction as he rolled past. Marie lifted a hand in silent apology, and his nod acknowledged it.

Heaving a sigh of relief that she hadn't pulled in front of him, she started to cross Main. But then something struck her, and she stared after the van. The driver had appeared to be Mennonite in his dark suit and familiar hat, yet vans were not on the list of approved vehicles. She had reviewed the list only last week, knowing she would need to trade her red car for something more conservative if she remained in Sommerfeld.

A feeling of dread wiggled down Marie's spine. Without another thought, she made a sharp left and followed the van toward the edge of town.

Twenty-five

Knowing her red car would be conspicuous on the brown landscape, Marie fell back, her heart thudding with fear of being spotted. When the van turned right on the second county road outside of town, her instincts told her to go to the next intersection and double back. She craned her head as she continued north past the intersection, watching. The van increased its speed, kicking up puffs of dust that nearly swallowed the entire vehicle.

Her hands felt damp and her stomach churned with nervousness as she increased her acceleration to reach the next corner. She made a sharp right, holding her breath as her tires slid on the gravel, but she clutched the steering wheel with both hands and kept the car on the road. Looking off to her right, she spotted the swirl of dust that indicated the van's progress.

She smiled. "Thanks, Lord, for the cloud." Speaking aloud offered some comfort, so she continued talking to God as she drove, the van's telltale cloud of dust pointing the route. The cloud disappeared behind the dilapidated barn of a farmstead long since abandoned and surrounded by scrub trees. If it weren't for the bare branches of winter, the farmstead would have been hidden by the barrier of wind-shaped trees.

Marie slowed to a crawl, aware that the same dust that had notified her of the van's progress would alert the driver to her presence. The crunch of the tires on the hard gravel road made her cringe as she let off the gas and coasted to a stop on the east side of the barn.

She found the van parked on the north side, its back doors standing open. The van's radio blared out a rock tune, which told her in no uncertain terms the vehicle was not being driven by a Mennonite, no matter how he was attired.

She sat in her car, leaning forward to peer around the corner, her heart booming so hard she feared it might burst. As she watched, the man came into view, carrying something that appeared to be heavy by the slope of his back and his staggered steps. He pushed the item into the back of the van, brushed his hands together, then turned toward the barn again.

He came to a halt, his head jerking sharply in her direction.

Marie sank against the seat, her mouth dry. She grabbed the gearshift with a trembling hand, prepared to ram the car into DRIVE and speed away if needed. The man rounded the corner of the barn and came directly to her window. Her jaw dropped as he leaned forward and tapped on the glass.

Rolling down the window, Marie gasped. "Mitch!"

He had the audacity to laugh as he snatched off his hat and ran his hand over his close-cropped hair. "Surprised you recognized me in these duds. I'm as stylin' as you, Miz Mennonite Lady." He struck an arrogant pose, his grin wide.

Marie opened the door and stepped out. "What are you doing?"

Mitch's grin faded, replaced by a sneer of displeasure. "Trying to load up and get out of here. I guess I should've waited another half hour. If you were already in that chapel, you wouldn't have seen me." A disparaging snort of laughter burst from his chest. "Guess I got impatient."

He slung an arm around her shoulders and herded her around the corner. "Well, c'mon. Might as well confirm what you're suspecting, huh?"

Marie's feet felt leaden as she moved unwillingly alongside Mitch. When they entered the barn, she nearly collapsed. The hodgepodge of items, stashed haphazardly, provided evidence of Mitch's illicit industry.

She swung to face Mitch, flinging her hand outward to indicate the collection of items. "You took all this?"

He crossed his arms and shrugged. "With a little help."

Marie stumbled forward, grasping the back of the sleeping bench that had been removed from the Dicks' home. Her disappointment was so deep she didn't know if she could form words, but somehow the quavering question came out in a strangled whisper. "Beth was in on this?"

Mitch's laughter rang. "You really think Lissie had anything to do with this? Oh no, Marie, you raised a real little goody-goody. Your darlin' daughter won't even keep an extra dime from a cashier who's too stupid to make correct change." He moved forward and stood at the other end of the bench, his grin mocking beneath the brim of the hat he'd slapped on at an angle. "No, I just took careful note of all her complaining about the stuff that got away. Then I went to the locations and made sure I got it for her."

Marie shook her head. Even with the evidence in front of her, the unreality made her feel as though she were caught in a bad dream. "So all this time. . . you haven't been in Cheyenne, you've been in Sommerfeld?"

"Well. . ." Mitch scratched his head. "Not Sommerfeld. I've spent most of my time in Salina. I knew Lissie was hanging out in Newton with some old lady, and I didn't want to accidentally run into her and ruin the surprise."

Marie's head spun, trying to absorb the truth. "But you met her in Kansas City Thanksgiving weekend. How did you explain being able to get there so quickly?"

Mitch released a snort. "Do you think I was dumb enough to *drive* there? Lissie's not stupid—she would've figured out I had to be close by to reach her in a few hours by car. No, I drove to Wichita, left my car there, and caught a plane."

He advanced along the back side of the bench until he stood only a few inches from Marie. "I've kept her completely in the dark on this. I knew she'd kick up a fuss, and I didn't want her knowing anything about it until it was all set up in our boutique back home. But boy, it's been tough being this close and not being able to spend time with her." He winked. "Thanks for getting in that fight with her so we could have our weekend alone."

Marie's knees went weak at his secretive grin. "You—you didn't. . . ?" She couldn't bring herself to ask the question.

Mitch laughed. He leaned forward and whispered into her ear, "You mean did we sleep together?"

She jerked back, heat filling her face.

His laughter rang again. "No. Little Lissie won't do that either." He scowled, surveying the items in the room. "She'd never approve of this, but I had to do it. It was too good to pass up. Plus there was no other way to recover the money I'd borrowed."

"You'd have the money from the sale of the house and café," Marie argued.

Mitch pulled his face into an impatient scowl. "Honestly, Marie, how far would that go in purchasing at auctions? Antiques are becoming harder and harder to come by. There's no way we'd pull a profit." He turned introspective, pinching his chin between his thumb and forefinger. "No, this was necessary."

Turning back to Marie, his scowl deepened. "And now I'm stuck. Because here I am, caught with the goods, and here you are, ready to talk."

Her breath coming in little gasps, Marie took an uncertain backward step. "W–what do you intend to do?"

He stared at her for a moment, his brows low in a scowl. Then he jerked back, eyes wide, and burst out laughing. "Oh, you think I'm gonna—"

Slapping his knee, he continued to laugh while Marie contemplated making a run for it. But her quivering legs convinced her she wouldn't be able to go ten feet without collapsing.

Mitch shook his head, bringing his laughter under control, and fixed her with a smirking grin. "Gimme a break, Marie. I might've helped myself to some things without paying for them, but I wouldn't resort to murder. Not when I know you're going to keep my secret."

Marie raised her chin and peered at him through narrowed eyes. "What makes you so sure I won't tell?"

Mitch's posture turned calculating, giving Marie a chill. "You wouldn't want to hurt Lissie, would you? She loves me. How would she feel, knowing the man she loves and wants to spend her life with is capable of"—he waggled one brow—"larceny?" Settling his weight on one hip, he crossed his arms and twisted his face into a knowing leer. "And based on our conversations of late, she isn't so sure you really give a rip about her. Just last night, in a weepy little voice, she told me how you chose the church over her. She's all broken up about it. You try to tell her I'm the Sommerfeld thief, and she'll just see it as a ploy to pull her away from me."

Another arrogant shrug made Marie want to slap his smooth-shaven face.

"It's a no-win situation for you, the way I see it."

Marie considered Mitch's comments, and with a sinking heart she realized he was right. Telling Beth that Mitch had been stealing from the citizens of Sommerfeld could drive another wedge between her and her daughter. Even if Beth believed it, it would hurt her deeply. Marie hung her head.

Mitch laughed again and brushed past her, heading toward the open doors. "That's what I thought."

Marie scurried after him, taking in great gulps of the cold air. "But you can't take these things!"

He whirled on her. "Why not?"

"They aren't yours."

"They are now."

"How do you plan to explain to Beth how you got them? She knows they've been stolen. You can't just put them in your shop and expect her not to recognize them. It'll kill her to know you took these things!"

Mitch paused, quirking his lips to the side as his gaze narrowed. "She'll understand. She'll know I did it all for her. Because I love her."

"Do you really believe that?"

He stared at Marie for a long time, the silence heavy between them.

Marie forced out a quavering question. "How could you hurt her that way? Don't you care for my daughter at all?"

Anger flashed in Mitch's eyes. "That's hitting below the belt, Marie."

"You know as well as I do, Beth is the one who stands to lose the most through all this." As Marie pled her case, she prayed for him to realize the extent of distress he would cause if he carried through on his plan to take the items to Cheyenne.

The look on his face changed from arrogance to regret, confirming to Marie that the Lord was answering her prayer.

"The only way to save Beth's feelings is for you to drive away. Leave all this stuff here."

"I don't know," he said weakly. "I've spent a lot of money on motels and food while I've been hanging around here, storing this stuff."

"I'll help you pay it back."

He raised one brow, his expression doubtful. "You'd help a thief?"

"For Beth. . .yes." Marie quivered from head to toe. Wrong or right, she would protect her daughter. She had no idea how she would come up with the money; she only knew she had to do it, for Beth's sake.

"What about all this stuff? How do you plan on returning it?"

"I don't." At his startled look, she said, "The acreage around this barn will be farmed, come spring. Someone will stumble upon these things and make sure they're returned to the rightful owners. I won't have to do anything except wait." Her chest felt tight. Keeping this secret would be deceitful, but she had no other ideas.

His eyes turned into malevolent slits. "You'll do that? Just wait, and not say anything?"

She looked him square in the eyes. "Yes."

"Okay then." He yanked off the hat and sailed it through the open doorway into the barn. Marie heard a light *clup* when it hit the back wall. "Help me put the stuff from the van back in the barn, and I'll head out."

Marie caught his sleeve. "And what about Beth?"

"What about her?" he snarled, jerking his arm free of her grasp.

"You. . .you plan to continue seeing her?"

"Why wouldn't I? We have our plans set, Marie. For the past year, it's all we've talked about—going into business together, combining our lives. That won't change." He glanced at the stolen items and smirked. "After all, what Lissie doesn't know won't hurt her, right?"

Having a boyfriend who would sink to the level of common thievery *would* hurt Beth! But Marie knew nothing she said right now would make a difference. So with a silent prayer that Beth would recognize Mitch's true character before it was too late, she moved woodenly to the end of the van.

Mitch had only had time to load a couple of antiquated washtubs and a beautifully carved mantel clock. When he set the clock on the sleeping bench's seat, Marie felt a pang of remorse. Surely being left in the weather—this barn was far from airtight—would ruin the clock's workings.

"Well, I'm outta here." Mitch clapped his hands

together and headed out of the barn.

Marie watched him swing up behind the steering wheel. He slammed the door, offered a mocking salute, and roared away in a squeal of tires and a wild churning of dust.

Coughing, Marie backed into the barn, waving her hands to clear the air. When she could breathe easily again, she moved slowly through the dimly lit barn, examining the items for damage. Although Mitch had stored them without much thought for orderliness—things stood helter-skelter—he must have exercised care when moving them. And everything, from old buckets to the Dicks' sleeping bench, seemed to be there.

Sinking down onto the sleeping bench, she traced the delicate rose petals carved on the face of the mantel clock, her heart heavy. Letting Mitch go hadn't been right, yet she couldn't bear the thought of Beth's broken heart if she learned the truth. Somehow she would have to keep this secret, let someone discover these things on their own. At least, she comforted herself, everything would eventually be returned.

"No real harm will be done." She spoke the words aloud, trying to convince herself.

A gust of wind burst through the open doors, and she shivered. She should shut the doors to at least provide some protection for the items inside. She stood and turned toward the doorway. And froze.

A man lingered in the open doorway. The sun

behind him put his face in full shadow, but when he stepped out of the bright shaft of sunlight, recognition dawned. Marie gasped and covered her lips with trembling fingers.

Twenty-six

"What are you doing here?" Her shielding fingers muffled the words.

Henry took one more step forward, his gaze sweeping the barn. His chest constricted when he recognized the jumbled scattering of stolen contents. Facing Marie again, he said through gritted teeth, "I was about to ask you that question."

Her face seemed pale in the barn's muted light, her blue eyes wide. Slowly, she lowered her hands and wove her fingers together, pressing the heels of her hands to her coat front. "I—I—" She clamped her lips together and fell silent.

Henry felt as though something hot and stifling rose up inside him, and his tone turned hard. "When you didn't show up at the meetinghouse, I got worried. Gil Krehbiel told me he'd seen your car heading north out of town. I was concerned, so I left to look for you. But I never imagined. . ." He broke off, unable to finish the thought.

All this time he'd felt sorry for her, defended

her, befriended her. . . and she had been stashing her neighbors' things away, one by one. The evidence shattered his heart. The years of loving her, praying for her, now seemed wasted. How could he have been such a fool?

"Now I know why you refused my ride this morning. So you could come out here, check on your *stash*." The harshness of his tone surprised him. Had he ever spoken to anyone the way he was now speaking to Marie? He didn't think so. But he'd never felt as betrayed as he did now. He had a right to be harsh.

Raising his chin, he fired off another question. "Did you burglarize another home on the way out, or have you and your daughter decided you've collected enough?" He glared at her, taking in her nutmeg hair combed back under the pristine white cap. What did that cap mean to her? Was it only a ruse to keep the community from pointing fingers of blame in her direction? Hadn't his and Lisbeth's prayers accomplished anything?

Pain rose from his chest, closing off his voice box. Spinning on his heel, he stomped toward the opening.

Marie flew up beside him, her slender fingers wrapping around his forearm. "Henry! Please. . .it isn't what you think."

He stopped, his body stiff, and glowered down at her. Her fingers, tight on his sleeve, burned him, yet he didn't try to shake loose. "Then tell me. Tell me how you came to be sitting here on Sunday morning while the rest of the fellowship—the fellowship you joined—sits in the meetinghouse in worship."

She blinked rapidly, her breath coming in spurts of white fog, but she remained silent.

Lifting his hand, Henry peeled her unresisting, cold fingers from his sleeve and took a step away from her. The depth of her deception created an ache in his heart so crushing he knew it would never completely heal. "It looks like your father was right. You didn't come here for the relationships—you came for whatever you could gain."

The knowledge weighed him down, the truth striking like the slash of a knife, searing his soul with anguish. "You said you'd do anything for your daughter. I guess. . ." His gaze swept across the items once more before returning to her. He forced his words past a knot of agony that refused to be swallowed. "I guess the world is too deeply ingrained in you after all."

He waited for her to speak, to explain, to defend herself. But she stood silent before him, tears trailing down her pale cheeks, her fingers twisting together. When several minutes passed and still no words of explanation spilled forth, he shook his head and stared at the spot of ground between his black boots.

"I'll go to the meetinghouse and let people know where they can find their belongings. You. . ." He tried once more, unsuccessfully, to dislodge the painful lump blocking his throat. "Go back to the house. I won't say anything except that I found the stolen goods."

"Oh Henry, you can't—"

He held up his hand, his head still low. "I'm not

protecting you. I'm protecting Lisbeth's memory. I won't have this shame attached to her in any way." Lifting his head, he met her gaze. "You leave with Beth when the time period of the will's stipulation is over." The words came out in a hoarse whisper, burning in his belly like an ulcer. "I'll stay silent about your actions only if you promise to take your worldliness away from Sommerfeld and never bring it back again."

She gasped, clasping her hands to her throat.

He waited, but she didn't answer. He thundered, "Will you promise?"

Still no words came, but she shrank away from him and gave a quick nod, her eyes glittering with tears.

"Now go to Lisbeth's." He made a deliberately insulting sweep from her toes to her head. "And remove that cap. You make a travesty of it."

A sob broke from Marie, stabbing all the way through Henry's chest. But he remained rooted in place as she dashed past him. He heard her engine start, heard the crunch of gravel, heard the car drive away. He waited until he heard nothing except the beating of his own heart.

Yes, it still beat despite his certainty that Marie's deception had split it in two. With a sigh, he straightened his shoulders, ran his hands down his face, and returned to his vehicle. He had a happy message to deliver to the congregation, and somehow on the drive he must find the ability to smile through his heartbreak.

Marie burst through the back door, stumbled down the hallway to her room, and fell across Lisbeth's bed. How could a heart that ached this badly still manage to pump blood?

The look on Henry's face. The tone of his voice. The emotional withdrawal. Marie hadn't experienced such a depth of pain since the day she learned of Jep's death. On that day she'd lost something precious, too. Something irreplaceable. Something that could never be restored.

Until that moment—that horrible moment when Henry's face reflected both the anger of accusation and the hurt of betrayal—she hadn't realized how important his friendship had become in her brief time back in Sommerfeld. But now she'd lost him as surely as she had lost Jep.

"Oh God, what should I do?" She wanted to pray, but no words would come. She merely groaned, the sounds of her distress stifled by Lisbeth's pillow. She thought her chest might explode with the force of her sobs, but holding them back was worse.

Her face buried and eyes closed, she gasped in surprise when hands closed on her shoulders. Someone pulled, rolling her to her side, and she opened her eyes to find Beth kneeling on the bed.

"Mom? What happened?"

Her daughter's concerned voice and worried face brought a new rush of tears. Beth reached for her, and Marie found herself being cradled the way she had held Beth when she was little and was afraid or hurt. She clung, sobbing against Beth's shoulder, all of the pain and frustration of the past several weeks seeking release.

Beth rubbed her back, murmuring in her ear. In her daughter's sympathetic embrace Marie finally brought her crying under control. Pulling back, she reached for a box of tissues on the corner of the bedside table and noisily blew her nose. Beth, still on her knees, watched with her brow furrowed.

Marie took in several shuddering breaths and sank against the pillows, closing her eyes. Her head pounded painfully, and her eyes felt raw. She brought up her hand and pulled the cap from her head, dropping it in her lap. When she opened her eyes and glimpsed the rumpled ribbons lying across the skirt of her simple dress, she remembered Henry's command that she remove the cap.

He'd said she made a travesty of it. A mockery. A pretense. He thought she put it on just to fool people into thinking she wanted to restore her fellowship. To trick people while she stole from them. Henry, her dear childhood friend, believed she was capable of such horrendous acts. And if Henry, who should know her, thought this, surely the town. . .

She would have to follow his demand and leave. She had no choice. Tears welled again, and she covered her face with both hands.

Beth tugged her hands down. "Mom, what in the world happened?" Beth's cold distorted her words and made her voice raspy, yet the concern carried through.

300

"Did they kick you out of church or something?"

Marie shook her head violently.

"Then what is it?"

Different explanations paraded through Marie's mind, but none could be shared without divulging secrets. She turned her face away, pressing her trembling chin to her shoulder.

Beth took Marie's hand between hers and squeezed. "Please tell me why you're crying. You're scaring me, Mom."

When Beth's voice broke, Marie's eyes flew wide. The purpose was to avoid hurting Beth, not worry her. When she saw the tears shimmering in her daughter's eyes, she reached out and stroked Beth's cheek.

Finally she forced a few words past the sorrow that tightened her throat. "I'll be okay. It's just. . ." Squeezing her eyes closed, she once more envisioned Henry's accusing glare, heard his command that she remove her cap, that she leave.

She shook her head, determined to dislodge the memories, and the movement loosened her hair from the pins. Locks tumbled against her cheeks, and she smoothed them away from her face, her gaze dropping to her lap. The cap still lay there, and suddenly another picture filled her head—Henry, wearing a smile of approval while tears winked in his eyes when he'd seen her in the cap. Pain stabbed anew, and she groaned out one word: "Henry. . ."

Beth leaped off the bed, her brows forming a sharp V. "Henry hurt you? How? What did he do?"

Marie couldn't speak, regret closing off her voice box.

Beth slowly moved toward the bedroom door, her gaze on Marie. Her expression remained hard, angry. But when she spoke, her voice held nothing but kindness. "Do you want some tea? Some of that spearmint kind from the café that you like so much?"

Tea wouldn't fix anything, but she sensed Beth's need to do something to help. So she nodded wordlessly.

Beth paused in the doorway. "You stay here, Mom. I'll be back with that tea. Just rest, okay?"

Marie nodded, and Beth slipped away. When she heard the *click* of the back door latch, she rolled over, hugged the bear that Beth had crafted from Lisbeth's quilt, and once more allowed the tears to flow. Henry's words continued to echo through her mind.

"Take your worldliness away from Sommerfeld and never bring it back again."

⁂

Beth turned the car onto First Street. Her stuffy head throbbed from her cold, but it couldn't compete with the pain in her chest. Seeing Mom that upset. . .it hurt. A lot. And Mom had said Henry was the one who had hurt her.

She clamped her gloved fingers around the cold steering wheel and clenched her jaw until her teeth ached. Who did he think he was, making Mom cry? She drove straight across Main Street rather than turning toward the café. The tea could wait. Her talk with Henry couldn't.

Henry put the plate holding a cold ham sandwich on the table, pulled out a chair, and sat. He sighed deeply, staring at the food. Although breakfast had passed hours ago, he wasn't really hungry. Food wouldn't fill the void he felt.

Loneliness overwhelmed him, as heavy and enveloping as one of the lap robes from his boyhood days. Grandmother had always made their lap robes several layers thick to block the cold wind that rushed through their buggy during winter rides. He'd never liked sitting beneath one—he preferred frigid air to the feeling of suffocation from having to crouch under that heavy square of layered cloth. But right now there was no escape from the smothering layers of loneliness.

At least the citizens of Sommerfeld were rejoicing. He had managed to deliver the message to the congregation: "The lost has been found." In their excitement, no one had asked more than where to find their belongings. While people bubbled with relief, he had quietly slipped away and come home. Yes, for the citizens of Sommerfeld the lost had been found.

He had used those same words when speaking of Marie to J. D. Koeppler. Now he realized nothing had been found. For him, everything had been lost. He fingered the top slice of bread on the sandwich. Maybe he should just wrap the sandwich in aluminum foil and put it in the refrigerator. The lump in his throat would surely prevent him from swallowing.

Before he could decide what to do, a pounding on his front door intruded. Frowning, Henry rose and crossed to the door. He peeked out the window and drew back sharply in surprise when he recognized Beth Quinn on his porch. When he opened the door, a gust of chilly air rushed in, followed quickly by Beth. She charged past him into the middle of the room, faced him with her hands on her hips, and attacked.

"Mister, you've got a lot of explaining to do."

Her words were colder than the December wind. Henry closed both the storm and interior doors, then stood in the misshapen rectangle of sunlight filtering through the door's window. "Good afternoon, Miss Quinn."

At his droll greeting, her gaze narrowed. "This isn't a social call and you know it. What did you do to my mom?"

Raising his chin, he spoke in a flat tone. "I did nothing to your mother."

Beth shook her head, her uncombed hair wild. "You must have done something. She's more upset than I've ever seen her, and all she said was your name."

Based on the girl's red-rimmed eyes and chapped nose, it appeared Marie had spoken the truth when she said Beth was ill. Henry gestured to the sofa. "Sit down, please."

"No!" the girl's voice croaked hoarsely. She angled her body toward Henry, her stance reminding him of a rooster preparing to battle for kingship of the chicken yard. "Tell me what you did to make my mother cry!"

The girl's defiance stirred Henry's anger. Marching across the floor, he captured her arm and propelled her to the sofa. With a slight push, he managed to seat Beth on the edge of the cushion. Jamming his thumb against his chest, he said, "I did nothing. If your mother is crying, it's over her own guilty conscience, nothing more."

"Guilty con—" Beth shook her head, her fingertips pressed to her temples. "Mom has nothing to feel guilty about."

Henry snorted. "Is your sense of right and wrong so distorted you can't see the truth? She steals, yet she shouldn't feel guilty?"

"Steals?" Beth's head shot up, her eyes wide. "What in the world are you talking about?"

Henry stared at Beth, unable to believe she didn't know. Was it possible Marie had acted alone? She loved her daughter desperately. Would she have done all this without Beth's knowledge as a way of protecting the girl should she be caught? It was the only logical explanation. For one moment, Henry experienced a twinge of sympathy for Beth. How would she feel when she discovered her mother's love for her had driven her to such extremes?

Sitting on the opposite end of the sofa, he linked his shaking fingers and rested his elbows on his knees. "I'm sorry to be the one to tell you, but your mother is responsible for the thefts that have been taking place in town."

Beth sat bolt upright, her eyebrows crunching downward to create a scowl of disbelief. "No way."

Henry admired the girl's loyalty, but she had to face the truth. "It's true. This morning, when she should have been in service at the meetinghouse, I found her in the barn of an abandoned farm about three miles outside of town. All the stolen goods were there with her."

Beth shook her head slowly, her breathing erratic. Holding up both hands, she said, "There's got to be some mistake. My mom wouldn't—"

"There's no mistake." Unintentionally, a hard note crept back into Henry's tone. "I saw her with the stolen goods. And she offered no explanation."

"But why would she steal?"

Henry drew a breath through his nose, gentling his voice. "For you."

Beth jerked to her feet, swaying. Henry rose, too, poised in case the girl fainted. But she held her footing. "You're wrong."

"How can you be sure? Isn't that why you came—to gather items for the business you plan to open? When people told you no, your mother found a way for you to have the things after all." Henry's chest constricted as he spoke the words. How it hurt to condemn Marie this way.

"You're wrong." Beth's voice quivered with conviction, tears glimmering in her eyes. "My mother is the most moral person I know." Her chin jutted forward. "Once, when I was in first grade, I took a candy bar from the store without paying for it. One of my friends from school was having a birthday, and I planned to give it to her as a gift. When mom found me wrapping it, she took me back to the store and made me apologize to the manager. I had to give the candy back *and* pay for it. When I told her I had taken it for a present, she said, 'You don't steal for *any* reason; stealing is wrong.' " Crossing her arms, Beth glared at him. "Mom wouldn't steal. I know she wouldn't."

"Maybe not for herself, but—"

"Weren't you listening to me? She wouldn't do it for anyone!" A tear slipped free and rolled down Beth's cheek, and she brushed it away with a vicious swipe of her hand. "I don't know why she was out there. I don't know why she wouldn't explain herself to you. But I do know my mom would not steal. Not even for me. She—"

Beth's voice broke, and she jerked her gaze away, her chin crumpling. She took a few ragged breaths, her shoulders rising and falling with each heaving inhale and exhale. When she was somewhat controlled, she looked at him again. "She taught me that the only thing a person can truly call her own is her character. Mom's character is as pure as anyone's. And since we've been back here, all her talk about God. . ."

Shaking her head, Beth fixed Henry with a look of pained betrayal. "You hurt my mom a lot. I've never heard her cry that hard—never. She wasn't feeling guilty. She was just. . .hurt."

Beth drew herself up, her chin high. "All this time, I thought you were her friend—someone she could depend on. But you're just like all the rest of them." She charged past him and slammed out the door before he could say another word.

Henry stood in the middle of the front room, staring at the storm door, his thoughts racing. His throat convulsed as he envisioned Marie crying harder than she'd ever cried before. Because of him.

Beth's description of Marie's moral character is what he wanted to believe. But the evidence was against her. He had caught her red-handed! And she hadn't offered any explanation.

A need to discover the truth drove Henry out the door to his car. Behind the wheel, he turned the vehicle toward the county road he had traveled that morning. He would search the barn for answers. *Please guide me, Lord.* He would not rest until he found the truth.

TWENTY-SEVEN

B eth slipped back into the house with her pocket full of packets of spearmint tea. She found her mother in the kitchen in front of the wall calendar, her fingers pressed to the square representing December 25. Beth crossed to her quickly and put her arm around her shoulders.

"You okay?"

Mom shrugged, releasing a dismal sigh. "I'll be all right."

After all that crying, Mom's nose was as stuffed up as if she had caught Beth's cold. Beth snatched three tissues from a box on the corner of the counter and pressed them into her mother's hand. "I'll get your tea started."

"Thanks."

Mom remained at the calendar while Beth filled the teakettle and set it on the stove. She lit a burner with a flick of a match, then returned to her mother's side while the water heated. For a few moments she stood silently, her gaze on her mother's profile. Mom simply stood there, her focus on the calendar, almost as if she were frozen in place. Beth touched her shoulder with her fingertips.

"What are you doing?"

Mom glanced at her, her tousled hair seeming incompatible with the Mennonite dress of hunter green. "Thinking. About Christmas." She heaved a sigh. "We haven't gotten a tree or anything, and it's only a week away. Do you want to drive into Newton tomorrow morning and find one? I'm sure they'll be pretty picked over, and we don't have any decorations, but. . ." Mom's eyes swam with tears.

Her chest tight, Beth put her arms around her mother's unresponsive form. "Don't worry about what Henry told you. He's just a jerk. Forget about him."

Mom pulled free and stared at Beth, her eyes wide. "How do you know what Henry said?"

Beth offered a quirky grin and scratched her head. "I went to see him. I gave him what for, too."

Sinking into a chair at the kitchen table, Mom continued to stare, wide-eyed. "Oh honey."

Beth sat, too, and took her mother's hand. "I know there's no way in the world you took that stuff."

Mom lowered her gaze to their joined hands. Her shoulders lifted and fell in a sigh.

Beth tipped her head. "But what were you doing out at some abandoned farmstead? I thought you went to church, but Henry said you didn't."

Mom turned her gaze to the window that looked over the pasture behind the house.

Her curiosity increasing with each silent second

that passed, Beth said, "It is odd that you knew where to find the stolen things. Did somebody tell you where they were hidden?" Her mother remained silent. "How did you know to go there?"

Mom's clamped jaw let Beth know she didn't intend to answer.

She gave her mother's hand a tug. "Mom?"

A soft whistle from the teakettle intruded. Mom removed her hand from Beth's grasp and rose. "The water's ready. Do you want a cup, too?"

Beth watched her mother cross the floor on stiff legs and prepare two cups of tea. But when she set one cup in front of her, Beth shook her head and rose, backing away from the table. "Why won't you answer me?"

Mom fitted her hands around the mug and lifted it, the steam swirling up around her face. Fixing Beth with a serious look, she said softly, "Honey, remember when I asked you where you were spending your time, and you told me I should just trust you?"

Beth gave a small nod.

"Well, now I'm telling you the same thing. You have to trust me." She sipped the tea, her gaze returning to the calendar.

Beth, her heart pounding, turned and quietly headed to her bedroom.

Henry stood in the middle of the abandoned barn, his brows pulled low and hands shoved deep into his pockets. The floor was stirred up, showing signs of recent activity. All of the items were gone, claimed by their rightful owners, but if he closed his eyes he could remember the scene he'd discovered earlier that day. Marie, on the Dicks' sleeping bench with her arm around Albrecht's mantel clock. Off to the side, the Flemings' Russian trunk had waited, and behind it, a stack of enameled pans.

Suddenly something struck him, and his eyes flew wide. He gaped, his gaze jerking here and there as other pictures cluttered his mind. The barn had been in disorder—no specific space designated for furniture, another for implements, all just thrown in with no thought given to organization. Even as a child, Marie's school desk had always been neatly arranged, the pencils here, the paper there. The restaurant was now attended with the same care. Would she have been careless in the storing of valuable antiques? That didn't make sense.

Henry ambled around the interior of the barn. So many people had come and gone this afternoon, the soft dirt floor wore scuffs and gouges. He came to a halt and crouched down, his heart skipping a beat, when he discovered, in one corner, a shoe print that didn't fit with the others. Wafflelike markings left by some sort of athletic shoe.

He swallowed. Like Deborah and Trina, Marie wore athletic sneakers in the café. He put his hand beside the print, measuring it against the length of his fingers, then jerked to his feet and placed his foot alongside it. He nodded, a smile of satisfaction tugging at his lips. A man made that print—a man who wore sneakers rather than the boots of a Mennonite.

Turning a slow circle, Henry's gaze meticulously scanned the floor for more prints matching the one he'd just found. He located two more complete ones and a partial one. His heart pounding harder with each discovery, he continued searching for clues. Along the far wall, in the shadows, he spotted something.

He crossed quickly to the item in question. A black hat, lying upside down in the dirt. At first glance, it appeared Mennonite, but when he picked it up and carried it to the yard, where the sun sent down its light, he discovered it was constructed of tightly woven straw painted black rather than felt. No man from town owned a hat like that.

Which could only mean one thing. At some point, a man wearing athletic shoes and a hat meant to look Mennonite had been in this barn.

An idea took shape in Henry's mind. He tapped his leg with the straw hat, his thoughts racing. From Lisbeth's letter-sharing, he knew Marie had no man in her life who would assist her in any endeavors, whether wholesome or unwholesome. However, Beth did—and that man had an equal stake in the business she wanted to open.

Maybe. . .just maybe he had forced Marie into helping him. Perhaps he had threatened her into silence.

Hope tried to blossom, but he squelched it. No more speculations. He needed truth. Tossing the hat into the backseat of his car, he headed to town.

With a heavy heart, Marie slipped the dress she'd sewn only last week onto a hanger. She placed the hanger on the closet rod, then lifted the sleeve, admiring the color. She'd chosen deep green because once Henry Braun, with his face glowing pink, had said green brought out the red in her hair. How foolish. She released the sleeve and closed the door with a snap.

Smoothing her hands along the hips of her blue jeans, a rueful chuckle found its way from her chest. Who would have thought that, after such a short time, blue jeans could feel foreign? Yet they did. She reached for the closet door handle, fully intending to put on the dress again, but she snatched her fingers back before they closed around the tarnished brass knob. No longer would she wear the Mennonite trappings.

But I'll still wear God in my heart.

The thought brought a rush of comfort. Moving to the window, she peered outside. Dusk had fallen, painting the surroundings with a rosy hue. Across the street, lights glowed in windows. Families were sitting down to their evening meal of lunch meat, cheese, crackers, and pickles. Always a simple evening meal on Sundays.

Marie's mind replayed other Sundays and their evening meals, some from her childhood, others more recently with Joanna's family. She shook her head, forcing the memories aside. It was best she start separating herself now. Less than three weeks remained before Beth could sell everything, and then they would return to Cheyenne. To their old life.

No Sommerfeld, no café, no Joanna and Deborah and Trina, no simple meetinghouse, no Henry.

A lump filled her throat. If she didn't think of something else, she would cry again, and that would only upset her daughter more. Worn out from her cold and her excursion to Henry's, Beth now slept. Determined not to wake her with another noisy crying jag, Marie searched her mind for something to do. Her gaze fell on Aunt Lisbeth's small desk, and an idea struck. A shopping list for Christmas items would surely occupy her mind and cheer her at the same time. If it were going to be the last one in Sommerfeld, she wanted it to be special.

Crossing to the desk, she pulled open a drawer and searched for paper. A tablet of white lined paper came into view, along with a half-empty box of envelopes. She lifted both out and sat at the desk, placing the items in front of her. Then she pulled out the center drawer and withdrew a pen. She gave the pen's push button a click and flipped back the cover on the tablet.

Her heart leaped into her throat. Writing went halfway down the page, obviously penned by Aunt Lisbeth. The first line read, "*My dearest Marie. . .*"

❦

Beth rolled over, and the cot let out a now-familiar squeak of complaint, bringing her awake. Yawning, she slipped her hands outside the covers, stretched, then balled her hands into fists and rubbed her eyes. Opening her eyes, she found the room blanketed in darkness. Apparently the sun had slipped behind the horizon while she napped. What time was it?

By squinting at her wind-up alarm clock—the one she'd purchased for her stint in this house with no electricity—she managed to make out the position of the black hands. Seven thirty. Her stomach growled, confirming the hour. But she didn't get up.

Instead, she slipped her hands beneath her head and stared at the white-painted plaster ceiling, which appeared gray in the absence of light. She wiggled, trying to reposition herself on the lumpy mattress provided by Henry Braun.

Henry Braun. . .

A picture appeared in her mind of his face when she'd stormed into his house that afternoon. She sure had surprised him. But that was only fair— he'd surprised her, too, by turning on Mom that way. After everything he'd done to help them out, too. It made her mad all over again to think about it. And confused.

Rolling to her side, she pulled the covers to her chin and stared across the room. At least she had accomplished one thing. Mom wouldn't be staying in Sommerfeld now. They'd go back to Cheyenne together after Christmas. Somehow the thought didn't cheer her the way it once would have.

Tears stung Beth's eyes as she realized her mother had seemed happier here than she ever had in Cheyenne. Mom had never been one to wallow in despair or complain—that wasn't her way—but here, in Sommerfeld, she exuded an element of deep contentment. Despite the conflict with her parents, despite the lack of enthusiastic welcome by the community, her mother had found something here that gave her joy.

How had Mom identified it? She pressed her memory, straining to recall the exact words. They came in a rush—*"a fellowship with God."* With the remembrance came a splash of regret. She and Mom had always shared everything. Big things like an apartment and a car. Little things like toothpaste and shoes and banana splits. But this God fellowship thing belonged to Mom alone.

Beth felt left out.

When they returned to Cheyenne, God would surely go, too. She recalled her Sunday school teacher saying God was everywhere. He didn't just live in Sommerfeld. Beth swallowed, her throat aching. Would she feel left out even in Cheyenne, when Mom took her fellowship with God home to Wyoming?

Then there was this thing about Mom being in a barn with a bunch of stolen goods. Why wouldn't she tell Beth what she was doing there? Sure, Beth had kept a few secrets since they'd come to Sommerfeld—she'd had to if she didn't want to ruin a good surprise. There was still one more she was saving for Christmas. But Mom had always been open with her. Holding back something as important as a reason that could exonerate her didn't make sense.

Tossing aside the covers, Beth sat up. She groped under the edge of the cot for the fuzzy socks she had discarded before climbing under the quilt—the wood floors were cold in spite of the blast of warm air from the iron heater grates. Once her feet were covered, she headed for the hallway. She needed her mother. And some reassurance.

Twenty-eight

"M om?"

Marie lifted her gaze from the unfinished letter at the sound of her daughter's voice.

"You're crying again."

She touched her face, startled to find tears. Wiping them away, she offered a tremulous smile. "Don't worry. I'm okay. Look." She held the tablet toward Beth. "I found a letter from Aunt Lisbeth."

Beth squatted next to the chair and reached for the pad. She read the brief passage quickly, then looked at her mother again. "It's not finished."

"No." Marie took back the pad, her gaze on Lisbeth's neat, slating script. "I'm not sure what interrupted her, but I'm sure she intended to finish it and get it mailed." Hugging the tablet to her chest, she closed her eyes for a moment. "Aunt Lisbeth never stopped loving me, Beth. Never. We didn't have to be together for our relationship to continue. And that gives me such comfort right now."

"Why?"

Beth's gently worded query brought Marie's eyes open. She looked at her daughter and forced words past a knot in her throat. "Because soon I'll be away again—away from Joanna and Art and the others—but somehow we'll stay in touch. Through letters, just like Aunt Lisbeth and me."

Beth took the pad and tapped one paragraph on the page. "This must have been written shortly after my graduation. She thanks you for a picture from my big day."

Marie laughed softly, looping a strand of hair behind Beth's ear. "I included her in all your big days—your first tooth, first haircut, first day of school, first ballet recital." Suddenly something struck her. With a frown, she began opening and closing desk drawers.

"What are you doing?" Beth stepped back, clearing the way for Marie to open the drawers on the left side of the desk.

"Through the years I sent Aunt Lisbeth enough photographs to fill a small album. It just occurred to me I haven't seen them anywhere." Looking up at Beth, her heart fluttered. "She wouldn't have discarded them. . .would she?"

Beth shook her head adamantly. "They've got to be in a box somewhere. Want me to look?"

Marie closed the last drawer and slumped back in the chair "No. That's okay. When we get things ready for the auction"—pain stabbed with the comment—"we'll probably come across them. Who knows where they might be right now?"

Beth hung her head. "Mom, about the auction. . ."

Her daughter's shamefaced pose brought Marie to her feet. "Yes?"

Meeting her mother's gaze, Beth licked her lips. "I–I've sounded really selfish about all the stuff in this house. I wanted to make as much money as I could so I would be able to do something nice for you. You've always put me first, and just once I wanted to put you first and pay you back."

Relief washed over Marie as the motivation for what she had perceived as money-grubbing became clear. Her heart swelled with love. "Oh honey."

"Now I think maybe I could pay you back the best by letting you keep the stuff from your aunt's house. It means a lot to you, I know. So maybe we should just forget the auction."

How much her daughter had matured over the past weeks. Marie embraced Beth, giving her a kiss on the cheek. "That is the best gift you've ever given me."

Pulling away, Beth offered a wobbly grin. "Even better than that ceramic frog I made in third grade?"

Laughing, Marie hugged Beth again. "I loved your purple, six-legged frog! I still have it tucked in the sock drawer of my dresser back home."

At the word *home*, both women froze for a moment.

Looking into her mother's eyes, Beth posed a quiet question. "Mom, do you want Sommerfeld to be your home now?"

To Marie's chagrin, tears stung her eyes. A deep part of her longed to remain in the place of her birth, but Mitch's actions—and Henry's accusations—had sealed her fate. What she wanted didn't matter anymore. She couldn't stay. Not now.

Blinking, she cleared the tears from her eyes and forced her lips into a smile. In the brightest tone she could muster, she said, "This was to be a three-month adventure, right? And it's nearing its end, so. . ." She flipped her wrists outward in a glib gesture she didn't feel.

Beth crossed her arms and quirked a brow. "You aren't fooling anybody."

"Well, I—" Before she could complete the thought, a knock interrupted. She glanced at her wristwatch and frowned. "Visitors at this hour? I hope nothing's wrong." She hurried down the hallway to the front room with her daughter on her heels and pulled the curtains aside. Seeing Henry and Joanna standing on the porch, she glanced at Beth, who shrugged and said in a hard tone, "Might as well let 'em in. Knowing both of them, they'll stand out there in the cold until you do."

Henry allowed Joanna to precede him through Marie's front door. In the past, he had always entered this house through the utility porch in the back. Coming in the front door gave the visit a feeling of formality that left him vaguely unsettled. Yet he knew, given the topic that must be covered, formality would be a good shield for the emotions that churned in his belly.

Marie closed the door behind them, then stood, hugging herself, her wide-eyed gaze flitting from her sister to him. His heart plummeted when he scanned her attire. Blue jeans and a sweater. Standing there with Beth, who wore similar clothes, she seemed oceans away from him again.

Joanna stepped forward and embraced her sister, her white prayer cap and neatly pinned hair incongruous to Marie's tousled, uncovered locks. Henry looked away, turning back only when Joanna touched his arm.

"Let's all sit down."

Henry appreciated her taking charge. His tongue felt thick, incapable of functioning. Fortunately he'd had full use of it when he went to Hugo and Joanna's and told them what he'd found at the barn. The need to confide in someone, to seek someone's advice, had overwhelmed him as he'd driven back to town earlier that evening. Not having Lisbeth to turn to, he chose the one who had most fully embraced Marie's return. In Joanna he'd found his advocate, and her presence now gave him confidence that, together, they would get to the bottom of things.

Beth inched toward the double doors, her narrowed gaze boring a hole through Henry. "If you don't need me, I'm going to my room." She pointed to her red nose. "Not feeling too good, you know?"

Marie crossed to her quickly and gave her a kiss on the cheek, whispering something to which Beth responded with a nod, before the girl disappeared around the corner. The evidence of Marie's deep care for her daughter twisted Henry's heart. It seemed to point, once again, to the extremes she would go to for Beth.

Marie sat in Lisbeth's well-worn rocking chair, and both he and Joanna took seats on the sofa— Joanna at the end closest to Marie, he at the farthest end. Joanna stretched out her hand toward her sister, and Marie reached back.

"Marie, Henry made sure everyone knew where to find their belongings today. So all of the goods are back with their owners."

Henry watched Marie closely. Her shoulders slumped slightly with the news, but she didn't seem dismayed.

Joanna continued. "When he told us at the meetinghouse they'd been found, he didn't tell us how he came to find them." She glanced at Henry, then turned back to Marie. "He only told everything to Hugo and me. The town doesn't know you were with the things when he found them."

Marie's face drained of color, and her gaze shifted in his direction. "Thank you." The words came out in a wavering whisper. "You kept your word."

He managed a nod. Yes, he had told her he wouldn't tell—to protect Lisbeth's memory. Yet he knew, deep down, he'd also done it to protect her.

"But Marie," Joanna went on, capturing Marie's attention, "we need to understand. You rejoined the church. You told us you wanted to stay. You—you weren't being dishonest with us, were you?"

Marie's pale face mottled with red. Henry's heart

pounded. Could that rush of high color indicate a guilty conscience? His body angled forward slightly, leaning toward Marie, inwardly praying for her to share an explanation that would set everyone's mind and hearts at ease.

"I wasn't being dishonest." Marie's voice was tight, as if she were being strangled. "I truly wanted to regain fellowship and remain in Sommerfeld. But. . ." She drew in a deep breath and released it slowly, the splashes of pink fading from her cheeks with the dispelling of breath. "But apparently it isn't meant to be."

Joanna turned toward Henry. Her brows were low, her lips pursed. "Henry, I'm thirsty. Would you get me a glass of water, please?"

Henry nodded, understanding the silent message. She wanted time alone with Marie. He welcomed the distraction and the separation. Marie's last statement had been like putting a knife through his heart. He headed for the kitchen with his head low, his heart aching.

The moment Henry disappeared through the dining room, Marie felt Joanna give her hand a sharp jerk. "All right, Marie," her sister whispered, "we're alone now, and I want the truth."

Marie reared back, sending the rocker into motion. She stared at Joanna, surprised by the vehemence in her tone. "I—I—"

"And no avoidance! I don't for one minute

believe you had anything to do with the thefts." Tears glittered in Joanna's blue eyes, pain evident. "So you must be protecting somebody. It was Beth, wasn't it? Beth and her boyfriend."

Marie yanked her hand free and clasped it against her ribcage. She felt her own heartbeat against her hand. "No!" She, too, kept her voice low, but she matched Joanna in passion. "My daughter is not a thief!"

Joanna's forehead crinkled. "Then who, Marie? Henry found footprints out there, man-sized, that didn't match the boots our men wear."

Even now, the reference to "our" made Marie's heart pine with longing to be a part of that "our."

"He suspects, as do I, that Beth's boyfriend is involved."

Marie looked away, certain her face would give away the truth.

Joanna leaned forward, capturing her hand again. "Are our suspicions true?"

Marie's chin quivered with the effort of holding back her secret.

With a long sigh, Joanna released Marie's hand and slumped back on the sofa. "Why are you protecting him?" Her voice reflected confusion. Suddenly she sat up straight again, her eyes wide. "Did he threaten you?"

Shaking her head, Marie faced her sister. "No. Not really. He just. . ."

Joanna leaned forward, bringing her face near. "What, Marie? Tell me."

Her body trembled. Marie drew up her knees

and wrapped her arms around them. Yet her voice quavered when she replied. "He just made me realize how terribly hurt Beth would be if she knew the truth about him. She loves him. . .and he's a thief."

Joanna sat in silence, her gaze never wavering from Marie's, her brow knitted and her lower lip pulled between her teeth. She nodded, the movement so slight Marie almost sensed it rather than saw it. "I see."

Marie thumped her feet on the floor and tipped the rocker forward, grasping both of Joanna's wrists. "I can't tell, Joanna—not without hurting Beth. And I can't stay here with Henry thinking—" A dry sob burst out, and she lowered her head, regret weighing her down. "If only it could be different."

Joanna raised her hands to cup Marie's head and draw it to her shoulder. Marie sat within the circle of her sister's arms, absorbing the love and understanding offered through the wordless embrace.

After long moments, Joanna spoke softly, her voice hoarse. "So you'll let the one who loves you think you are capable of being involved in something morally and legally wrong in order to protect Beth's feelings?"

Slowly Marie removed herself from Joanna's hold. Settled against the back of Lisbeth's wood rocker, she answered, "Yes."

"I think you're a fool."

Marie nodded. "You're right. I'm a fool for thinking I could come back. I would be miserable, trying to live here and attend the meetinghouse regularly with Dad feeling like he does. Maybe this is God's way of sending me back to Cheyenne. That's where I belong."

Joanna's eyes flooded with tears. "No, Marie. *Here* is where you belong. I've seen you blossom here. We all have —Henry and Hugo and Kyra and Deborah. How can you even think of leaving?"

"How can I even think of staying?" Marie countered. She released a sorrowful sigh. "No, God brought me back for a reason—to rediscover my relationship with Him. I've done that, and I know I'll never let Him go again. So. . .at the end of Beth's and my three-month time period, I'll move on."

Her sister stood, glaring down at her. "You're just as stubborn as our father. Well, I'm not going to argue with you. But I am going to pray very hard, between now and the end of the month, that God brings you to your senses." Moving to the doorway leading to the dining room, she called, "Henry, I'm ready to go."

Henry returned and followed Joanna to the front door. Marie remained in the rocking chair as he opened the door. Poised in the doorway, Joanna looked back.

"We're all meeting at Mom and Dad's after service Christmas Day for dinner and presents. This is your official invitation. You and Beth are my gift to me this year, so I expect you to be there." She stepped outside. Henry followed, pulling the door closed behind him.

Twenty-nine

Through the wall, Beth heard the front door latch and knew the guests had left. She flumped back on the creaky cot, her thoughts racing. No doubt Joanna and Henry had come to harass Mom about the stuff in the barn. She hoped her mother hadn't told them anything. Not because she didn't want the truth to come out, but because she wanted Mom to tell her before she told anyone else.

Her relationship with her mom had gone through some rough water lately, but once they were back in Cheyenne, things would settle down again. Maybe her business wouldn't start off with the bang she'd imagined, but it would still start. Things would be okay. Especially with the new skills she'd picked up from Mrs. Davidson over in Newton.

A smile formed as she thought about the surprise she had waiting for Mom, thanks to Mrs. Davidson's tutelage. Slipping from the cot, she tiptoed out the door and down the hallway. She peeked into the front room and spotted her mother in the rocking chair, head back and eyes closed. Satisfied she wouldn't be caught, she returned to her room and opened the closet door.

On the floor, wrapped in old towels, waited the gifts she had made of stained glass. For Mom, a two-foot square of bright tulips, with the sun beaming down from the upper left-hand corner. She had drawn the pattern and chosen the colors herself. Pride welled as she remembered Mrs. Davidson's words of praise for her accomplishment. Beth's heart lifted, imagining her mother's pleasure. Mom loved flowers and bright colors.

Several smaller pieces also waited, all made of the same design—a frosted-center cross with brightly colored beams shooting from behind it. She had fashioned each in a different color scheme and had enough for Joanna, Kyra, Trina, and Deborah, plus one more. She had toyed with the idea of giving the last one to Henry, to thank him for his help. But given his recent actions, she was not about to follow through with that idea.

Folding the towel back around the colorful window, Beth wondered if this type of craft would sell well in the city. Mitch would have an opinion on that. She slid her mother's gift back in the closet, closed the door, and picked up her cell phone, eager to discuss the possibility with him.

The phone rang four times before Mitch's voice answered. The line was staticky, with wind noise in the background. He sounded harried.

"Hey, what're you doing?" Beth greeted.

"Driving—snowsto—"

The connection broke in places, and Beth frowned, struggling to comprehend. "If there's a snowstorm, don't go out."

"—ing home. I—to get there—ly."

Beth sat on the edge of the cot, pressing the phone to her ear while she ran her free hand through her hair. "Can you hear me okay?"

"—es."

"Then listen, okay? I need to talk to you about making stained glass windows to sell in our boutique. When you're not driving, call me back, okay?"

Between breakups, she heard his laugh. "Our— still on?"

"Our boutique?"

"Yeah."

"Of course it's still on. Why wouldn't it be?"

"—eason. Th—mom for me, huh?"

Dread was in Beth's stomach. "What about Mom?"

The line disconnected. Beth sat, stunned, thoughts whirling through her mind like the snowflakes she envisioned swirling by Mitch's car. Mitch wanted her to tell Mom something. . .thank you, maybe. . .but why? When had he been in communication with Mom?

A sickening picture began to take shape. She shook her head, an attempt to keep it from forming. Despite her efforts, little bits and pieces of conversations with Mitch from the past several weeks whizzed back, dropping into place like puzzle pieces.

"So tell me, Lissie, where did you see that mantel clock?"

"Don't worry, baby—we'll get your antiques."

"They've formed a community watch, huh? All the time? Well, yeah, of course not during church."

And that weekend in Kansas City. At one point he'd chuckled for no reason she could discern. When she questioned him, he'd said, "Oh, I was just thinking how quiet it is in good ol' Sommerfeld right now." At the time she'd thought he was unfavorably comparing the tiny town to the bustling city. But now the choice of words—it *is* rather than *must be*—haunted her.

She leaped up, her heart pounding. Charging out of the bedroom, she sobbed out one word: "Mom!"

On Christmas morning Beth joined Marie in attending the special service at the meetinghouse. Her daughter looked so nice in a simply styled blue skirt, white blouse, and loose-knit blue sweater, with her long hair pulled into a sleek bun on the back of her head. Not quite as conservative as Marie's hunter green dress and white cap, but it thrilled Marie that Beth had selected the outfit herself, giving careful thought to what would be appropriate for the service.

The past week had been a time of talking, crying, and praying together that had bonded mother and daughter more firmly than ever before. Just last night, seated with Beth at the little table in the corner of Lisbeth's kitchen, with the glow of the lantern illuminating the pages of Lisbeth's Bible, Marie had guided her daughter through the steps necessary to become a child of God. When Beth prayed the sinner's prayer, inviting Jesus Christ to enter her heart, Marie's heart soared with a joy beyond description.

After Beth went to bed, Marie wrote a note to her daughter on the inside cover of Lisbeth's Bible, wrapped it in shiny paper of the brightest red, and placed it under their Christmas tree with "To Beth, from Great-Aunt Lisbeth" on the tag. She knew Lisbeth would approve.

Gratitude filled Marie so completely, she felt she would burst from happiness. With God in her heart and Beth at her side, she could face her parents today with a sense of peace.

During the closing hymn, she stood between Beth and Joanna, holding their hands, linking her past with her future. With God at the center, everything would be fine. Of that, Marie was certain.

When the service concluded, she and Beth exchanged wishes of Merry Christmas with worshipers as they made their way out of the meetinghouse. Her gaze collided with Henry's, and it lingered, her heart straining toward him. Although they had seen each other in the café every day since his visit last Sunday, they hadn't spoken.

She longed to bridge the gap between them, especially now that her leave-taking was just around the corner, but a part of her feared reaching out to him. If what she suspected was confirmed—that she had grown to love Henry in the past weeks—then leaving him would be impossible. The gap must remain, no matter how painful.

She allowed her lips to form the words, "Merry Christmas," waited for his answering nod, then forced her gaze away. Taking Beth's arm, she said, "Let's get to your grandparents' place, shall we?"

Neither she nor Beth spoke on the short drive to Marie's childhood home. Turning into the lane that led to the house, she broke into a cold sweat. How she wished this homecoming was like the story in the Bible about the prodigal son, with the father watching, waiting, arms outstretched, an embrace and celebration at the end. Her gaze swept the house, the yards, the outbuildings. With a chuckle, she observed, "It all looks so much smaller."

Beth sent her a sympathetic look. "You know, Mom, we could just go back to Lisbeth's and have a quiet day together."

Marie considered Beth's suggestion but shook her head. "As tempting as that sounds, this may be my last Christmas in Sommerfeld. I really want to be with my family—my whole family—and I want all of them to at least meet you, see what a beautiful daughter I've raised."

"Aw, Mom." Although her tone sounded embarrassed, Beth grinned. She looked out the window and frowned. "Looks like we're the only ones here so far."

"They'll be here." Marie got a sudden idea. "While we're alone, let's snoop."

"Snoop?" Beth released an amused snort. "Seriously?"

"Seriously. Come on." Marie swung her door open and stepped out of the car. A light covering of snow dusted the ground, but the sky was clear and bright, and no wind whipped from the north. "I'll show you around—let you see my childhood playing spots."

Beth grinned. "Okay."

Knowing time was short, Marie chose her favorite location first—Dad's woodworking shop. Linking arms with Beth, she guided her to the cement-block building behind the barn. "We kids were never supposed to play in here because some of Dad's tools could be dangerous. But I never touched the tools, and he knew it, so he let me go in. It made me feel special."

Releasing Beth, she turned the knob on the heavy wood door and swung it open. The hinges groaned in the cold, and a familiar smell greeted her, sending her back a quarter of a century. Marie closed her eyes and inhaled, allowing the odors of cut wood, leather, paint, and turpentine to fill her senses, igniting memory after memory.

"Mom?" Beth's startled tone brought Marie's eyes open. She turned and spotted Beth at one end of the long, homemade workbench that stretched along the entire north wall of the sturdy building. "You've got to see this."

Marie crossed to Beth, and her jaw dropped when she realized what her daughter had discovered. Pictures—dozens of them—tacked to a board that had obviously been mounted for the sole purpose of displaying them. Marie touched the crisp, white pine board. It had been recently erected.

Stunned, she turned her attention to the array

of pictures, recognizing every one. The photos she had sent to Aunt Lisbeth, arranged chronologically, starting with the snapshot of her and Jep on the steps of the courthouse where they had recited their vows and ending with the day of Beth's graduation from junior college. Marie's life laid out in silent snapshots.

She stared, unbelieving, her heart thudding out a message. *Dad, Dad, Dad.*

"Why would he have done this?" Beth asked.

The groan of the door intruded, stopping Marie from answering. She turned to face the entry, and her heart doubled its tempo. Her father stood framed in the doorway, his face unsmiling.

"Dad." Marie took a step away from the workbench, her fingers linked together. "I—I just wanted Beth to see the places where I spent time as a child. I didn't—"

He moved over the threshold into the building, closing the door behind him. "I always trusted you not to touch things in here." His voice rumbled, low and stern, yet Marie sensed no anger in the tone.

She gave a quick nod. "And I haven't touched anything today either. I didn't abuse your trust."

His gaze shifted from her face to the wall behind her, and his chin quivered.

Marie's heart melted. "Dad. . .you took Aunt Lisbeth's photos?" She made certain she spoke softly, gently, with no hint of recrimination.

"I did."

"Is it because. . . ?" She held her breath, waiting, hoping, praying. *Please, Lord. Please.*

Tears glittered in her father's blue eyes. His face crumpled, and he lowered his head. His gaze aimed downward, he rasped, "I missed so much. I needed to—to somehow know you again."

Marie heard Beth's sudden intake of breath, felt her daughter's hand on her arm. The desire for reconciliation was so strong it became a flavor on her tongue. Giving Beth's hand a quick squeeze, she stepped forward, making the first move.

"Dad, I'm right here. And I want to know you again, too." Her breath came in tiny spurts. "Can we let go of the past and start over?"

He stood so stiff and unresponsive, Marie wasn't sure he'd heard her quiet words. Her heart pounding with hope, she waited.

Slowly her father's gray head lifted, his tear-filled eyes meeting hers. His hands quivered, then inched upward, reaching, the hands open and inviting.

With a little cry of joy, Marie ran across the concrete floor and flung herself against her father's chest. His arms came around her; his head tipped to rest on her white cap. Warm tears soaked the top of her head.

His "Please forgive me" and her "Oh Daddy, I'm sorry" spilled out at the same time. They broke away for a moment to look into each other's faces. They both released a brief laugh before embracing once again.

A second pair of arms came from behind Marie—Beth, joining the hug. Marie felt one of her father's arms slip away, and she didn't have to look to know it now enveloped her daughter.

Marie closed her eyes, memorizing the moment. The smells of the shop blended with the smell of snow trapped in her father's suit coat. Beneath her cheek, she heard the thud of her father's heartbeat; on her head, she felt the pressure of his jaw. The sting of cold against her bare legs juxtaposed the warmth of the embrace, becoming a symbol of the sting of resentment being replaced by the warmth of acceptance. Silently she praised her Father God for allowing her this precious time of communion, of connection, of bygones becoming bygones, of hurts melting away.

They stood in a tight circle, with Marie at its center, for long moments until finally, reluctantly, her father's hold loosened and he stepped away. Looking down at her, he said, "I can't let you go again without saying. . .I love you, Marie. You—you're still my girl." He grazed her jaw with thick, callused fingers. She clasped his wrist, pressing the broad hand to her cheek.

His fingers quivered. "Your mother has a dinner waiting. . .and presents." His gaze turned to include Beth. "For both of you."

Beth smiled. "Then let's go in, Grandpa."

THIRTY

Marie allowed Beth to drive back to Aunt Lisbeth's from the farm. A light snow fell, the tiny flakes taking on the appearance of tossed glitter in the headlights as they drove along the silent country road toward town. She leaned against the headrest, tired yet blissfully happy. Her prayers had been answered—her family's full acceptance was the best present she could have received this Christmas.

The gift Beth had given her was a close second, however. Although she had already thanked her, she took advantage of their time alone to express her appreciation again. "Honey, I love the stained glass window you made for me. I'm so impressed with the arrangement of colors—it almost looks as if the tulips are in the foreground and the sun far behind. I've never seen stained glass with the illusion of depth before."

Beth shot her a quick, quavery smile. "Mrs. Davidson said I had a rare talent—that creating three-dimensional stained glass art is difficult."

Marie's eyebrows shot high. "Honey! Perhaps you've discovered a gift."

"Could be." Beth turned her attention back to the road, but Marie could tell by the way she nibbled her lower lip that her thoughts drifted beyond the dirt pathway.

Marie sighed, settling back in the seat again, reflecting on the teary good-bye at the farmstead just a few minutes ago. Leaving town would be difficult, but miles could be traveled both ways. She would be back, frequently. The next twenty years would be different from the past twenty.

The headlights scanned the front of Aunt Lisbeth's bungalow as they turned into the drive. Beth slowed, leaning forward over the steering wheel to squint out the windshield. "Mom, is there something on the porch?"

Marie looked. It appeared a square package had been wedged between the front door and storm door. "I'll go see what it is." She hopped out and stepped under a shimmer of moonlight that created a bluish shadow of her form as she crossed the snowy yard. When she lifted the box, her fingers slipped, surprised by the heft. She hugged it to her chest and returned to the vehicle.

Inside the car, she shook snowflakes from her hair and read the printing on the brown paper wrapping. "To Marie, from Henry." She stared at it, unmoving, wondering what it could be.

Beth nudged her. "Well, open it!"

Her stomach jumping nervously, Marie did as her

daughter hid. Under the brown paper, she discovered an age-yellowed box. She opened the box and released a gasp.

"What is it?" Beth asked.

Marie slapped the lid back in place. "Honey, I—I need to go see Henry."

"Now?"

The girl's incredulous tone made Marie smile. "I'm afraid so. Do you mind being alone for a little while?"

Beth's slack-jawed expression changed to one of understanding. "I'll be fine, Mom." She put the car in PARK and slipped out the door. Leaning back inside, her lips formed a quavering smile. "Good luck."

Marie's face filled with heat as Beth laughed and closed the door. Sliding behind the wheel, she reversed the vehicle and headed to Henry's. She used one hand to drive; the other caressed the box on the seat beside her.

Henry ran his hands over his face. Fingers pulling at the skin along his jaw, he looked out the window. Again. Then glanced at the clock. Again. Grimacing, he turned away from the snow-laden night and released a groan.

It had been a foolhardy thing to do, leaving that package. It probably embarrassed her. Or scared her. Or both. While it had seemed a good idea at the time, he now realized it could lead to more heartache and regret. What had he been thinking?

Well, he'd just have to go get it. Maybe she hadn't returned from her folks' place yet. He could fix this if he could get there before she did. He hurried across the room to the coatrack in the corner, but as he raised his arm to lift down his coat, he spotted headlights. He froze, watching, as the car turned into his driveway.

Marie.

Too late.

His legs turned to jelly, but he managed to move the few feet needed to reach the door and open it just as she stepped onto the porch. Snowflakes graced her head and shoulders, glistening under the light of the moon. Her blue-eyed gaze met his, and although she didn't smile, neither did she frown. His gaze dropped to her hands. She held the box. He swallowed.

"May I come in?"

Her tremulous voice spurred him to action. Jerking out of the way, he said, "Yes. Please." With an awkward bob of his head, he gestured to the box. "You found the gift."

She stood hesitantly in the doorway, her coat buttoned to her throat, her sweet face lifted to him. "Thank you, Henry. It means so much to me to have it."

He nodded, unable to find his voice.

"You've kept it all this time?"

"I couldn't take it back. I wrote in it."

At her crestfallen expression, he could have kicked himself. Why had he blurted out something like that? Shaking his head, he took hold of her arm. "Come in, please, and sit." He guided her to the sofa and waited until she perched on the center cushion. He sat on an overstuffed chair at the end of the sofa, clasped his hands together, and pressed them to his lap.

"I wouldn't have taken it back anyway." What a relief to see her expression change. Her blue eyes flickered in his direction. He found the courage to finish what he wanted to say. "It was meant for you. You should have it."

She nodded. Her graceful hands lifted the lid on the box and set it aside. With her chin still low, she glanced at him. "May I read what you wrote inside?"

She hadn't done that yet? His neck and ears grew hot, but he nodded.

He sat in silence while she peeled back the cover of the white Bible and read it out loud. It only took a few seconds—he'd never been a man of many words. But he sensed by the way she traced her finger over the writing that she found pleasure in the brief message. She faced him again, and he swallowed.

"Henry, thank you for this Bible. That's why I came here tonight—to say thank you."

He nodded stupidly. Of course that's why she'd come. What other reason would there be?

"But may I also tell you thank you for so many other things?"

"Like what?"

She tipped her head back a moment, as if gathering her thoughts, then met his gaze once more. Tenderness showed in her expression. He tightened the grip of his fingers, the tips biting into his own knuckles.

"Thank you for being such a wonderful friend to Aunt Lisbeth. She loved you like a son. You were very special to her."

As she was to him. He nodded.

"Thank you for your prayers over the years. Most people would have given up, but you didn't. And now I am reaping the benefit of your steadfast devotion."

His second nod was jerky, his neck muscles so stiff he felt he had no control of them.

"And thank you for your efforts to reunite me with my family. They were successful. This was the best Christmas I've ever had. I'm a part of the family again, welcomed by every member."

"*Every* member?" his voice croaked out hoarsely.

Her smile told him she understood the simple question. "Even Dad. We made our peace. It was precious."

Henry blew out a breath of relief. "I'm so glad."

"Me, too."

They sat in an uncertain silence, with their gazes aimed at their own laps. Marie seemed to examine the Bible she continued to hold; Henry begrudged the grease he could never completely remove from beneath his fingernails.

After a long while, Marie set the Bible aside and looked at him again. "Henry, about last week. When you found me—"

He held up his hand, meeting her gaze squarely. "It doesn't matter."

"It *does* matter. It must. You haven't spoken to me all week."

Henry ducked his head. He hadn't known what to say to her. If she were innocent, his accusations were inexcusable. If she were guilty, he couldn't reconcile himself with it.

"I need to tell you the truth, and I hope you'll forgive me for being less than honest with you when you found me."

Raising his head, Henry said, "I'm listening."

Briefly, Marie explained how she had come to be in the barn that morning and why she had kept the details to herself. Henry remembered his promise to keep silent in order to prevent any negative light being cast on Lisbeth. He realized, with a start, that Marie's motivations for silence were no different than his had been.

She finished quietly. "So now that you know it was Mitch, charges could be filed by everyone who had items taken. I'll understand if that's what you choose to do. And I'll accept my responsibility for letting him go. I won't lie about it anymore."

Henry thought carefully before speaking. "Thank you for telling me. I think, since everyone has back what was taken, they would be willing to let the matter lie. We could talk to the deacons if it would make you feel better."

"What would make me feel better," she said, her eyes flooding, "is if you would forgive me. I don't want to leave again with regrets between us." Touching the Bible with her fingertips, she licked her lips. "You meant to give this to me before I left. . .with Jep." She looked at him, her expression uncertain. "I don't want another message to go unstated."

Henry drew in a ragged breath. "Marie, my biggest regret right now is having, for even a brief time, believed you capable of thievery. I should have known. Please, will you forgive me?"

Her eyes sparkled, her lips tipping into a smile. "Yes. And can you forgive me?"

"Yes."

Her smile grew, and she released a light bubble of laughter. "Oh, that feels good."

Henry smiled. Yes, it felt good to have past mistakes erased, to start with a clean slate. Another silence followed, but this one lacked the unease of the last. Instead, it was a time of settling, of finding a comfortable ground together. It made his heart feel light, and although he hated to interrupt it, he had a question he wanted to ask.

"Marie, do you think Beth would be willing to sell the café to Deborah and Troy?"

She tipped her head, her fine brows coming down for a moment. "Deborah is interested in running it?"

"Yes. She and Trina would keep it going. She's come to enjoy being there."

Another light laugh spilled out. "Well, this is a day for surprises. I'll have Beth get in touch with Deborah. I'm sure they can work out the details with the Realtor."

"Good." He cleared his throat. "And when it sells. . .you'll be leaving?"

For several seconds she seemed to hold her breath, looking at him, something in her expression making his heart increase its tempo. Then, in a hesitant voice, she said, "Do I have a reason to stay?"

Slipping to her side on the sofa, Henry took her hand. "I hope you do." Reaching across her, he lifted the Bible from its box and put it on his knee. He opened the cover and read the words he had penned there the week before Jep Quinn arrived in town. "What God brings together, let no man put asunder." Giving her hand a squeeze, he said softly, "Marie, can I hope that. . .perhaps. . .I might be a reason for you to stay?"

Tears blurred his vision as he admitted, "I've never stopped loving you. Lisbeth knew it. She hoped, like I did, that one day you would return. I know you loved Jep--I wouldn't try to replace him in your heart or Beth's. But if you gave me a chance—"

Marie touched her fingers to his lips. "Henry, I would never see you as a replacement for Jep."

His chest constricted as he waited for her to continue.

"Jep was the love of my youth, and I don't regret loving him. He once told me I helped bring him back in step with the Lord. He gave me Beth. I can't imagine my life without her. Our relationship had a purpose."

Her tender tone, her gentle expression—even though she spoke of another man—held Henry captive.

"But you've been faithful to me, expressing care for me, even when I didn't return it. There is no substitute for that kind of dedication and love. Jep was the love of my youth. But you, Henry, are the love of my life."

He opened his mouth, closed it, swallowed, and finally formed words. "Do you mean. . .you love me, too?"

A tear burst from its perch on her thick lashes and spilled down her cheek with her nod.

He scooped her into his arms, pulling her against his shoulder. "What about Beth? Will she return to Cheyenne alone?"

She made no effort to extricate herself from his embrace. Her face against his neck, she murmured, "God has brought us back together. He'll take care of Beth—I trust Him with her."

He crushed her close, burying his face in the scent of her hair, before setting her aside. Tears trailed down her smiling face, and he brushed them away with his thumbs.

Her sweet lips curved into a smile that sent his heart racing. "Merry Christmas, Henry."

For once, Henry's clumsy tongue found the perfect words. "You are my God-bestowed gift. I love you, my Marie."

About the Author

Kim Vogel Sawyer, a Kansas resident, is a wife, mother, grandmother, teacher, writer, speaker, and lover of cats and chocolate. From the time she was a very little girl, she knew she wanted to be a writer, and seeing her words in print is the culmination of a lifelong dream. Kim relishes her time with family and friends, and stays active in her church by teaching adult Sunday school, singing in the choir, and being a "ding-a-ling" (playing in the bell choir). In her spare time, she enjoys drama, quilting, and calligraphy.